Mystique: A Bitt

"Being a vampire who kills other vampires doesn't go down well in that specific society. With a bounty on my head, trying to keep a low profile and keeping the existence of vampires a secret, I'm bound to run into a lot of complications."

Mystique is a vampire with skill; able to use witchcraft and her survival instinct to avoid the death sentence. On a personal hunt to find the one who murdered her parents, Mystique begins to discover that the past is never forgotten and danger is always lurking in the shadow of her decisions.

And when her sister suddenly disappears, the search becomes more deadly than ever...

To Tania,

Hope you enjoy my book!

MYSTIQUE
A BITTEN PAST

AJ WOOLFENDEN

APS BOOKS

APS Books,
4 Oakleigh Road,
Stourbridge,
West Midlands,
DY8 2JX

APS Books is a subsidiary of
the APS Publications imprint

www.andrewsparke.com

First published worldwide by APS Books in 2019

ISBN 9781789960914

Thank you to those who supported me in the process and those who gave me more confidence to achieve this goal. You know who you all are.

"For you, I'd give anything.

My money, my possessions, even my very last breath if that's what was needed to make sure that you stay alive, safe and remain with the life that I have taught you.

The life where you can escape the monster,

Not a death where the monster consumes you."

"A vampire's life is already decided and the path we go down has no left or right.

Fear, bloodshed and death is inevitable."

Chapter 1: Promising Start

The icy air stings my skin, my breath turning to fog and evaporating into the night as I calculate the next step as I stand over the bloodstain snow on the ground, watching the injured monster struggle to catch his breath, slumped against the cold alley wall.

The winter night is anything but quiet within the city of London. The drunken party celebrations nearby from the popular hotel on Bow Street, evade the dimly lit night as people shout and sing in their drunken haze, trying to keep their balance as the snow crunches beneath their feet. Instead of joining them, myself and the vampire are deep in an ally way, shielded from anyone's curious gaze. My attention firmly on interrogating the monster for information.

His blood red eyes cast themselves up to meet my own, as I crouch over him; blood he doesn't own stains the corners of his mouth. My coat elopes my hourglass frame as my golden blonde hair is pulled back, so he can clearly identify who has interrupted his dinner time.

A street light close by clicks its tongue as it flickers, the timid yellow glow not giving us much light which aids in us being undisturbed.

Scrutinizing over his appearance; broad stature, skin head, blood red eyes, misshapen nose, my eyes cast themselves to the raven beauty victim he pulled from the hotel just over the way; her body discarded in the disturbed snow.

"Well if she liked danger, she certainly found it with you... along with the definition of ugly but I cannot judge."

"You little bitch... You were... you were waiting for me... weren't you?" The vampire stutters his words, trying to recover from the broken ribs he acquired from me.

Reaching out, my fingertips press against his chest as I allow the power of paralysis to channel to my hand; the bright green energy crackles like electricity as my blue eyes are replaced with jade green, matching the power's colour. The paralysis quickly consumes his nervous system, stunning him into admission. The blood of his victim trickles from his chin as I glare in disgust.

"Yes. However, I had hoped you would be alone... yet you had to drag her into it." I retort.

Caging his face with my other hand, I thrust his head to the left to convey the scene.

"Look at her." I snarl. "Look at what you did!"

The victim's body lies twisted in an unnatural pose just a few feet away from us, her face portraying the fear she went through for this vampire to feed upon, her wide empty eyes gaze in our direction.

"I fed from a human." He states matter of fact; spiting the young woman's blood that continues to drip from his lips. "What the hell do you want from me?" Whipping his face back, my eyes slowly return to the original colour by cancelling out my power that has now done its job; a deep ocean blue washes over the jade green.

Travelling my hand to rest on his shoulder, I focus on the task at hand. "I want information. I know you work for *them*. So, give me what I want and I may let you live. Unless you want to be like your friend over there –" nudging my head in the victim's direction "- Do you believe in an afterlife? Every part of the world and religion has some form of it."

My eyes catch his arm spasming in pain as his efforts to punch me are rendered impossible. My lips shift up into a smug smile. "The more you try to move the more the paralysis hurts. I could not risk you recovering from your injuries and attacking me."

The vampire tries to move his arms again but to no use. He swears under his rapid breath as the pain surges through his chest.

"It is funny how easy it is to kill vampires. For me anyway." Gesturing my hand up and down his body to prove an obvious point, the vampire tries to spit at me but it just trickles down his chin. His stone wall poker face is trying to mask his pain as the vampire speaks; his voice cracks but his brisk sarcasm tone still rings clear.

"Yes, because you are the... the great vampire Mystique. Blessed with... with many abilities... for a blonde bimbo."

A half-hearted laugh jumps from my throat in amusement. "You are a risk taker, aren't you?"

"So are you." He spits out as I observe his bear like body convulses in pain. "You see yourself as, as a God. But you are no diff-different then I am. You are a monster. Like me, like them... Like your sister."

A snarl rips from my throat as my hand springs like a cage from shoulder to neck; his pulse throbbing beneath my fingers. "I would be very careful with your next words..." growling deeply "-especially since you know who I am. You must be aware of my reputation. I don't leave vampires who cross my path alive."

My available hand comes down onto his leg and the snap of his bone like a brittle twig causes him to choke out a scream. "You... You... You broke my leg... You fucking bitch!"

"Pain helps to gain information. Little fact, it has been used for decades. Now... tell me... Does Edward still have a bounty on my head?" Cocking my head to one side, I arch my eyebrow waiting for an answer.

"For leaving... Yes. For hunting us down... He raised the price. Told everyone that if we could kill... kill you and bring back your head, he would pay us for our... our service."

"No change there. Bloodshed, butchery and bleak is how I have always described them... and money? Can't he do better than use greed to motivate you?" Rolling my eyes and sighing.

His voice trembles with the pain in his leg but his eyes widen with panic. "You got it all wrong! He- he didn't send me. I'm not looking for ... for you."

"No but you found me anyway... Actually, I was looking for you so that statement isn't really valid. But thanks for telling me he didn't send *you*... because that means he *has* sent someone." The sound of a young man and woman stumbling down the road approaches my ears as I slam my hand over his mouth, staying still as stone as they scutter by; their laugh echoes down the darken ally way with the stinging alcohol aroma wafting in the cold winter breeze. Once out of sight, I remove my hand, giving him an exaggerated expression of impatience.

"No...No." He stutters as I push the weight of my body through my arm slowly on the fractured leg, causing him to grit his teeth to stifle a scream of agony, his eyes squeezing shut as if in attempt to block out the pain. "No vampire... will go... go near you."

"Is that a lie?" Arching my eyebrow in suspicion as a few strays of blonde hair fall to the side of my face, free from the ponytail.

"The Royal Order hasn't ordered anyone... to come after you."

My patience is drifting away, much like this vampire's survival rate. Knowing I need this information with time running away, I swallow the developing lump in my throat, trying to ignore the swirling sickness in my stomach as I give my best poker face.

"I find that hard to believe. Edward is the head of the Royal Order and it is common knowledge that he doesn't like me. You realise the longer this takes..." opening up my powers again, the colour melts away like ice within my iris as a ruby red fire takes its place, channelling my aura to my hand on his leg. Flames manifest from my skin burning the denim jeans, melting the material into his flesh "-the more impatient I become." I keep my eyes trained on him, ignoring the increasing flames and heat beneath me.

His face screws up in agony, his screams stifles as he clamps his teeth shut to contain his cries within his chest but the effort is very much in vain.

"See this is another reason why I paralysed you. You cannot heal any injuries I give to you." I mock him, trying to distract myself from the flames.

"Ok, ok please stop! Edward has someone after you but I don't know who he is! I swear. Please let me go! Let me go! Let me go!" He begs as the smell of burning flesh lingers in the air. Retreating my hand back, distinguishing the flames as I do so; the blackened skin sizzles and parts of flesh begin to break off his leg, leaving a black palm sized hole. Staying crouched in front of the wounded vampire, watching tears stream from his eyes as he struggles to catch air into his lungs that is not filled with the gut-wrenching smell from the new burning wound, I try again.

"I need a name." I state, leaning closer. The smell of the girl's blood just a few feet from us is sweet and potent as the cold winter breeze brushes it by our noses, whereas the blood from his wound smells sour.

"You can't do this...You can't... You can't play God." Each word is a struggle; his body trembling with the fresh sizzling burn on his leg as his nerves are exposed to the cold temperature.

"Why has he sent someone after me?"

"I don't know."

"Don't make me ask again." I snarl, articulating every word. His lip trembles as his wide terror filled eyes stare at me.

"I don't know much. I wasn't told. All I know is that someone is after you. He sent him about a week ago." His voice quivers unable to mask his fear.

The cries of drunken laughter from the street catches my attention once again and I know time is quickly slipping away. My craving for blood is elevating with passing minutes.

Shit, I haven't had blood since this morning! Maybe I can drink his if he becomes useless to me. I quickly sum up.

"Thank you. Now answer me this and I will let you live." My words give him hope as his eyes light up like a candle in a church, praying for a miracle, praying for a way out of this darkness.

"Who was my creator?"

That candle lit hope in his eyes whisks away like a gust of wind; his hope melting like wax from my question that was already clear he could not reveal the answer I desired.

His lip trembles with fear, his head shaking weakly from side to side. "I-I don't know. I swear. Please." His voice cracking like ice as his eyes dart to his left, seeing his victim, remembering the promise I had made to him at the beginning of our encounter. "Please, I beg you. I don't know!"

"Who killed my parents?"

"I don't know... Don't kill me! Please don't kill me! Don't tear me to pieces I beg you! I beg you!"

With his life in my hands he now reminds me of a child, begging for a toy back I am now playing with. Shushing him, my hand strokes his face, my thumb removing some of the blood from his chin. My lips move close to his ear. "You said it yourself. I can't play God."

Before another word escapes his lips, I sink my teeth into his neck. Smelling his blood is too tempting even with the sour notes. I have the willpower to walk away but tonight I am choosing not to. Besides I have no regret in taking this vampire's life. He killed an innocent woman.

The warm blood pours into my mouth, some of it spilling onto the white canvas around us tarnishing its purity. His body convulses at the sensation of having large amounts of blood drawn from his body forcefully. The warmth of the blood radiates like the sun's glow from my stomach through every vein and muscle. I close my eyes as the ecstasy consumes my senses. Like a flame diming out into nothing, his life is taken away by my hands.

Soon, his shaking body comes to a standstill but I continue feeding not focusing how much I drink as usual, draining his body of blood so there was nothing left but his empty corpse. Wiping the blood from my mouth as I drop the vacant vessel, I stand back to view the mess.

His body is in an awkward position; his leg unnaturally lying in a twisted pose. His mouth hangs open and his eyes are vacant. The blood stains his neck and the snow around him much like his victim. Knowing from experience leaving an empty body would raise suspicion, I go to pick the bodies up when the sound of three sets of footsteps find my ears.

Having no time to cover up the blood or hide the bodies, reluctantly I twist my hand and the colour of my eyes changes again so the flames rise from my palm. Shooting two balls of fire at both the corpses, quickly setting them ablaze.

This is the best I can do for now; I hope the fire will destroy the bodies before anyone sees there was no blood left.

Turning to the alley walls, I propel myself, leaping from wall to wall to get positioned on the roof. Landing with a muted thud, I find myself needing to look one last time at the scene. Looking down once more, I see the mess I have created.

The burning bodies of vampire and victim lies on the white snow; their blood still warm is beginning to melt the crystallised water, their corpses turning black from the flames and the burning smoke rising into the air. Some teenagers approach the alley way and upon seeing the flames they manage to pull out their phones and ring for the police. I can hear them saying stupid remarks about the fire and "how cool" it is but I ignore their idiocy, knowing they have no comprehension that I have just removed a dangerous vampire from crossing their paths. I turn my back on the scene and fade away into the silver lit night.

Jumping from building to building, I get to another alley way and jump down, landing silently and make my way out onto the public street. It is still quiet and checking my watch, it is now midnight. After just feeding I can feel a lot of energy coursing through me, begging me to put it to good use.

Catching my reflection in the window of a parked car, I admire what stares back; my blonde hair that hangs from the ponytail to the middle of my back is now shining with health, my white skin seems to glow against the navy-blue outfit which is very practical for my hunting nights. Eyes sparkle back in the reflection and a wide smile beaming in the moonlight. The teeth are no longer pearl white; the blood give them a monstrous stain. I drop my smile, looking away from my reflection.

Turning to the road, I know no one will see me running if I go full speed, everyone in this part of London is asleep; I can smell the aroma coming from the buildings; soft sweet lavender.

Needing no time to count myself in, I dash down the road with full speed; the wind and buildings speeding past my vision. My heart rate only increases slightly. This isn't a work out for me, it is just like walking. My vampire lungs and muscles are designed for speeds like this. Racing home to my own solitude, I can't help but know I will never be praised for ridding vampires in this city, making innocent people safe for another night. If people knew they wouldn't even have the decency to call me a hypocrite.

Chapter 2: Solitude

My house sits outside the busy city of London. By car it would have taken about an hour to get there, running only takes me 15 minutes. It sits along an excluded road which is rarely used. It had a lot of land for sale so I bought a bit of it and built my own house. Keeping to the Tudor design with the typical white outer walls with black beams, elongated windows and elegant doors suits me well as it's still 'in fashion' so changing the building design hasn't been an option yet.

Anyone who sees the house most likely thinks a wealthy family lives here; our money comes from our inheritance as well as my every day job. I've made my money last well, and investing in some businesses helps to top up the pot too.

Opening the door with my security pin, I walk into the reception area and slip my long coat off, hanging it up on the old rustic coat rack. The bruises and scratched paint on the legs shows its true age. The 100-year-old paintings of sceneries, lovers and dancers hang with pride on the mauve purple and cream walls, the small floral sofa in the corner next to a wooden desk has collected a bit of dust due to lack of use. The grandfather clock stands tall and proud, showing its cuts and bruises off with pride as its ticking voice scatters through the room. The wooden stairwell leading upstairs has recently been polished; the smell of pinecones dance in the air. Every part of this house is traditional and contemporary in design.

"Ah Miss Field! You are home." Laurence's voice trails from the top of the stairs as he exits one of the rooms, carrying a basket of clothes and blankets in his hands. "How was your night? Any luck?" His voice is deep but warm, like a hot spring.

"When it comes to being me luck has a tendency to cower or turn a blind eye, when it sees me walking down the street."

"So, you retrieved no answers?"

"Only one. The Royal Order has sent someone after me. Couldn't get a name though." I sigh with frustration as I walk across the room, halting in the centre for Laurence to greet me. As he descends the stairs his swollen belly jiggles beneath his black jumper with each step until his feet touch the bottom. He probably would not look so round if he was taller but his short stature reminds me of a blow-up beach ball with a pebble grey balbo beard attached; one prick and he would pop!

"Maybe the answers you seek are not meant to be yours." His old words of wisdom are never too far from his lips as he greets me. He certainly looks like a wise old man, physically looking about 70 years old but of course looks are very much deceiving in terms of being immortal. I look to be 26 years old, of course it is an illusion.

"Neither is this answer but you need it. Black is sliming but not on you... also you look like an old man trying to recapture his youth wearing all black and sporting a man bun. Your youth went flying by centuries ago."

Laurence laughs heartily, rubbing his free hand on his stomach as he greets me in the middle of the reception.

"I agree that maybe it does not give me the trimmed down look I need... but everyone is wearing them!" His smile flows across his whole face; deepening the laugh lines and wrinkles evenly imprinted on his face.

"Also, for once, I would love to come home from work and not have an irritating speech from you." My annoyance sprouting in my chest as my impending urge to sit down and relax grows.

His untamed bushy eyebrows bow together. "I have barely given you one. However, I would like to remind you that going out hunting our own kind for information is not what most would consider work... or honest work at that." His red eyes lovingly look at me with sadness and I detest it.

" *Vampires*" I harshly correct him.

"We *are* vampires... or have you forgotten?" His words in a desolate tone fuel my rage. Turning my back on him knowing a nagging pep talk is inevitable, I focus on my breathing as he continues talking. "Master Field you cannot ignore that fact. I understand you wish you were human again. But what is done is done. You cannot unburden yourself with the card you have been dealt with, but you can unburden your own anger and grief."

Silence consumes the room with a heavy weight of contemplation; however, I am sure I am the only one to feel this weight. My anger, like a dragon, uncurls itself from my stomach as Laurence continues.

“If what you say is true and the Royal Order has sent someone after you... You need to tread more carefully.” His words send the dragon up my spine; my body growing hot from its flames.

“I can handle it. I’ve handled everything before and I can handle everything to come.” The dragon takes place in my head; its heat burning up my ears almost muffling the sounds with its flames. My eyes squint from the pulsing pain in my head.

“Amanda,“ Laurence begins to speak in a tone expressing concern and worry. I quickly inhale to try and douse the dragon before interrupting his lecture.

“How has Hilary been today? Any progress?” Sharply changing the subject as I look over my shoulder. He stares back at me for a moment, his face showing concern but acceptance that I don’t wish to talk about this subject. He nods his head, indicating the change of topic. The dragon slowly begins to ease off, gliding back down my spine.

“She did very well. Her training is going steadily. She is succeeding in mastering her strength and power however... “

“Is she ready to leave?” I cut him off, impatiently waiting for the only answer I want for hear, turning my body back to face him. Laurence shakes his head disheartened.

“I do not believe she is safe yet. Give her time. She will get there... On a more positive note she helped me with some of the housework. I asked her to clean the desk in the reception but she conveniently forgot about it. She also kicked my butt at chess. But I promise you I have a trick up my sleeve for next time.” He chuckles as he winks at me with a wide smile streaming across his face, knowing that Hilary can hear him.

I smile at the thought of Laurence and Hilary playing together. It reminds me how lucky I am to have Laurence around. He is able to give Hilary personal time when I cannot.

Taking in a deep breath, I smile gratefully as I speak calmly. “Forgive me, I have had a stressful day. I just want to rest.”

“You are forgiven.” Nodding his head as he smiles sympathetically. “I don’t mean to make you angry. I just want the best... for both of you.”

“I know.”

The sound of the television drifts through the house and Hilary's laughter chimes like music following the comedy show she is watching. That laugh causes my eyes to break from Laurence and look in the direction, bringing a joyous smile to my lips as I bow my head to him.

"Thank you. I will spend some time with her now." From the corner of my eye he bows his head back, smiling warmly.

"Of course, Master Field."

Turning towards the living room to the left side of the reception, Hilary's laughter is infectious as I enter smiling to see her curled up in her pjs, holding her Victorian doll Milly. Its purple and white dress is a little torn and seen better days but we have done a good job keeping it intact; its black bouncy curls still firm and full of colour. Milly has needed to go to a repair toy shop a few times but she's holding in there. Hilary's golden blond hair is like a curtain around her face, hiding her smile away.

The big open fire crackles away as if it was laughing at the T. V's jokes as its joy spreads warmth through the traditional styled room. Everything has been cleaned thoroughly with evidence from the smell of lemon scented chemical cleaning products. From the dark mahogany bookshelf on the right of the white marble fireplace to the picture frames of traditional art work that place themselves evenly on the dark emerald walls above the wooden panels that meet halfway. Not a speck of dust can be seen anywhere. The TV sits on a unit to the left of the fireplace where Hilary is curled up on the far-left side of the sofa.

Each move I make is slow and precise as I creep my way forward into the room, my eyes set on Hilary with my arms outstretched, fingers reaching out desperate to touch her. Just as I make it to the back of the sofa, she catches me.

"I know you're there." She giggles, twirling Milly in her hands.

My hands lunge for her regardless, my fingers tickling her weak spots. Her laughter and high pitch squeals of delight contagiously make me laugh too.

"And yet I still got you!" I laugh back, as I slide myself beside her on the sofa, pulling her close as she fights to get away.

"S-stop tick-tickling me-e-e!! I'll g-get you back- back for this!"

"Oh no! Whatever shall I do?" Easing off my tickling attack but dramatically raise my hands to my face in a scared look. Hilary sees this and, still bouncing in fits of giggles, starts snorting like a little piglet which makes me burst out laughing as her face turns red.

"Oh no the piglet has been let loose! Quick, catch her! Catch her." My arms wrap themselves round Hilary's waist and this time she doesn't struggle, allowing her little body to be cradled by mine. Once we both calm down from our fit of giggles, the sound of the TV finally being heard again, I smile softly as I kiss her cheek, allowing myself to sink back into the brown leather sofa. Hilary lies beside me, her fingers tracing the buttoned texture of the sofa.

"So, you finally decided to help Laurence with the housework Cherry? I think you missed a spot though."

Cherry was my nickname for her as she loves the flavours. When she was ill it is all she would want to eat. If you give her a choice of any food in the world and cherries, there was no competition.

The pointed-out fact catches her attention but only slightly, as she uses her normal excuse.

"It has felt no touch upon its face with every summer day and winter fall. Why take that dust away when it shall fall forever more feel no touch?"

The old poetic English roles off her tongue and for a moment I feel transported back in time. But it is not a lifetime I wish to remember, so I change the subject.

"Watching some comedy, I see. What happened to your action films?" I ask as the open fire continues to crackle in delight, the portrait of our once happy family hangs above it. Hilary gazes at me; her own eyes beaming wide with humour. If it wasn't for those bright blood red eyes, she would look like your normal every day 12-year-old child and not as a monster... her true self... a vampire child. She is more dangerous than me. Children are cute, sweet and innocent, capable of doing no wrong. Everyone is drawn to children like moths to flames. A vampire child is worse. Our bright eyes, strong features, swift and graceful movements will make everyone fall at their knees to Hilary and coo over her. One minute they are admiring her, the next she's feasting on them.

She has powers too although unusual; if she touches an item, she can see the occupant who owned it and for a brief moment, can see what happened with each person. It was amazing to see this when we once went into town. She found a lost toy on the floor in the centre and when she picked it up, saw the baby who had held it and which shop the mother had gone into. Within half an hour we managed to return it as well as a lost watch dropped by a bustling businessman. Of course, this was a time when Hilary could leave the safety of our home.

With our abilities between us I cannot help but see the connection. Hilary is the past, I am the future. It's almost quite fitting to us actually. She speaks about the past often, almost being stuck in it, whereas I can see the future and am always searching for our next move.

"I'm really enjoying thou laughter one brings from such amusement. The action films were becoming somewhat a bore to me", Hilary dramatically yawning as she speaks.

"Your modern English is getting better..." rolling my eyes as I speak "-soon you'll be talking like a proper 12-year-old."

She giggles and nudges my arm forcefully. "You know I can talk modern, stupid. I just sometimes like to speak normally. The way we use to."

My heart sinks once again at the thought of our old life. Our time. I kiss her forehead, her hair smelling of roses and tulips. "I know, I miss speaking that way too sometimes."

We both drop to silence as we watch the comedians stand up and tell their jokes. Laurence makes us a pot of tea, as usual I take a cup but Hilary does not. He joins us in watching TV, making his own jokes while we laugh at the good ones or 'boo' him for a terrible one.

As the night progresses, Laurence declares himself done for the night. He kisses Hilary on the forehead, wishes me a pleasant night as always and leaves the room. The memories of another life try and flood back into my mind but I shut the door and bolt it up. The light patter of rain on the window drifts through the room harmoniously with the dancing fire.

"Out hunting were we tonight?" Her voice pipes up from beneath my arm. "You wear the same outfit every time you go out."

"They are comfortable and easy to move around in". Nudging her shoulder, she giggles and runs her hand over my black denim trousers. Her fingers then caress my midnight sleeveless jumper, feeling the softness of the fabric. Hilary has always preferred to wear skirts or dresses, sticking to the colours of green, yellow or pink in different shades. Her pale green with pink flowery PJs are no exception.

“You look nice in it too... and I love your black boots.”

“I’ll get you a pair when I next go shopping.”

“Can I come with you? Laurence said I was doing much better.” My eye catches hers and her expression is one of hope. “I have to call you Mystique out in public right?”

“That’s right. But he said you needed a bit more-”

She scoffs and rolls her eyes, cutting me off. “You know I can’t remember the last time I went out... I think it was like the 1900s.” Shifting her body away from me, her arms cross over her chest in a stubborn manner; an argument is about to break out and I can already feel the headache approaching.

“We’ve talked about this.” I state as her body tenses. Another argument hangs over us and it feels like the air has gotten heavier.

Her voice comes out in a whisper. “I’ve gotten better with my strength.”

“I know you have. But your strength and speed can pose as a danger if you accidentally slip up in public. Do we really need to go through this again?” Sighing in frustration, two times a week now we have this conversation.

Jumping up and turning to face me, Milly doll cast aside on the sofa, her red eyes try to stare me down but as usual it doesn’t work.

“I can control my hunger too! Today a cat got in through the open window and I didn’t kill it even though I’ve wanted blood all day!”

A sense of pride welled up within me, but deep down knowing she would not last five minutes out in public. In a soft voice, I speak calmly.

“You know I want more than anything to take you out of this house. But in a crowd of people, you wouldn’t stand a chance. A cat’s blood is nothing compared to a person’s... You know that.”

Her eyes cast down, anger and shame fill her face. I speak more softly. “You are much too wise and strong... far beyond your physical years. When out in public you need to act your age and speak your age as well as controlling your hunger and powers. It’s difficult to do and- “

Hilary's voice goes higher and louder, the air almost shakes with the vibrations. The rain has become more intense; striking the windows like bullets being fired; loud and heavy.

"I've been out before! I need a life!! Being trapped in this house all the time isn't helping me! It won't happen again! I swear! I'm better now!" A flash of lightening crosses the sky and the sound echoes through the night; as if agreeing with Hilary's anger. The memory flashes across my mind of when she was first turned and the people she killed. My mind automatically shreds it up like paper.

"You're being over protective!" She screams at me, her hands curling into a fist and her teeth bare, like an animal ready to pounce.

Standing up in anger, I raise my voice to match hers; matching her animal instinct, snarling my words. "There is no such thing as over protective when it comes to us Hilary! *We* have to protect ourselves from our own nature. Don't you get it?! How many more times do I have to say this before you will listen?" The dragon inside me returns, quickly going up my spine and nestling in my head.

Hilary turns on her heels and storms off but I follow, quickly matching her stride.

"I've heard it a million times, but that doesn't mean I can carry on like this! I'm not an animal!" Her words screeched through me and I clench my jaw in response. Making her way up the stairs in thunderous steps, I stand my ground at the bottom, letting my hot words breathe out and up towards her.

"No, you are not but you have the power and deadly nature of one. That is what I am trying to help you with! Why can't you understand?"

"Oh, look at me! I'm the world's most stupid vampire who needs to be locked up because my stupid tiny brain can't understand anything!" Animating her arms to be dramatic and having the sarcasm spit from her words joined with a childish tone of voice is like nails on a chalkboard to me. I snap at her again, screaming at the top of my lungs, breathing the raging fire I can no longer control.

"You have sneaked out plenty of times before and look how that turned out! You came running back within minutes because you couldn't handle the public like you use to! You keep trying yet you know you are not ready! But fine, go! Just walk into the middle of the city like it is no problem.

You'll take the phrase 'paint the town red' to a whole new meaning and when that happens do not come crying to me!"

Hilary turns on her heels to bite back, her face flooding red. "I'll start with your blood then! Seems fitting for the monster to turn on its own master."

"I'm trying to make you less of a monster than me, you stupid girl!"

"Yeah well you didn't have to let me change into this! You could have let me die! I'd rather be dead!" The burning ember words scorch my heart. My anger fizzles out into ashes as I gaze at Hilary's shaking body at the top of the stairs.

"You know it wasn't my fault. I did not have the knowledge I do now. They never told me..." my burnt words catching in my throat but Hilary cut me off, her voice cracking like glass.

"I never wanted this to happen Amanda! What did we do wrong? Why are we meant to be like this?" Hot tears roll down her cheeks before burying her face in her hands, sobbing quietly and muffled, her animal persona vanishing as she sits herself on the top step. My heart feels like it has been rescued from the fire but is now drowning as I watch her little body shake. The sound of the rain becomes the only noise to be heard.

Walking up towards her and wrapping my arms around her, pulling her close to me I let her tears fall; stroking her head four times before breaking and doing it again. I hold back my own tears, stinging my eyes.

"You remind me of mother when you do that." Hilary's voice comes through, calmer than before.

"You were too young to remember her." I whisper.

"I know...but I like to imagine that's how she would have stroked my hair... I'm sorry for acting like a child."

"I'm sorry for calling you a silly girl... You aren't silly, you are frustrated like I am too. That is why I am trying to get answers... who turned me into... this. They destroyed our lives and so I will take theirs."

A moment of silence fell on us as the rain continued to pour down. I continue to stroke her hair; the rose and tulip scent strongly noticeable and I am sent back to our magical garden that was full of apple trees and flowers of every kind. Roses and tulips are Hilary's favourite flowers; as a baby, mother would cradle her by these flowers, pointing the colourful ones for Hilary to see. Again, my mind shuts the memory away.

"Do I still have training tomorrow with Laurence?" Her voice squeaks from my stomach and I can feel her smile slowly growing. The rain continues to hammer down so I suspect this will last all night.

"Of course, you do soldier. No slacking!" I bend down and wipe the tears from her eyes, smiling softly. She smiles back, knowing there was no point in being upset for long.

"But I've got a bad stomach ache." She backs away holding her stomach while groaning in pain dramatically. She pulls it off well. I laugh at her fake act of illness.

"You're a vampire, we don't get sick." I point out as I raise myself up, indicating towards the kitchen as I walk and she follows me; her feet on the stairs mimicking the patter of the rain.

"Well I'm a special vampire that gets sick." She jokes as we enter the kitchen. I flick on the lights for the room to welcome us. The cream cupboards against the stone-grey walls stands out with touches of raspberry in the characteristics of the décor such as pictures, cups and decorative items placed around the kitchen. It was Hilary's idea to add the raspberry colour and I grew to like it. The room opens up by the breakfast bar into a cream dining room which follows the colour scheme.

Hilary jumps onto the marble counter next to the fridge and kicks her legs out, scuffing the cupboard doors as always. I've surrendered in repainting as Hilary states the marks add character. Reaching into the fridge, I grab a bag of blood and pass it over.

"This ought to settle your stomach." I wink.

Holding the bag up, she sneers at it with a look of disgust. "Yay... old man blood. How I can't wait to sink my teeth into that!"

"Just have it will you? Or would you prefer the cat blood?"

Putting up her hand, she signals me to shut up. "No, no. It's fine." Quickly, and literally, sinking her teeth into the bag. She drains all the blood in a matter of seconds.

"Dessert?" I ask, throwing her another bag knowing she won't refuse. She takes her time with this one, having a few sips here and there. "There are a few bags left in here. It should last you until I go back to work."

"It's naughty to steal blood from the hospital, nurse." Hilary jokes, smirking at me while sipping on the red iron liquid.

Flashing a smile and a wink, I lean in and catch some of her hair between my fingers and twiddle it around. "What they don't know won't hurt them."

She smiles but only half-heartedly, her eyes cast themselves to the dark wooden floor, her swinging legs falling silent. "So, are you pleased with me that I managed to not kill the cat? Isn't that proof that I can control my hunger?"

Pushing the boat a little again, as she always does.

"You know the difference between the two is like a puddle to the sea... But it is a very good start." Leaning against the adjacent counter, I find myself admiring her. She looks so much like mother. Behind those crimson red eyes, I can still see the meadow green that matched mothers.

Hilary eyes the bag of half full blood... seeming lost in her thoughts. "I don't mean to rush things. I just want a normal life."

"I know Hilary. I do too... but this is the best life I can give you... For now. I know it's not much... but it's all I can give." Finding my arms wrapped around her in a close embrace, smelling the soft flowers once again, my words softly and lovingly come from deep within my heart.

Hilary brings out such a motherly side of me. I think to myself.

"For you, I'd give anything. My money, my possessions, even my very last breath if that's what was needed to make sure that you stay alive, safe and remain with the life that I have taught you. The life where you can escape the monster. Not a death where the monster consumes you." Stroking her hair again, I whisper softly. "You know I love you."

"Even after I go to the sky". She replies, nestled in my chest.

"Or across the seas without a goodbye."

"You only have to close your eyes."

"And I will be by your side". Our own personal phrase finishes from my lips and sealing it with a kiss to her head.

Hilary looks up at me from my chest; worry and sadness filling her eyes.

"Amanda... do you really think things will get better?"

I gaze back, whispering softly as my forehead meets hers. "What is my favourite Latin phrase?"

Hilary smiles as a tear falls down her cheek. "*Dum spiro spero.*"

"While I breathe, I hope." I translate, wiping the fallen tear from her cheek. "As long as I breathe, there will always be hope for us."

We settle back down on the sofa and continue to watch the program for a while. Soon enough I feel the heavy weight of sleep forcing my eyes to begin to fall. Looking to Hilary, she has already fallen asleep, the blood bag empty on her lap. Switching off the T.V and throwing the empty bag away, cradling Hilary in my arms as I take her up to her bedroom with Milly doll in her place on her lap.

The green and white walls welcome her back and the bed wraps itself around her with a 'missed-you' hug. A meadow of different flowers artistically painted flow across the wall beside her bed; saturated in all the colours imaginable. Her blush pink desk sits in the corner, next to her mountain of cuddly toys. As I sit and study her features, it's almost as if I am looking at a painting of mother. Same shape eyes and cheekbone. Her lips thin, perfectly shaped and her freckles she inherited from our father. People often stated I looked like a feminine version of my father. Hilary is most certainly the double of our mother. I kiss her goodnight and slip into my bedroom across the landing.

My room greets me with a sense of calmness with the deep teal walls promising to keep me safe. The large bookshelf stands stern taking up an entire wall; its mass overwhelmed with books, CDs and DVDs. A large oak wooden desk sits strategically in the corner.

As I walk in, removing the clothes from my body I scan the shelves for something to read for a while, some figures draw my interest in. Sitting on one of the shelves stands a theatre mask, a mermaid with a blue and green tail sitting on a big clam and a witch sitting on a pumpkin with a black cat. My fingers reach out to caress the items individually. They were gifts from Hilary when we were able to have our family day outings. The memories flow through my mind; the theatre, the Aberdovey beach and Halloween trick or treating. Each time she brings me a gift with a little note that always read 'Thank you.'

Exchanging clothes for pjs, I sink into bed and flick through the T.V channels instead, finally settling on CSI. But my mind swirls with memories that are trying to break free from their chains. I urge them back as remotely as possible. The programme quickly loses my interest. Slipping further down under the covers, I switch off the weary T.V and shut my eyes, allowing myself to drift into slumber; a surprising but happy discovery when I was first beginning my vampire years. Evidently the memories of my past life break out of their chains and attack, with the vampire's words echoing in my mind.

"You see yourself as a God. But you are no more different then I am. You are a monster like the rest of us. Like me, like them... Like your sister."

Chapter 3: Responsibilities

My small fingers glide across a piano, the melody drifting through the luxurious living room as I look up to see a woman gently dancing. A champagne Tudor dress with red silk embroidery woven through frames her body, hair like a waterfall of gold, smiling sweetly. Her eyes as green as the emeralds that she wore round her neck. My young innocent voice drifts out to her.

"How was that Mother?" My voice is that of a child.

Her hand cups my face gently and lovingly. "It was perfect dear."

A hand that feels too big for my shoulder sits itself there as I look to see father, kneeling down to my level holding an open book, his finger guiding my eyes across the page, his lips moving in time with the words written. His mud brown hair combed back neatly as his warm blue eyes shine with pride. His lips find my cheek, kissing it softly as he hoists me up, cradled by his arms. My young arms wrap around his neck in security as I hear him speak. "You are my perfect little girl."

My whole world shifts into darkness as I suddenly find myself now older, standing alone in our family study. As quick as turning on a switch, the room catches fire. The flames lick the walls like serpent tongues and I cry out for my parents. My eyes dart around the room for an escape.

Concealed within the flames is a man with no face; darkness hiding his features. Through the flames I spot a bassinet just behind him and I fear for Hilary. As I try to step forward to reach her the flames prevent me; lashing out at my feet like whips. The man slowly turns to the bassinet and my heart jumps into my throat.

"No!" I cry out, but the fire is too great. It draws closer to me, threatening to consume me.

My eyes tear open, quickly adjusting to the dark room, my heart pounding like a drum is the first thing I hear. Propping myself up on my elbow, a bead of sweat drips down my forehead, my mind feeling like it is been inside an open fire.

Turning my head to see the clock quietly ticking away, showing the time of day to be 3am. I decide it's pointless trying to get some more sleep. My body twitching with being on high alert from the nightmare, I inhale a large breath to try and stop my jumping nerves.

Where did that come from? I wonder. Jumping out of bed, my mind is still trying to reinforce the nightmare as I dress into a red wool jumper, jeans and black boots. My hair looks more like a haystack from the tossing and turning, my fringe flicking up in different direction. Scratching a hairbrush through it, tidying up the blonde mess as best I can, leaving it to fall down my back as I head downstairs to the kitchen, trying to leave the nightmare behind me.

Switching the light on, the room awakes from its darkened sleep. A stifling yawn breaks free as I rub the sleep from my eyes. The sight of French doors in the dining room welcomes me to a show of snow in the garden; big balls of powder and snowflakes re-surfacing the ground.

"Beautiful morning isn't it?" Laurence states as he suddenly stands silently beside me.

"When we have fresh snow like this, it's inevitable." I smile, not looking away from the white scenery.

"Shall I do the honour of a pot of tea so we can talk about why you are up at this time?" Laurence heads to the kettle not needing my reply; it was a rhetorical question. In a blur of motion, a flash of green shoots across the room with an excited voice bouncing off the walls.

"IT'S SNOWING! GUYS! LOOK! IT'S SNOWING!" Hilary squeals in giddy excitement, pressing her face against the glass doors, looking out into the garden. She didn't even change out of her PJs.

"No second guesses as to why she's up." I laugh lightly.

"They say three is company anyway." Laurence chuckles as I head to the refrigerator and pour myself a small glass of orange juice. Taking a seat at the breakfast bar, I sip the sharp sweet juice, watching Hilary gaze in innocent awe at the falling white snow.

Laurence prepares the tea; his burgundy dressing gown swaying as his body jiggles around the kitchen, deeply humming a little tune as he does so. His silver hair pointing in all directions looks worse than my own did and I can't help but try and hide my amusement. Hilary hears me quietly laughing and skips over. She notices too and starts giggling.

“Did you look at yourself in the mirror this morning?” I ask him humorously.

“I awoke as usual and heard you moving around, so I admit I did not. Why do you ask?”

“Cause you look like you’ve been dragged through a hedge.” I chuckle as Laurence temporarily abandons the tea, blindly investigating his misshapen hair.

“You look like that mad scientist who made Frankenstein.” Hilary giggles. “Oh, I know!” Racing out of the room and returning in seconds, with a comb; wooden carved with lilac daisies delicately painted on. She holds the item out with a Cheshire cat smile.

“Would you like us to groom you this morning like a doll?” I mockingly ask as Hilary mischievously giggles.

Laurence smiles as he finishes making the tea and placing the tray down on the breakfast bar. He sits in the chair between myself and Hilary.

“I will allow you to do so on one condition.” He announces with a loud voice.

“What’s that?” I question suspiciously.

“That you make me look as pretty as Hilary.” He reveals, trying to batt his eyelashes like a woman. Before I can respond with a quick remark, Hilary beats me to the punch.

“Laurence we are *vampires* not magicians!” Rolling her eyes dramatically as I snigger at his slightly offended reaction. Laurence happily sits still as myself and Hilary make a start on fixing his hair, taking a drink of his tea as I brush the comb rhythmically, while Hilary places ribbons or hair clips in his hair she secretly stashed in her PJ pockets.

“I feel like a cat being groomed.” He announces with a little too much content in his voice and we laugh at his comment.

“You are too wise to be a cat Laurence... You are more like a silver fox.”

“I like that better! It makes me sound more charming and mysterious.”

“Whatever you say Mr Fox.” Hilary lightly mocks as I work the comb through his long silver (and surprisingly thick) hair.

Laurence takes a slow sip of tea, deeply sighing in content. "You know Amanda... you and I must be the only vampires who still enjoy the taste of food and drink." Chuckling to himself as I note he is using his favourite teapot; burnt orange with elephants carved delicately into the side. Collecting tea pots was always a little hobby of his.

"I miss cherries. But that's it. I don't really miss anything else." Hilary pipes up as she clips a black glittery hair clip into place. "Why do you guys still eat human food?" She questions with a wonder fuelled voice.

"It gives me a sense of normality." Smiling a half smile as I pause to take a sip of the hot liquid.

"I just enjoy the taste." Laurence lifts his cup up to toast, smiling a huge smile. "To appreciating the little things in life."

I touch my cup with his. "To being awake at 3am." Adding on sluggishly as we both take a deep sip of the delicate liquid while Hilary continues her work. Placing my cup back down, I work on the last section of his hair silently, brushing it into place.

"Ta-da! What do you think?" Hilary giggles, holding a mirror up to Laurence as she beams with hope of positive news. Laurence tries not to laugh at the reflection before him. His hair still pointing in different directions except sleeker with more sparkles and ribbons.

"I look so pretty!" He chokes up jokingly as Hilary smiles with joy. "I look wonderful! Thank you so much my little hair stylist!" Picking Hilary up and swinging her about, she laughs loudly as they almost dance about the kitchen, twirling into the dining room. Hilary catches sight of the snow again and calls out to me.

"Can we go into the garden and have a snow ball fight? Please! Pretty please!" She begs as Laurence puts her down.

"I have work soon but I promise when I come back, we will."

"Can I go out into the garden now and build a snowman?"

"As long as you don't sing the song then yes." I begrudgingly state as Hilary darts towards the door. "Put your coat on!" I yell, stopping her in her tracks; her mind contemplating.

"But I thought we can't get sick so why can't I go out in my PJs?"

“Because I said so... and you still feel the cold regardless.”

Hilary flashes me a sheepish grin before dashing off in a blur. She returns in a rose red hooded coat and her glittery rainbow coloured boots.

“Scarf and hat?” I question in a motherly tone of voice.

“I don’t have it! Come on I want to go outside!” Stamping her feet and puffing out her cheeks as she protests.

“Oh well funnily enough-” Racing out to the coat cupboard in the reception and back within a couple seconds, I hold up the winter wear as I approach her. “I do.” Winking as I wrap the emerald green scarf around her neck and pulling the black sparkly hat over her head. Giving a kiss on the nose, my hand finds the handle of the door.

“Go on.” Flashing a smile at her as I open the door. Without a second thought she bursts through, already using her vampire strength to gather huge amounts of snow. I smile for a moment as I watch her, before returning to my chair.

“Now that it’s just the adults in the room...shall we talk about why you are up earlier than usual?” Laurence questions, his fox-like eyes studying as he takes his place in the chair next to me, unbothered by his new look to fix it. I let out a deep sigh paired with a smile.

“When I saw you were using your favourite tea pot, I knew we were going to have one of your deep spiritual talks.”

“I’ve been living with you for too long.” He laughs, his hand tapping the tea pot.

“It is normal for us to sleep for short periods.” I answer, purposely avoiding the word I detest. “Just a bad dream,” I mumble. “It was nothing.”

“Are you sure you don’t want to talk about it? Opening up allows us to let go of the pain.”

“But I am not holding in any pain. I’m fine.” I smile weakly. Taking a mouthful of tea to empty my cup, abandoning it as my hand reaches over the counter, grabbing a handful of red grapes from the fruit bowl. I pop them in my mouth one by one. Laurence pours me another cup silently, returning to his own to top it up with the hot brew.

"You have always been holding on to pain. Even when I first saw you, I could tell. You walked into the Royal Order's chambers carrying the weight of your world on your shoulders. For the short time you were with us, I saw something in you. I saw someone who not only had a great deal of pain but it did not tarnish your sense of justice and humility. You hated fighting. You hated using your powers; one in particular. You hated your hunger for blood. You hated killing innocent vampires or people when Edward commanded you to. Despite all this, you showed inner strength."

Swallowing a grape, I do not meet Laurence's eyes as the memories creep up into my head.

"I had no choice. With your brother it was either kill or be killed. I quickly learnt to pretend."

Laurence's eyes look up to mine in a way that seems to question my statement. "Forgive me Miss Field but do you truly believe you are still pretending?"

My face screws up as I reply; my fists balling up as my dragon stirs within.

"I don't enjoy killing innocent people. I kill vampires."

Stroking his beard, Laurence looks away with a stone face. "My brother has a very twisted idea of how vampires should be. To him, not everyone who is made into one deserves the title. If a vampire can't fight well, or kill without a second thought, or even have a monstrous nature then they are not deemed an original vampire. They are a mockery of the name." His disapproving voice seeps with the sadness he clearly feels.

"That's why he wanted me to stay. The day before I escaped, Edward told me I must have been destined. I excelled in my powers. Controlled my skill to kill unsuspiciously. I proved I was smart. He wanted me to join permanently."

Nodding his head, he takes another sip of tea before answering. "But you left. You left because of your sister."

My eyes cast themselves out to Hilary building her second snowman, placing stones and twigs on the shapely blank canvas.

"I thought he had taught me everything I needed. I feared if I didn't leave soon, he would force me to stay or have me killed."

"He certainly would have." Laurence states with a matter of fact tone.

"Since then they have tried and failed to kill me." I chuckle to myself, grabbing more grapes from the bushel. "You left too you know. Yet you aren't on his hit list."

"My brother may have his faults but family was always important to him... When it comes to achieving his goals, he doesn't give up. He may not think clearly at times but he is not one to back down and surrender defeat."

"Neither am I," I add as the cup finds my lips.

We sit in silence for a while, the clock clicking its tongue as the seconds pass and the humming of the fridge quietly sounds. Swivelling round, I scan the room, noticing the raspberry splashback behind the cooker could do with being repainted.

"Stop trying to find a distraction to our conversation," Laurence states as I turn in my chair back to him stubbornly. "The past can be a wonderful teacher. However, we must not forget to focus on the present. So...what is your plan with this vampire who has been sent to kill you? Any thoughts on that?"

Rolling a grape between my fingers, I lazily inspect it. "The same plan as always. Any vampire who tries to kill me, I'll kill them first."

Laurence's fingers run along his beard, looking not at all convinced. "What about Hilary's safety?"

Glaring at him with daggers, clashing against his words as I weigh in on his comment. "Hilary is my number one priority. I have taken down hundreds of vampires before and I will do it again."

His mouth presses into a thin line. "Be careful Amanda. You are over confident. You shouldn't underestimate the Royal Order-"

I scoff, cutting him off; "The Royal Order has wanted me dead for centuries. If you haven't noticed, as time passed, they found it harder and harder to get vampires to come after me. Your brother and his disciples will not chase me down because they are too...how did he put it?" Tapping a finger on my chin repeatedly for a few seconds. "Oh, that's right. Valuable."

Laurence retreats to his cup, watching the steam rise. His words are slow and steady. "You detest the fact you are a vampire yet you have built up a reputation of being untouchable. Tread carefully. I would hate to see you lose the ones you love for the sake of your stubbornness."

"I have three abilities." Holding up my fingers, I count them off. "Paralysis, sleep and fire. No vampire has been able to kill me because of this. I have been able to control my powers and I have been fighting for mine and Hilary's life since the 1500s. What you call 'reputation' I call survival."

Laurence's hand hugs mine, his other hand nestles on my shoulder. "Survival doesn't mean revenge! You have been unable to let go of your past and this has caused dangerous situations."

"All of which I have handled," I answer in a raised voice.

Laurence shakes his head in concern speaking again in a stern and slow manner. "You are confident but arrogant. All I ask is that you stop and think about what you are doing here."

As I feel a fire starting in my stomach, I imitate his slow and steady tone. "Everything I do...I do to protect the ones I love." Standing up, I throw the hot tea to the back of my throat, slamming the cup down, cracking it in the process. Glancing at the clock on the wall, it shows it is just turning 4am.

Good, the home won't be waking up their residents for some time and this anger is making me hungry.

Making my way out of the kitchen and towards the front door I call to Laurence over my shoulder.

"Do some training with Hilary today." My feet stop for a moment. A rope of guilt tugging at my heart to not leave like this. I call out again, calmer, feeling Laurence's presence behind me. "I want to take us all out on a family trip soon. I think we need it...I will see you and Hilary when I return from work." Grabbing my beige wrap coat and quickly pulling it on, I open the door to the cold air and lock it behind me securely.

The Pine Care Home is just a ten-minute drive from my house and it is my usual feeding ground. Pulling up my car down the road, I jump out, making my way to the nursing home. The building is pretty typical; large and worn in filled with rooms and nurses, carers and other staff members running about taking care of everyone's needs and demands. The building looks repainted and revived; the pale green windows standing out against the fresh white walls, the broken roof tiles replaced and some fake plants have been assigned along the front to make it seem 'homely'. However, it is poorly guarded with a simple alarm system that is easy to avoid setting off. It is designed for humans to break in, not anything else. Coded doors are also in place to stop residents making a dash for it, but there is no need for me to use the door.

Scanning the building, I see a window left open on the top floor.

They probably thought no one could get up there to break in, but then again it is winter. Do they want their residents to die from hypothermia?

Bending my knees to give me some power, I catapult up and slip inside through the break-in invitation. My feet landing on the carpet floor, but not a sound is made. I stay still and listen, making sure that no one will interrupt on my feeding. Hearing a nurse walking on the ground floor, I wait to see if they would come on to the top floor or go into the staff room that I know is located in the middle of the building. The person turns to the staff room, hearing the door creek open and close so I begin to walk down the red carpet hallway; the simple paintings of flowers in fields, sunset at a beach and forests paths hang on the pale cream walls and a lonely table and vase with no flowers stands alone and seemingly out of place.

It is rare times like this when I think about being immortal; remaining 26 forever. I won't ever grow old and stay in a dull place like this, to sit in a chair all day watching endless T.V, listening to nonsense chatter and then to be medicated to sleep all night by staff. This will never be my life. Forever I will be maintaining my independence and seeing how the world evolves like it has through the decades; how society changes, new laws coming into place, technology, fashion and our way of life. I would trade it all in a heartbeat to reclaim my humanity.

The snores of the elderly can be heard throughout the home. Walking past the rooms reading their names clearly marked on their bedroom doors.

Ben Neil. Hilda Turner. Lucy Muller. Robert Hill.

The elderly here have nothing to live for, dying of illnesses or diseases, being neglected by staff and family members. It's easier for me to take their blood to satisfy my hunger rather than an innocent person.

Stopping outside a door, the scent of an ill, dying body fill my nostrils. The scent is very strong; an earthy musk mixed with a sweet pear drop smell. From life experience due to my job and my way of life, I know the pear drop scent comes from the dying individual's breath, as an indication to their kidney's shutting down.

This one will do.

Looking at the name tag on the door, the person is *Cathy Jules.* I slip into the room unheard and unnoticed. The elderly woman, fragile and thin, is lying in her bed, tossing slightly in her sleep. Her hair up in pink and lilac hair curls, her bronze glasses placed on the bedside table. The curtains flow in the cold chill wind from a window that has been left open.

Clearly the care from this home is not improving. Are they not going through enough without the coldness threatening to take them to death's door in the night?

Feeling sorry for the shaking woman, I close the window and the sound of it shutting causes Cathy to stir but she doesn't wake, mumbling in her sleep about someone named George. My eye catches a chart that has been left by one of the staff on the little desk by the bed. Picking it up, I read through the medical notes, picking up on the main points.

Cathy is aged 85. Mesothelioma Cancer. Palliative care needed. Arthritis and signs of Alzheimer's. Bed bound. Vomited three times today. Eaten only quarter of lunch. Refused all other food and fluid.

Placing the chart back, next to black and white pictures sitting on the desk in shiny frames of different colours and sizes. Children, babies and adults smiling and happily hugging each other or looking up at the camera while being caught doing something like dancing to some forgotten music or having a friendly fight. A picture of a young Cathy sat on a piano, smiling with glee as she plays a piece of music. She seems to have had a good life. A young musical woman, who fell in love, married and had children who then became a grandmother. Now she's in a home where the staff only see her as an empty, fragile old vase whose personality and needs have withered away like the dying of flowers, wrinkled and unappealing to look at. Maybe one or two staff members would treat her right but this home's reputation was falling.

Placing one of the pictures back down, I walk over to Cathy, seeing her mumble in her sleep. Her wedding ring shines in the dim light and so I figure George must have been her husband. In her hand, a teddy bear with a golden ribbon wrapped around its neck is being held onto tightly. She reminds me of a child; dependant on others, having simple things to make her feel safe and comforted when she feels nervous or unsafe.

Slowly, I concentrate and channel my energy, a purple aura illuminating from my hand and camouflaging my eyes. Touching her forehead gently, the aura spreads across her like a purple fog. Once it takes effect, I wait silently watching as she slowly stops mumbling and stirring, slipping into a deep coma. I didn't want her to feel anything. No pain, no suffering. My nocturnal energy is strong enough to make people feel sleepy and to put them into comas.

Lowing myself to her, I sink my fangs into her neck and drain her blood. It is bitter with a hint of tobacco and the dry taste of chemicals from paracetamol and sleeping tablets. After feeding, I lick the wound on her neck.

A vampire's saliva has been evolved to not only drip venom but also to heal bite wounds. It is a little method that stops the belief of vampires arising within the human society. If every dead person had two puncture holes in their neck, people would get suspicious. The wound heals up and I move back, wiping the blood off my mouth.

The elderly are easier targets for vampires as most people don't question their deaths, especially if they have terminal illnesses. Vampires should always leave a little bit blood in the body for there to be no suspicion of any kind. The body cannot be drained of blood, it has to look as natural as possible. But some don't and when this happens it causes a problem. If the body is found it will be reported on the news and so panic and suspicion will rise. There have been cases where it has happened too often and the vampire causing it has been hunted down by the Royal Order and killed on sight, on the grounds of violating concealment of vampires. Their way of killing is not a pretty sight.

Leaving the room quietly, I search for another elderly who didn't have long left. Finding a man who suffered a stroke and had a bad heart, I feed from him too. Another resident who also has cancer is fed from. Her last breath whispering into the night as I leave the room quietly.

The door has only just closed as the sound of feet walking to the door behind me catches my attention; light weight feet and slow moving, the sound of fabric brushing their skin as the door opens slowly. An elderly woman stands before me, in a mint green dressing gown, the fabric as thin as paper. Her vacant hazel brown eyes stare at me, almost looking past me for a moment. Her brain has lost the battle of capacity; memories lost and wandering, her mind slipping, reality losing its grasp.

"Who are you?" Her deeply lined face sinks in more as she speaks, her lips dry and rough. A large bruise on her arm indicates she must have fell not long ago.

Smiling gently at her, I whisper. "Just visiting."

A memory comes back to her mind, she smiles widely. "Are you my granddaughter? Poppy?" Her eyes fill with happiness, as if she has seen Poppy for the first time. Walking forward, her hand reaching out shakily to touch my face but doesn't quite make it. My heart jumps out for her. I can't help it. Taking a step forward to allow her hand to touch my face, as it does, she fills up with such love and joy I can't help but smile widely.

"Oh, Poppy where have you been? I missed you," she cries quietly as she hugs me; her arms carefully wrap around my figure. The name on the door is Dorothy and I knew I couldn't leave Dorothy now. Pulling away I smile, leading into the bedroom and closing the door behind us. We sit on the bed and talk.

She tells me, through the haze of the Alzheimer fog, of Poppy and her memories as a shop assistant, a family orientated woman and wife. At times she stops and stares at me or the ground, losing track of her thoughts. Then the Poppy motion came flooding in again, and I allow her to go on.

Other times her memories get mixed up and it doesn't make sense. Smiling and holding her hand, listening and asking questions was all Dorothy needed. She made me laugh with some funny stories, or something silly as a reply to a question. She talks about her husband as if he is still alive and then a few minutes later became consumed with grief when her memory of his funeral pass through her mind.

After thirty minutes, I knew I had to leave. Giving Dorothy a hug and a kiss on the cheek, I smile and stand up.

"I've got to go, but I will see you tomorrow." I state as Dorothy smiles and stays sat on her bed as I exit through the bedroom window. There is a small garage by the side of the building so I quietly land on it. I hear her door open and a nurse walking in.

"Dorothy what are you doing awake at this time in the morning?" His concerned voice whispers.

"I've just seen Poppy; she will be back soon."

As I leave, I hear the nurse sadly say "Poppy died twenty years ago when she was nineteen. A car accident. Remember Dorothy?"

As if she would want to remember something like that... and the grief starts over again.

Driving to the hospital, I switch my brain back to normality, getting myself ready for the day ahead. The hustle and bustle of a busy city within a ward. It's like New York without the flashing lights and attractions ... just demanding patients, stressed out staff and the hard sounds of the bells shrieking in your ears. The morning has been very busy as usual, doing the drug round, helping the HCA's with the patients to give personal care and needing to give four IVs of antibiotics for chest infections and infected injuries. To top it off another patient is being admitted into my bay as I am the only one who has an empty bed.

"It's IV day today I think." I mumble to myself as I stand in the treatment room checking the patient's NHS number and details in order to give him pain relief with Holly, a nurse whose chirpy nature reminds me of a bird. Her long cherry red hair tied in a bun clashing against her navy-blue uniform. The sound of the AC humming quietly as we talk.

"Could be worse, you know... could be D&V day! No one wants that." Her voice chirps as she checks her own drugs simultaneously.

"Oh God no! If we get a case of D&V now, I will blame you for jinxing us!" I exclaim in horror as Holly laughs, holding up her fingers in a cross position, as if warding off the jinx.

"Oh, let me tell you about my date I went on last night... Talk about D&V!" Holly laughs with embarrassment and now it's my turn to hold up the cross.

"Please tell me it wasn't you! I don't want to end up in the toilet all day!" Grabbing a disinfectant wipe with a mischievous grin, I quickly wipe it over the surface that she has touched in a humorous state of panic.

"No, no not me. My date! He turned up white as a sheet and clammy. We never even made it to the restaurant... we were both embarrassed... It was ... oh man... Just don't. If I wanted to look after someone I may as well have come to work".

Grabbing another wipe, I playfully start wiping her arm and uniform to decontaminate her. She jumps back, laughing and playfully shoving me away.

"Oi cut it out! I said it wasn't me!"

"I cannot take the risk. Infection control Holly! Infection control!" I laugh mockingly, continuing my decontamination. The treatment room door swings open and Matron Bridge looms in the doorway, her piercing eyes stare at us with shock at our amusement.

"Uh ladies-" her dry monotone voice interrupts "-less of that please. I can hear you laughing from outside."

"We were just having a bit of fun." Holly squeaks from under her breath; her bubbly persona quickly withdrawn back into her shell as it does whenever Matron appears.

"This is a hospital girls. Professional at all times, remember." As she speaks, she shakes her head, sticking her nose in the air so high you could count her nostril hair.

Deciding to have a little fun, I reply back. "We are aware Matron. However, I couldn't help but notice in the office you have put up a poster declaring your retirement party." Matching her monotone voice, smiling sarcastically. Naively unaware of my point, she smiles widely, exposing her cigarette stained teeth.

"Oh, you saw it? Will you be attending Amanda? Holly?"

"No unfortunately not. But that is not very professional is it? A party is a personal affair. It has nothing to do with work." Raising my eyebrow to her as the corner of my mouth inches up into a smug smirk.

Matron straightens her posture to try and look more threatening however she refuses to meet my gaze. Knowing she has lost; she tries to keep the high ground the only way she knows how to; using her high position to outrank everything that challenges her.

"My poster is quietly sat in the office and isn't drawing any attention unlike you two with your squealing... and you, Holly, with your hair!" Her bony finger stabs the air. "I've told you time and time again. It's too bright! Dye it a different colour or tone it down."

"You're right. Your poster is not drawing *any* attention," I counter smugly.

Her face begins to burn with embarrassment. Scoffing begrudgingly, she waves her hand to dismiss my words like flies around her ear. "Just be quiet next time ladies." She leaves the room allowing the heavy door to slam behind her.

"Her retirement can't come quick enough." Holly growls, grabbing the sharps box and some gauze from the cupboard behind her.

“She is just grumpy cause no one likes her.” Chuckling to myself as I give Holly a sympathetic smile.

“Well with that bitch ruining our mood, I’ll get back to work. Andy wants his cannular out, well demanding more like! He’s such a vile man! You know he hit me the other day because I was putting a catheter in due to retention. Called me whore! The bloody cheek of him! I told him I wasn’t doing this for the pleasure of it.”

Giving a sly smile, I turn to her and wave my hand in an overdramatise manor.

“Oh, I know... You are only a whore on the weekends Holly - everyone knows that!” I laugh as Holly gives me her ‘innocent’ look, shrugging her shoulders and laughing with me.

“*Ssshhhh* If we laugh too much Matron will appear again and suck the fun out of our souls!”

Holly laughs again at my statement, a tear escaping from her eye. “Stop making me laugh! Let’s change the subject... speaking of whore - Amanda how has your dating life been? Got any yet?” Her smile is one of mischief and adult humour.

“I keep telling you I’m not interested.” Finishing up my checklist, I pick up my equipment and head for the door to avoid the conversation, but Holly blocks me in.

“Yeah I know. You have your sister and you’re busy all the time with work but come on girl, you are still human.”

If only that was true.

“I’m just not interested in dating.” I reply, trying to shrug it off.

“You haven’t met the right guy yet. What about Dr Bale? I know he has a thing for you.” She winks at me with mischief and I just roll my eyes.

“Not my type.”

“Dr Goodwin?”

“Too old.”

“Dr Stew?”

"He looks like a child... and acts like one."

"Oh, oh! What about Dr Morgan?" Chirping and waving her hands like a bird trying to take off.

"Stop trying to set me up with everyone in this hospital - you'll give me a reputation."

"To match my own." She smiles slyly, nudging me in the ribs as she allows me to leave the room. The ward's chaotic atmosphere greets us. Holly grabs my elbow to prevent my escape once again.

"You spend all your time looking after your sister and working here. It's not healthy. Do you even have a hobby?"

"I go jogging, I read, I shop for clothes. It's all I really have time for."

Not necessarily a lie. I jog after vampires. I read their expressions as they die. I shop for clothes with no blood stains.

"Not even a cup of coffee with a handsome man?" Holly smiles wickedly as I ignore her remark.

"Don't you have some work to do Holly?"

"Ok, ok I'm going. Just think about it will ya?"

"Yeah, yeah ok." Dismissing her as she walks off, leaving me to get on with my busy day as I push away her remarks for dating.

Arriving home after stealing some blood from storage, my dragging feet enter the house to signs of Hilary keeping herself busy clear as can be; clean floors, TV left on and the ocean breeze air fragrance drifting above my head. Heading into the kitchen I find Hilary sitting on the dining room table staring out the kitchen window in her plum t-shirt with a white star on the front and olive-green trousers.

"Midnight snack is here! Well 9pm really." I call to her, throwing one bag onto the counter as I place the others in the fridge. Hilary doesn't even look at me, her gaze focused on the snow now falling from the sky.

A note from Laurence on the kitchen counter states that Hilary did well in her training and he has gone out to hunt.

"Laurence went out to hunt." She announces as her flexes her feet forward and backwards; a sign of agitation.

"Yes, I can see that... What are you nervous about?" I ask, walking over to her.

Shrugging her shoulders, Hilary keeps her face away, her hair acting like a cover.

"Laurence is my only friend. We could do with some friends." When Hilary says my name, I know she is being serious and I note the loneliness in her voice. Walking closer, my arms become a blanket, wrapping themselves securely.

"You understand why we have to do this. Remember when you lost control-"

"I won't lose control this time. I promise."

"You said that before... both times."

Hilary falls silent to my answer.

I take a deep sigh before speaking. "But... I know I can't keep you locked up in here forever. You need to try again at some point. So, here is what I propose-" Looking into her eyes there is a gleaming of hope shining through. "- We will go out tomorrow for the day. We'll go to the museum. You drink as much blood as you can, to the point you can't stomach it ok? We will stay out for as long as possible. The *second* you feel like you are losing control you tell us and we leave."

Her arms grasp my waist before I even finish speaking.

"I promise! I promise I will do it! Every day since that train incident I've practised and I know I can do it! Thank you! Thank you!"

Happiness washes over me as her squeals of laughter fill the house, pure joy and excitement that the house has been deaf to for some time.

"You have to promise me you will tell me or Laurence when it becomes too much. We don't want another relapse." My voice goes hollow at the word relapse as I know she regrets every day what happened.

Her laughter dies down, lowering her head in shame, she stares at the floor for a second before whispering under her breath.

"If I could give all those lives back I would."

Holding her close, I stroke her hair, the floral scent floats off her. "I won't let it happen again. *Dum spiro spero.*" I place a kiss on her head before nudging her.

"Now, I thought we were going to build snowmen? Race me outside?"

Hilary beams with excitement as she races off to get her coat and boots.

Sighing loudly, I lean against the counter and think about my next plan of action.

The Royal Order has sent someone after me. But I still don't have an answer to what happened to mom and dad. What if the person responsible for their murder is dead? What if the vampire who turned me was killed by the Royal Order? There is no way to deny that may be the case. But that churning in my gut tells me otherwise. None of it adds up. I cannot think of a single person who would want to harm me... before I became like this, before I met the Royal Order our family had no enemies.

Hilary runs through the kitchen, torpedoing my black quilted jacket at me. "Hey!" I yell as I shrug it on and chase after her. We run out into the snow but immediately start having a snowball fight. I land a few hits before she gets me back. She tackles me into cold white snow as it gets into our hair and inside our coats.

"Cold! Cold! Cold!" She yells in glee, as I ignore the iciness, spreading my arms and legs to start making snow angels. Hilary starts gathering snow to build a snowman. "Come on! Let's see who can make the better one!" She challenges me with a starry twinkle in her eyes.

After a few minutes we stand back and admire our creations. Hilary's snowman was certainly better than mine; it stood up straight for one thing and its arm hadn't fallen off.

"Looks like mine is better than yours!" She smiles with pride. I kiss her on her cheek, feeling the snowflakes stuck to her skin.

"It most certainly is."

The sound of the doors bursting open cracks in the air and I jolt at the sound, spinning round to see Laurence, hunched over in the doorway, his eyes wide with fear, dark stains visible on his slightly torn clothes.

"What happened?" Racing up to him, I guide him inside to rest as Hilary grabs him a wet cloth to wipe some of the dried blood off his cheek.

"I was attacked... by a ... by a Royal Order member. He mistook me for a ... a human regarding my old age. My healing ability is slower than most. I managed... managed to get away." Huffing and puffing his words as his hand cradles his side where the pain sits.

"Where were you attacked?" Questioning him, already planning an attack but Laurence is three steps ahead of me.

"You will not go after him." His eyes stare at me with determination as he wipes the blood clean.

"He attacked you."

"No, you think he will have an answer to your past but he won't!" His voice booms with anger, his fist coming down hard on the table, causing him to jolt in pain. "You need to give up this pursuit before something bad happens to you or to Hilary!"

Ignoring his words, my only focus being on this Royal Order vampire, I swiftly walk past him, heading for the front door.

"I'm going after him. I'll be back soon. Stay here." I call out, slamming the front door behind me.

Chapter 4: Acquaintance

The streets are the same as they always have been with the night life on its high wave. My feet pace the streets, searching for the smell of Laurence's blood which will still be fresh from his recent attack. The snow crunches under my boots as I take short cuts and alleyways; places I know Laurence takes care in not being seen and is a good chance of finding homeless people who are a source of blood. Getting deeper into the city of London, the drunken teens and partyers make their way out onto the streets as well as the substance abusers trying to sell whatever they can.

Doing my best to avoid them, I take another short cut, the sound of the snow crunching under me echoes down the narrow street. My eyes catch on to a red stain in the snow. Getting closer I can smell that it belongs to Laurence.

Ok, time to follow the blood trail.

Spotting another blood stain heading into an even narrower street, I follow eagerly, keeping my wits about me. The blood stains start to get larger as I go deeper within the trail. The laughter and energy of the London night begins to fade as I seem to be walking into the belly of city. Finally, I stop, with a large amount of Laurence's blood staining the snow in a little alley way. The snow is clearly disturbed, some blood stains the brick wall which doesn't belong to Laurence and a couple of bottles of beer smashed up shine in the moonlight. The scent of dead bodies engulfs my nostrils harshly; they are new, only a couple of hours old.

Looking further down the way, there is an opening where an old building stands; clearly deserted and bordered up. The sound of a car approaching grabs my attention and I crouch down, moving closer to the end of the alleyway staying out of sight. A black Land Rover pulls up, two big burley men jump out; their vampire scent potent. One vampire opens the door to the abandoned building as the other goes to the boot of the car. From the driver's side emerges another vampire; a grin on his face and a cigarette in his hand. His shaven head reveals a little scar in the shape of an untamed 'L'.

My heart accelerates. My eyes widen.

That's Luke! He's one of Edward's executioners.

The memory replays itself; when I was with the Royal Order, I noticed how him and Edward were close. Luke was always the one to be ordered to kill the vampires Edward deemed too weak. But Luke never showed mercy. Instead he would make a show out of it, slowly torturing his victims.

The other vampire opens the car boot door and drags out two people; a woman and a man appearing to be about in their mid-30s. Dragging the victims into the warehouse, they lock the door behind them and I jump up onto the roof of the warehouse, careful not to alert my presence.

The sound of my boots on the roof is quiet, muffled by the thin snow. The sound of the Luke's laughter and the woman's shrieking crying can be heard. A broken window on the top floor is my only silent way in. Slipping through it, I can hear the banter of the vampires as I scan for a way into the ground floor. The second floor is completely vast and almost vacant, cobwebs hanging low, dust covering every inch of space. A couple of wooden chairs left behind stood weak, looking as if it is about to collapse at any minute. It's clear this building was under construction but was unable to complete it. An explosive hole in the centre provides me a view into the warehouse below. Quietly moving closer, grateful I am at an angle where I can see everything; I wait for my moment to crash the party.

At the back of the room are the corpses of two victims; both female. Their eyes colourless, lifeless and their mouth hang open; still portraying their pain and fear. The two that are alive are being dragged like rag dolls, fighting against the strength of the vampire as they are forced inside the warehouse. Luke follows behind, smiling a devil's smile and a killer's lust shining in his eyes.

I have to laugh slightly; he hasn't changed one bit. He is clearly still the psycho that I remember. His gleaming eyes dance with excitement as his muscles flex under his deep wine-red shirt; preparing themselves for the 'enjoyment' to come. Twirling the cigarette between his bony fingers, Luke takes his place leaning against a wooden table, theatrically positioned in the centre with the large damaged window framing him from the background and allowing the moonlight to dramatically shine in.

"Now, stay there." Vampire one orders, his big, steroid arms flexing as he throws them on to the concrete floor. The woman is hysterical; sobbing and shaking on the floor with her brunette hair shrouding her face from the childhood nightmare, too afraid to move or beg for her life. She screams a blood curdling noise as she spots the corpses and the red-haired man turns to see the lifeless bodies, but he doesn't make a sound.

He's a fighter. I note.

He stands up and searches for something as a weapon to protect himself and cause damage if needs be, not being aided by the poor lighting from the worn out, artificial buzzing ceiling lights.

Either he doesn't know what they are yet or he is just being desperate to fight regardless. I think to myself trying to figure the man out.

The two vampires laugh brazenly, amused by the man's fighting nature as he picks up a pipe that lies by some abandoned crates.

"I am a policeman and you, my friends, are in serious trouble." His voice trembles with fear but despite this, puts himself as protection in front of the woman. His tall and thin stature isn't much of a barrier but the woman who has now curled up into the foetal position in shock with her green dress stopping at her grazed knees. She is in no state to fight let alone protect herself.

"Oh, trying to ruin my fun, are you?" Luke speaks for the first time, puffing on the cigarette watching them both with a glint in his eyes.

"What the fuck do you want?" The man shouts, his voice echoing in the vast warehouse.

Leaning slowly forward, Luke flashes his white fangs at the man. "I want your blood." He states clearly, pointing to the red stains on the man's elbow, clear on his white shirt. Luke laughs harshly as what he wants drains from the supposed policeman's face.

His sturdy legs now shake as his voice indecisively wavers between pitches. "Are you a killer? Like... Like cut me up into little tiny pieces... Put my head on a spike... killer?"

He can't be a policeman. He's too afraid. It must be a cover.

"No, I'm a vampire." He laughs again, as if it was a normal statement.

The man shows signs of trying to make sense of the situation and the mortal danger he is in; his breathing increases and the sound of his heart pumping more furiously could be heard by every vampire within the building. Luke stares at the man with amusement in his eyes, raises himself up and starts edging closer towards his victims. The two vampires decide to leave him to it, shutting the warehouse door behind them and the sound of them running back into London reaches my ears.

"Vampires are not real!" The man shouts back, tightening his grip on the pipe.

"Oh, but we are. The story of the vampires were not mere horror stories to scare little children, they are a fact of history. Humans just chose to not believe it."

His heart is pounding loud and fast, his pulse elevates, adrenaline shooting round his body.

"Well... if you really are a vampire..." The man mumbles, broadening his fighting stance as Luke closes in, his grin wide, his eyes lit up.

The pipe shines in the moonlight, the man's hands twists as he prepares himself. "...Then this shouldn't hurt."

Swinging as hard and fast as his strength can allow, the pipe crashes against Luke's head and the sound of a cracking skull explodes through the vast warehouse. Seeing blood cast off on to the floor and on the pipe, I know the man thinks he has caused enough damage to render Luke immobilised so they can make a break for it. But he knows nothing about vampires, he isn't aware that even though they can be injured, they heal faster than anything on this earth.

A paralyzing silence remains for a few seconds as time seems to stand still. The only sound is the man's breathing; the woman too, has been silenced by the impact. The sound of pieces of bones being healed and slotted back into place inside Luke's skull fills the silence with a stomach-churning noise and I see the man going ghostly white at the sound; almost trying to not throw up.

Quickly and quietly, I grab one of the chairs and tear off one of the legs, finding a large piece of discarded glass, I sharpen the one end of the leg into a spike, all the while keeping my eyes securely on the events unfolding.

Luke's wounds heal within seven seconds, his head returning to the original shape as his sturdy sharp smile never vanishing from his face. The pale, frightened man drops the pipe with a clanging noise, as he realizes that no weapon is going to stop this monster from killing him. He stumbles back, shaking in fear.

"N-No. Please. I have a son. I have a little boy!"

Positioning myself, getting ready to propel the hand-made spear, I allow the green aura to possess it.

I focus on Luke's shoulder and prepare to launch. His manic laughter is filled with desire; desire to watch the man's blood spill and his screams to be heard.

My arm releases. Launching the spear towards his shoulder, aiming perfectly. But the next sound to reach my ears is one I didn't want. Ever.

The crack of the spear being snapped fills me with dread. His dark eyes cast up, burning into mine as he locks onto me. A wide fanged smile grows over his face as his arm, outstretched, holds the broken spear in his clutched hand.

He knew I was here all along!

His demon grin never left his face, his eyes glow with anticipation of me being here, challenging him. "Come on, Mystique. You have to do so much better than that."

Sighing, knowing I am caught, I jump down, landing expertly on the ground floor. The man is now shaking his head, not believing what is happening, disbelieving the events unfolding. His confused and worried expression latches onto me, not sure if he should be happy to see me or not.

"Let them go." I demand, my voice harsh as I stand upright. Luke stands between me and the two victims.

"Hmmm ... no." His voice is confident, playful. He is, of course, going to make a game out this. Still holding the broken spear, he examines it, taking in the structure of the broken weapon.

"It's amazing isn't it? We are powerful, dangerous beings... yet we can still be killed by the same things a human can... but of course it takes luck-"

"And skill... and trust me, I have plenty of it."

Smirking, he can see he isn't the only one with confidence in the room. "Oh, I know. I remember everything about you Mystique. I helped train you. Your skills and ability... Can I say I was jealous? Witchcraft splits into many different elements. You are lucky you are blessed with more than one power."

"If your game is to bore me to death, you're doing a fine job." My voice almost neutral in tone as I keep my awareness on the two humans in the room.

The quickest opportunity I have to get them out of here, the better.

His sarcastic laugh is short and sweet; his eyes glaring into mine as he moves, slow and steady, not moving closer nor moving back, as if marking off his own territory like an animal in the wild protecting his meal.

"Don't you miss it? The young rich blood, being with a family of vampires, working for Edward... Do you not regret walking away?"

"I regret not drinking *your* blood when you found me on the street. You attacked my friend."

Confusion sweeps across his face for a moment until the realisation hits. "Laurence is with you?! ... Pfft, but of course. Two traitors living together. It makes sense."

"Rather be a traitor than a monster."

"But we made you, Mystique, aware of the vampire laws and regulations! Without us you most likely would have broken the rules and been killed. I made you aware of your powers-"

"And I thank you for that-" I interject harshly. "-Now I will get what I want from you and kill you." I state matter of fact.

His eyes twinkles as he knew what I have come to obtain. "Ah, yes. Your creator is a very interesting person."

He's toying with me. Trying to lead me on.

"Don't mess with me Luke! Tell me what I want to know and I *might* let you live... That is not a guarantee though."

"It never is." He states, throwing the broken hand made spear to the ground; the light patter of the broken pieces is like the patter of rain. His eyes shining with blood tells of his hunger growing as time slips by.

"Let them go. I won't say it a third time."

The man is afraid still, his ghost like face is locked in on the scene; his eyes focusing on me. I can see his pleas of life behind his green eyes; almost seeing the thought of his son in his mind; hoping he would live to see his little man grow up.

"No." Blunt and quick, it dances from Luke's lips.

Bringing up my knuckles, I crack them as I stare at his wild ruby eyes; determined to win this fight. "Fine, you want to play? Let's play."

His smirk is the trigger. Luke runs towards me; fast and quick. But I am confident. His fist flies towards me, but I dodge underneath it, side step and leap back, putting myself between the victims and him. We have now swapped positions.

"You know, I actually forgot how fast you are."

"Good. I have more up my sleeve."

He charges towards me again and grabs my shoulders. Before he can throw me, I slam my fists into his stomach and face. Throwing a right kick into his chest, he flies across the room and slams against the wall. He falls to the ground with a loud groan, clutching his chest.

Don't let him recover!

On top of him in no time, I pick him up and stay close to his body. Throwing close body shots, swift kicks and uppercuts to weaken his ability to recover. Throwing hit after hit, Luke couldn't get a move in and with a final kick into his ribs, the snap of the bone like thunder, he slides across the warehouse floor coming to a painful stop. Blood trickles down his mouth, his eyelid has been cut, one of his ribs has broken and he is winded, unable to move for a few minutes.

Turning and scanning the room, I find the man picking up the woman to stand on her feet and struggling to carry her towards the door. Running over, swinging the woman's arm over my shoulder I push for them to get to the door. The woman starts to scream at my presence, throwing a few slaps on my face.

"N-No! Monster! Demon! G-Get away from me! Stay away!" Hysterically screaming in a terrified daze as she tries to push me away.

“Listen I’m trying to help you! Stop shoving me and let me get you both out of here. Go to a hospital, both of you. Do not tell anyone about this otherwise it’s not the psycho ward you should be worried about.”

The man stares at me with confusion as we both hurry the girl to reach the door. “What do you mean?” He asks, grunting under his breath carrying the woman’s weight and trying to tread quickly.

“Just leave it as this; you have a government, right? So do vampires.”

“So... you are a good one?” His voice quivers at the question.

“Somewhat.” Is all I manage to get out. He nods his head, understanding, not wanting any more detail. Reaching the door and opening it with one kick from me, the woman escapes from our grasp, stumbling out into the snow and runs towards a phone booth.

“Go and make sure she says nothing ab...” A shot of pain rushes through my back and down my legs as something powerful hits me. Suddenly all my vision is distorted as the whole room spins frantically. Realizing I have been thrown back further into the building, before I can correct myself, my back hits the concrete; pain spreads like lightening as I freeze up on the floor, my sight almost going black with the pain as I am weakened temporarily. As my body begins to recover from the impact, the sound of someone else hitting the floor grabs my attention.

I look up to see the male victim on the floor, sprawled out in agony of the harsh impact. A growing red stain on his upper arm catches my attention as his blood gets absorbed into the shirt material. In a desperate attempt he begins to crawl away but Luke is right beside him, his smile clear as crystal and his eyes full with hunger. His hand comes down on the victim’s leg and a sharp snap echoes through the air. My heart stops for a second as his crying screams of red hot agony blasts through the warehouse. Luke’s red eyes catch mine and he quickly bits his victim’s wrist. The cries of pain escalate.

“NO!” Pushing myself up, I dart towards Luke and body tackle him, grinding his body into the concrete floor. Wrapping my hand around his throat, hoisting him up as the green aura passes through to his body, a small sense of relief passes through me as Luke’s body becomes loose and limp like a child’s doll. His eyes are wide as he struggles to breathe, his skin starting to become pale.

"Give me the information I need and I will let you live." I snarl at him baring my teeth. Releasing his throat, his lifeless body falls to the floor like a rag doll. Needing him to speak, I lift his chin up off the floor.

"I ain't giving you shit!" He spits out, the man's blood dripped down his chin. The man's cries of pain ring in my ears, tearing me apart as I remembered the same torture when my mind was going in and out of consciousness as the venom worked its way around my own system.

Slamming my fist into his jaw, it relieves me of my anger for a second but then it returns as he laughs in my face, spitting out his own blood now.

"I'm giving you nothing Mystique."

A snarl seeps from me as I glare at him. Even now, knowing I will kill him, he still laughs and mocks me like this is all a game. Grabbing his chin, I force it up as I growl, "I won't stop and you know that. I will find everyone related to the Royal Order to get this information. So, save me the hassle and bloodshed and tell me!"

A weak smirk crawls across his face, his eyes light up as he jokes. "Give me a kiss first sweetheart."

Once again my heart drops and a lump grows in my throat at the realisation I have no choice but to use my fire energy. My confidence drains from me. As calm as I can make my voice, I whisper slowly, trying to sound as intimidating as I have been.

"How about I give you this instead?" Holding up my hand in front of his gloating, cocky little face, I channel my aura and a hot fire shines around my hand and fingertips. Making sure I don't look at the flames, my hand rests on his chest. The fire blackens his skin. His cries of pain send shockwaves through the building. Twitching in fresh agony, he tries to escape from my grasp but his body stubbornly won't listen. The smell of burning flesh starts to fill the room, choking him as the aroma fills his lungs.

"Do you want to suffer the same fate of a vampire I burnt a while back?" My voice threatens to shake but I manage to contain it.

The guy is running out of time as the venom spreads. I need to heal him quickly.

Luke's mouth twists up in a smile as he sees through my mask despite the piercing hot wound in his chest.

"You... You hate using fire." He pauses as he watches my mask crack into pieces; my right cheek twitches, my bottom lip begins to shake, my eyes glaze over with tears.

He laughs mockingly, finding this new toy to play with, perhaps as a distraction from the agony to his chest. "Yes... your creator told me how he killed your parents. Fire ... Fire is a terrible way to die. Does it remind you... of your... of your dead parents? Burning away... in the flames... as your creator walked away... from their... blackening corpses." Every grunted word adds pressure on my chest, filling my throat with a lump of pain threatening to suffocate as the memories try to come flooding back. Tears sting my eyes as I clamp my teeth shut, in an attempt to stop my own cries of suffering showing face. Forcing myself to turn up the heat, the inflicting fire to his skin increases and Luke screams again in agony.

"You will die tonight. How you die depends on you. You can die burning and screaming like a pathetic pig or you can die with a snap of your neck. Make your choice." My voice trembles slightly but I hold my tone steady and sturdy.

My threat seems to anger him, or maybe the scorching pain becomes too much, as he hisses through bloodied gritted teeth.

"Your creator... He... He goes by the name of Great Fang. He is a powerful vampire who will work for the Royal Order if they pay him enough-"

"So, he is the one who is after me." I move my hand away; a black clear hole revealing some of his ribs has manifested.

"I know what you are going to ask... I don't know... why... why he made you into one of... us. He never told me." Luke's breathing is sharp and quick as he tries to control the pain.

"Does he have an ability?" I ask, making sure the threat of the fire on his chest again was still reliable.

"If he touches you, he can copy your ability... and make it stronger."

The screams from the bitten man, if it was even possible, intensifies and I knew I have to leave now.

"Where can I find him?" I growl, moving my still glowing hand closer to his chest.

"Only our Leader knows where he really is... but I've heard he visits ... the Lost Angel. But that's just a rumour." Staring into his eyes, I see he knows no more and channelling my aura back, I feel a sense of hope. I am now a step closer to finding him and having my revenge. "Please... let me go. I won't tell-"

"Oh, by the way, there was a secret third option". I interrupt his words; words he will never finish as the slice of his neck opening up is my choice of death for him, with a piece of the broken spear that was within reach as Luke surrendered the information. His lifeless body motionless in the pool of his own blood.

Sending a ball of fire to the body, it catch's alight and I leave it to burn as my focus shifts to the cursed man, who is still going through the searing pain of the venom. His cries of torture have not changed and he looks at me with only distress and fear. Hoisting him up and slinging him onto my back, I run out the warehouse and head in the direction of home but not before seeing the escaped woman's lifeless, twisted body in an alleyway; her hair is mangled and wet from the snow, her mouth left open from screaming and blood seeped down her neck and arms. Two bite marks visible on her neck.

One of the minions probably had her after she left. Poor soul, I hope she wasn't of importance to this man.

My muscles are working harder than ever to get to my house in time, listening to the man's heart rate and predicting how much time I have to get the venom out of his system. At the speed his heart is pumping and the time the venom has been in his system now, he only has two minutes before there is nothing I can do to save him from this curse.

Arriving at my home, swiftly kicking the door open, I race into the living room and place him on the sofa, darting into the kitchen to get the first aid kit and a bowl of water with a flannel. His screams have faded from a lack of energy. Hilary races into the room, stopping short of the sofa, astonished at the man present in the room.

Returning, I see the moisture on his forehead and his skin becoming paler, his eyes droop and his breathing has become shallow. The "flu signs" are presenting themselves. Looking at the bite on his wrist, my battle was far from over and the bitter spicy aroma of the venom fills my head like a fog. Hilary backs away from the sofa, the smell of blood catching her off guard. Laurence enters the room, his face still bruised and his cut eyelid still slowly healing, conveys the scene and places a firm hand on Hilary's shoulder for support and also restraint.

"I can't come near... I'm afraid..." Her voice is one of uncertainty and I nod my head to her in understanding but looking at the wound with uncertainty myself.

Can I possibly do this? I've never sucked venom out of a person before. What if I take too much blood and kill him?

"If you take your time and do not rush you can save him." Laurence's advice is of sombre tone to try and keep a calming atmosphere for Hilary's benefit but I can feel the urgency behind the words.

The man opens his eyes for a moment, trying to make sense of his surroundings; bloodshot and swollen. They fall upon me seeming to be screaming at me to kill or save him. Whichever it is I can't tell. His strangled words are muttered harshly.

"Kill me."

The words send my blood cold. Killing isn't new to me, I kill anyone who does not deserve to take a breath of oxygen... but to kill a healthy man with a child and possibly wife... To me, that is murder. To me, that would make me a true monster.

"No... I cannot do that."

His hand clutches my coat and wrenches me forward, so close I can feel the warmth of his breath, his eyes pleading with me, begging me to relieve him from this sheer agony.

"Kill... me." He stutters again. Hilary edges closer, every few seconds she dares to take a step closer with Laurence following her like a shadow. Her big red eyes balloon with shock at the words escaping his mouth; her own hangs open as if wanting to say something but is left defeated.

Making a quick decision and placing my hand on his tightening grip, my words are calm and soft. "I can try to save you... for your son's sake."

A gasp forces itself out at the mention of his son and he shakes his head franticly indicating yes.

"My-My-My son! Y-Yes I want to see... see my son." His words stutter as the venom begins to affect his lungs and throat. Inhaling deeply, channelling the purple aura into him through the contact of his hand, panic consumes him as he feels it's effects. Watching my eyes haze over into a deep purple, weakly he tries to jerk his hand away. Trying to subside his fear, I smile and rub my hand over his in comfort.

"It's okay, this is so you do not feel anything. You will feel sleepy but also numb. It will only last for a minute."

His whole body goes limp and his face relaxes as the searing pain melts away. Dipping my head to his wrist, I begin to suck the venom out of his system; its bitter spicy taste combined with his blood isn't very nice and I am momentarily grateful. The sound of a gasp from Hilary makes me look up to see her anxiety-stricken face; her hand covering her mouth.

The blood slowly becomes cleaner, the pain subsiding from his body and once the contaminated blood is pure, I lick the wound allowing it to heal. Hilary hastily leaves the room, not being able to handle the smell of blood anymore. I nod my head to Laurence to stay with her and he follows. The sleep energy wears off and the man is clearly exhausted from the events; his eyelids fight to stay open, his body battling against exhaustion.

"I will keep my eye on you, now rest. I will make sure you're okay." I promise and stroke his face for comfort. Now that I am closer, I can't help admiring the fact he has cute features. His red hair is short and wavy, his high cheekbones prominent and sculpted with a single mole just to the left side. The man drifts off into a deep slumber and I watch his heart beat in case he slips away. But it is beating strong.

"I was right. He clearly is a fighter." I whisper to myself; a sense of relief fills my chest washing away the sense of fear and dread.

The clock shows it is 11:10pm. Knowing he will sleep for most of the night, I prepare a sleeping arrangement for myself on the sofa closest to him. Grabbing a blanket and pillow from the spare closet, I place them on the sofa quietly.

Hilary is sat on the stairs, knees up to her chest. Laurence sits beside her, rubbing her back in comfort. Taking my place next to her I explain what had happened and what I was doing.

"You saved his life." She whispers. "I couldn't have done what you did. Never."

Wrapping my arm around her shoulder she leans her head against my body. "It would be silly to say you never will, but one day you may have to choose whether someone lives or dies... or becomes one of us. Whatever decision you chose is the right one. Okay?"

"Yeah, ok." Hilary returns to her room quietly as Laurence stays with me.

"You would be ok with the idea of Hilary allowing someone to turn into a vampire if she was ever in the same situation?" He questions as he stands up, facing me.

"No, I wouldn't. I would hate it. But I cannot force my own view and opinion onto her. She is her own person. She needs to make decisions on her own."

"That is very wise Miss Field." Laurence half turns to peer into the living room before turning back to me. "What are you going to do once he wakes up?" His voice isn't judging or unhappy; simply wondering.

My eyes cast to the floor, shaking my head in worry. "There is a good chance he will remember everything. Too much happened for me to be able lie in a way that is believable. I have no choice but to tell the truth."

"And if he goes telling people?"

"I'll keep an eye on him." I exhale deeply, moving my fingers across the temple of my head.

"Protecting Hilary, watching this man, watching out for the Royal Order's hitman on you, getting your revenge and the answers you seek while maintaining your work life and normality... You will start to struggle with balance. If you try and maintain it all, something will slip."

My head begins to ache with the thought of it all, my hands twitch and become clammy with sweat as I can feel pressure building inside me. Not wanting to answer his statement, I ascend the stairs making a bee line for my bedroom.

"I'm going to have a shower. Keep an eye on him."

"Does he have a name?" Laurence calls up.

"We didn't have time to exchange common courtesy".

The hot water pouring down almost feels like a baptism; washing away my sins and giving me a sense of peace. In my shower there are no vampires or people, no blood or spit. No one to remind me of my mistakes or choices.

No one who looks up to me with admiration so everything I do must be perfect. No one who looks at me as equals so I must never fall down. No one who looks down to me so I need to rise up and over to show no weakness. In my shower, in my room, with the hot water washing over my body, I am neither human nor... monster. I am just me. Existing. Absorbing the warmth of the water and feeling the sensation as it streams down my skin. I am here. Alive.

Slowly opening my eyes, the water dances with the blood of Luke and my unexpected guest swirls into the drain of the shower. Washing my hair with my favourite shampoo and conditioner fills the room with an aroma of fresh lilies and strawberries.

I must ask his name once he wakes up.

The hair products run down my bare back and my mind involuntarily goes to Luke, remembering when he taught me about the way vampires have lived for generations, how the Royal Order moved from place to place, how the laws always remained the same. He had explained how some vampires are blessed with "gifts". Once mine were shown and developed, it became clear of Luke's curiosity and jealously of my powers. He made it clear to Edward and anyone else within ear shot.

Shutting off the water, I step out, rubbing a soft cotton towel over my body as I walk back into the bedroom, throwing on black PJ shorts and a mint green top lying discarded on the bed.

The door creaks open to reveal Hilary's face peaking in; displaying alarm.

"What's wrong Cherry?"

"I don't like this man being here... I want him gone. I'm afraid... I'm afraid I'll... You are right... I'm not ready... I'm not ready." She trails off as she nervously walks into the room, rubbing her hands together with agitation.

Kneeling down and wrapping her in a tight embrace, stroking her platinum hair gently as it gives me time to compose myself.

"I'll give you three bags of blood tonight. If you feel like you need more get Laurence or me to go to the kitchen and get you another one. Stay in your room if you feel safe. If you want to come out, let us know."

Her red eyes are wide with fear but full of tears as she pulls away, taking a deep breath to calm herself before squeezing her eyes shut and balling her fists up. When her eyes open, I am smiling widely.

“Why are you smiling at me?” She asks with childish annoyed tone.

My hand encloses hers as our eyes connect.

“I’m just happy you are able to talk to me, to be able to say when you are afraid. It’s ok to admit it. I was afraid of saving that man’s life in a way I had never done before.”

“I thought you were never scared.” She looks at me, confusion sweeping her face.

“I get scared about a lot of things. I am always afraid of losing you. But you know what, fear can be a good thing. It can make us stronger. We do things in the face of fear that we may not be brave enough to do otherwise.”

Casting her face down to look at our hands, she contemplates for a moment.

“I understand.” Raising her head up, a smile plays on her lips as she again wipes her cheek with the back of her hand. Giving her a hug and a kiss on the head, Hilary returns to the sanctuary of her bedroom as I make my way back into the living room, relieved that Hilary isn’t trying to push herself too much and also that my new guest’s breathing is getting stronger as every minute passes by.

Laurence enters as I take my place on the adjacent sofa, watching our guest’s chest heave up and down slowly as my own tiredness sweeps over me like a blanket.

“Would you mind taking three bags of blood to Hilary for me? I need to rest.”

“Of course.” From the corner of my eye I see his bruise is now turning yellow; a sign of healing.

“You seem better.”

“I feel it, now that I have had time to recover. It’s unfortunate that fate was cruel to me. Making me a vampire at an old age means I am slower and weaker than most. But I should be thankful that I can heal at all.” Laurence answers me as he grabs the bags from the fridge.

“You are lucky you survived.” I state, feeling my eyelids getting heavy.

"Do you want to explain to me what happened?" Laurence stands in the door way, his eyebrows folding together in concern, the wrinkles deepening on his forehead.

"In the morning." Mumbling my answer as my eyes begin to shut. Sinking low into the cushions, I have no idea what to expect in the morning. *Will he freak out? Become scared? Order me to tell him what happened to the brunette? I really do hope she wasn't a friend or a girlfriend, it would save me delivering the bad news.*

Sleep shrouds my mind and I fall into a dreamless sleep, the last thing I hear is the man's breathing and the mutter of a name. "Jack."

Chapter 5: Human Endurance

The sun rises up from its slumber and with it, I awake too. The sunlight breaks through the gaps in the curtains allowing the warm light to welcome us to the day ahead. The sound of the clock ticking and the man's breathing is the only sound to be heard. The clock hanging stubbornly on the wall shows it is now 7:30 in the morning. Rising from my slumber, I stretch my muscles and rise up from the squeezed up foetal position of trying to sleep on a small sofa.

The man is still resting, his chest rising up and down slowly, his dream causing his eyelids to twitch in motion. His face is calm, peaceful, his laughter lines and faint wrinkles slightly smoothed out to give me a glimpse of a much younger man. A beauty mark beneath his left eye somehow compliments his face.

Trying to piece together bits of information to get a better understanding of this man isn't easy, as what I have is next to nothing.

A man who looks to be mid-30s, has a child - glancing at his finger to see an absent gold band *-no wedding ring so he hasn't got a wife. Divorced or separated from child's mother. Claims to be a policeman but his actions last night did not strike me as a man who has dealt with dangerous situations.*

Rolling over onto his side, the man sighs heavily as his dream continues and once again, I find myself admiring his handsome features; like admiring a piece of art in a gallery. The injury to his arm is exposed and I quickly shuffle the material up, to inspect if the venom managed to heal it. Three long scratch marks glowing on his skin are visible, however they are already close to healing. The venom in his system did good work to that before being removed.

Rising up and needing to stretch my aching muscles I head to the kitchen, switch on the lights and put the kettle on to make some coffee.

Maybe offering some food will make me look like less of a threat... As long as he doesn't remember me killing anyone. I can only hope saving him from his fatal fate will be enough. I hope.

His body shifting and the sound of groaning catches my attention as the kettle begins to boil and I pop some bread into the toaster.

Turning back, I see him sitting up with his head in his hands, rubbing his forehead, recovering from a headache caused by the venom.

"What... What happened?" He mumbles his question, still massaging his forehead.

I lean against the entrance of the kitchen, looking at him and waiting for the screaming and chaos to begin as he realizes he hasn't had a bad dream; it was reality.

"Headache?" I ask softly.

He looks up, locking onto me with fear and I can almost see the memories of the events flash across his eyes; fear rising in his chest.

"Oh fuck!!" Jumping to his feet in shock, he takes a step back, his foot stumbling across the rug. It catches a raised corner and he loses his balance, hitting the wooden floor hard, all the while the stream of panic swear words doesn't ease off.

"Oh fuck! Shit! Fuck! You! Fucking you! ... Stay away! Don't you come any closer!" Scrambling to his feet, he searches the room for a weapon in blinding panic, grabbing an ornament from the fire place. All the while I haven't moved a muscle.

"I am a policeman and you, my friend, are in serious trouble." He replays his statement, his hands shaking.

"Is that your catchphrase whenever you are in danger?" I can't stop a humorous smile playing on my lips as I try to contain my laughter.

"N-No! Of course not."

"Are you sure? Because you said the same thing last night."

Twisting the ornament in his hands, he tries to get his words out. "I know what I said you... you stupid... whatever you are!"

"Ok look, take a deep breath. You obviously remember last night. So..." I take a step forward, holding my hands up in a non-threatening manner to try and show I have no intention of harming him.

"I said stay there!" He threatens, holding the ornament out in front of him.

"- Let's use some logic here..." I hold up the relevant fingers to count down my points. "- One; I saved your life. Why would I do that if I didn't care what happened to you?" Lowering a finger, I take another step forward.

"Two; I brought you to my home to keep you safe. The same point as number one." Another step closer. The man stands firm, listening to my reasoning, slowly becoming less frantic.

"Three; If my intention was to kill, you wouldn't have woken up this morning. The fact that you have and are standing there right now is proof of that."

Standing in front of him, eye to eye, his breathing still heavy with panic, my hand slowly pushes the ornament away all the while I smile softly, letting my blue eyes conceal the true red to keep him calm.

"I am not going to hurt you." Softly whispering as I ease the item from his hands and place it back where it belonged.

"You're not going to kill me?" He mumbles, not being completely convinced but it's a good start.

"No. No one knows you are here. Its 7:30 in the morning, you have been resting."

"Oh." He begins to calm down, going through the memories slowly, his eyes shifting as he stares into space as if watching the memories play across the empty air.

"I... was bitten." He states, his hand instinctively moving towards his wrist where the mark once was.

"Yes." I answer automatically.

"I was in pain... It was like fire."

"The venom does that, yes."

His hand reaches to his upper arm, noticing the wound is almost healed. Within his eyes I can almost see the whirlwind of information spinning round his head. His eyes meet mine, full of surprise and confusion.

"But you are a vampire too... and you saved me. How did you do it?"

"I sucked the venom out of your system."

His face drops in shock, his skin turning slightly pale. “Why? Just... why?”

I shrug my shoulders and smile at him in a sarcastic manor.

“Oh, I don’t know, suppose it was because I thought you were cute.” Chuckling at my own joke as he stares at me with a blank expression on his face.

A sigh drifts from my lips and I explain my reasons, my eyes meeting his. “Just because you are forced to become a monster, does not mean you have to take the path of one.”

The kettle pings, announcing the water is ready and the toast jumps up, warm and golden. The man looks towards the sound of the kitchen.

“Let’s start over. What is your name?”

His eyes return to mine again; they are full of concern and worry. Clearly saving his life has not earned me *all* of his trust. He coughs, clearing his throat but his eyes do not reach mine again.

“Karl Cooper.” He pauses for a moment, perhaps taking in the idea of him talking to someone like me. “You?”

“Call me Mystique. Everyone does.”

Nodding his head, his eyes cast over to the kitchen again as the smell of fresh toast warms the air. Gesturing with my hand in the direction of the kitchen.

“How about a peace offering? Coffee?”

By everything I have seen of this man he should have ran out the door by now crying in hysterics. But here he is, sat at a table, in a house alone, with a vampire, well three vampires but he’s not aware of that, drinking a cup of coffee and eating toast.

His eyes still surveillance me; every movement he checks to see I won’t pounce like a tiger after her prey. My eyes scan him, checking for any more wounds I may have missed.

“Why are you studying me?” His voice is guarded, poker face in tow.

“The same can be said to you.” I reply, taking a mouthful of hot tea.

“You’re not human. You?”

Swallowing the hot liquid, I stay leaning against the marble counter, matching his poker face. "So, the fact that I saved your life means nothing?"

"You can still kill me at any minute – no offence."

I scoff as he takes a bite of toast, my bright blue eyes shining and burning into his, like the sun. He shifts his body weight to try and avoid the heat.

"Yes, because I save you to just kill you later? I thought I went through this quite well with you? Did I not make it clear enough?" Questioning him, I raise a brow.

We stare at one another for a moment, him analysing me, but I have no need to analyse him as I know his curiosity will get the better of his logic. Finishing off his toast, he takes the empty plate to the sink, carrying his cup of coffee in the other hand and then leans against it, his back resting on the marble surface still on the defence.

"So, you are not like most vampires?"

Hello curiosity. "In terms of my choices, yes."

"So, you can walk around in daylight?"

I laugh, shaking my head slightly in disbelief. "Ah, the myths of vampires, of course this would show itself at some point."

"So, no bursting into flames in the sun?" He continues, wanting to know what he's going to have to deal with. The sunlight comes in through the kitchen window; between us is a wall of golden light. To answer his question, I raise my hand to it, feeling the warmth on my skin. To add salt to the wound, I let out a sarcastic "Ouch." With a smirk on my face that I cannot control.

"Oh right, um, what about turning into a bat?" Clearly, he doesn't like to be proven wrong; jumping into the next question quickly.

"Would you like to know where that idea actually came from?" I ask with a humorous smile.

"Not really." Karl mumbles.

"If I am going to default these vampire myths isn't it interesting to find out how they came about?"

The corner of his mouth turns up into a smile as he sighs. "Ok fine. So, where does that myth originate from?"

"Like a lot of myths, they are either based on a bit of truth or just a simple scary story twisted into something worse. That particular myth comes from Vlad the Impaler who Dracula is loosely based on. It was said that he used the sun to blind his enemies and used rabid bats, who flew away from the sun to infect his enemies to win a battle."

Thinking about it for a moment before taking a sip of coffee from the cup, Karl looks into the garden at the rising sun, possibly imagining a flock of bats appearing in the horizon.

"I take it you know that because you were there that day?" He asks innocently.

I stare at him with a blank expression. "No, I Googled it."

"Oh... But I thought-"

"-That because I have lived longer than you that I know everything that happened? In every part of the world, every battle or war, every historical person to walk the Earth I *somehow* know everything about them? Also, in this modern day, that I don't know how to use the internet?"

Karl stares at me with a look of bewilderment, possibly by the realisation of the absurdity of his statement. "I think Hollywood really messed us up in terms of vampires... what about sleeping in coffins?" Reeling off his next question, clueless to his statement moments before.

"Vampires sleep for only a few short hours; everyone is different so for how long depends on them." Rolling my eyes, answering regardless.

"But no coffins?" Karl raises an eyebrow, as if it's something blatantly obvious, abandoning his cup as he pulls his arms apart to stretch.

"The theory for the coffins comes from us being the undead... Can I not enjoy the comfort of a bed?" I state, taking another sip from my cup.

He stares at me, all his "vampire knowledge" that society has given him must be racing through his mind.

"So, do you live forever?"

"Yes." I answer begrudgingly.

"Never aging? Never getting old? You just... live forever?"

"Unfortunately." My voice dull and this causes Karl to tilt his head curiously.

"You don't like immortality?"

Shrugging my shoulders, I cast my head to the side, away from him. "It can become exhausting."

"Oh..." He pauses for a moment, "So how old are you?"

Laughing slightly, placing my cup back down I sense his fear growing; his heart accelerating, afraid he has now offended me. "Karl, don't you know it's very impolite to ask a woman her age?"

"So you are *that* old?" He laughs but it stops short, as if he's caught himself doing something inappropriate. Laughing with someone like me is perhaps something he considered... unethical.

"I am 26 in human years... I was born in the 1500s."

His mouth drops open; disbelief stunning his face into a frozen state of shock. "You... wow... you've been alive since..." He exhales sharply, "-Wow, I can't even begin to imagine being alive for so long. I'd get so bored with living I mean..." Catching his words, his eyes dart to mine in panic as I try to convey my desolate smile to a happier one.

Giving out a nervous laugh, his hand trembles slightly as he goes to pick up his cup of coffee from the counter, his alarming sense of dread still clear although he tries to stay composed.

"Karl, please, I am not going to harm you."

His eyes glue to his cup, watching the steam rise from the hot liquid. "Sorry, you know, vampires and all."

"Hmm." Taking my last sip of tea, I place it on the counter and watch as he stares off once again into space. "Got any more vampire theories you wish to have answered?"

Karl snaps back from his short daydream and goes through the myths. "Garlic and crosses?"

"Are you terrified of food and wooden objects?" Sarcasm thick in my voice.

"... Does sea food count... and my mother's wooden spoon? It gave me headaches more than I care to mention." A smile cracks from his lips.

"Got disciplined much as a child?" I ask, smiling.

"A little." Karl smirks and laughs slightly, but again it stops short. His eyes look at me with caution. It's almost like I can read them. "What about your parents?"

The mention of my parents brings a pain to my chest and an attempt of flooding my eyes with tears, but I push them back, not wanting to show weakness.

"They were... great parents. They taught me a lot." The woeful sound of my words causes Karl to tread further.

"How did you deal with them not finding out... about..." He leaves the obvious statement to his sentence open.

"They were murdered beforehand." I state as I hear Karl swallow the lump in his throat.

"Oh... I'm sorry I asked. I shouldn't have asked... It was stupid of course, being what you are."

Shaking my head, I give him a half smile to try and ease his fears. "You are allowed to have a conversation with me. If it eases you, then fine. I am still a person... even if you choose not to believe so."

Karl looks away from my eyes, as if ashamed of himself. "Okay, what else... Um... Stake through the heart?" He continues our previous conversation.

"A close truth but not exact. If the stake was left in and not removed then yes, they would die from that. But if the stake is removed, they will heal."

"You can heal?" His eyes widen in shock as I find myself staring at him in disbelief once again.

"You smashed a heavy metal object over a vampire's head and watched his skull be put back together like a jigsaw puzzle-."

"Oh... yeah... Thanks for reminding me." He goes pale again, almost trying not to retch.

I continue, "-Vampires can be injured and killed in every possible way a human can. A bullet through any limb will injure them, a bullet through the head. Bang, dead. Being hit by a train or a car, drowning, burning in a fire... you get the idea. But you have to be really lucky. As you so politely stated, vampires are not human and so are very quick. Heightened senses, ability to heal and physical strength are what makes them deadly. They are very good at avoiding death."

"What about breeding?" his voice is cautious again, "-Some myths say you can, some say you can't. Which is true? Cause I got to be honest, the thought of vampire children running around... doesn't sit well with me." Roughly rubbing his hands together as he cracks his knuckles.

"A vampire child is possible... but not through breeding. No one is really sure why. Even the Royal Order doesn't have the answers... Not that they really care about breeding. They see themselves as monsters. Why should monsters have families? It's seen as a weakness." Each word grows in resentment as I speak.

"Why are families a weakness?" Karl questions, perplexed by my statement.

"Families, children, friends, are all leverage to weakness. If the Royal Order finds weaknesses, they exploit it." Silence elopes us for a minute as my words hang in the air like a noose around a neck, as he watches the ticking clock.

"So, who exactly is the Royal Order?" Karl dares to ask, needing more information to understand.

"They are the leaders in our society. They are fully aware of everything we do. They make the rules, we follow them. Only one rule reigns above all; keeping vampires a secret." My fingers draw patterns into the kitchen counter as I explain. "Their regulations are not looked at carefully and they are certainly not known for their... sympathy, for a situation or their need for justice. They are a group of corrupt vampires, who think they can do what they want and it doesn't matter about anyone else. They have spies working for them, hundreds, making sure rules are obeyed. If not, they report it and then send someone to kill you or drag you back to them... then they kill you."

"The death penalty is high then?" His voice is neither humorous nor surprised; just dull.

My words stab into the air. "It's their only penalty." Silence washes over us again as my words sink in, the information giving him the true view on vampires. Karl's eyes keep looking at the clock, his hands wrestling with one another.

"Would you like to ring your son? The phone is just behind you. I can only assume that's why you are keeping a watchful eye on the clock."

Karl turns to his right to see the phone hidden away in the corner of the kitchen. He stares at it for some time but shakes his head, turning back to me. "No, its fine. To be honest these things have happened before where I haven't called him or showed up at an appropriate time. He will just think I've been called in to work early."

"Is your son's name Jack? You mumbled it in your sleep."

"Yes, it is. He's a sweet boy." Karl smiles, his eyes glistening with pride.

"How old is he?"

"Just turned 12. It was his birthday a few weeks ago. Football party. Unfortunately for me it rained. Getting mud out of clothes is a nightmare." Scratching his fingernail along a coffee stain on the side of the mug as if replaying the muddy scene.

"No wife? I couldn't help but notice a lack of gold on your finger." Pointing to his wedding finger to state my comment.

"No... we divorced. She moved away. That's why I was on a date with Lucy..." He stops short, like catching a frog in his throat. Closing his mouth, he doesn't continue and I decide to not press on. His eyes cast themselves to the clock once again, showing it is approaching 8am.

"What is your job if you don't mind me asking? I assume you said police officer to just scare them."

I'm hoping it is anyway.

"It wasn't a lie." He says calmly but a sting of fear shoots through me.

Oh, bloody great!

"How can a police officer act like a scared little child in the face of danger? Surely you are trained to deal with situations like that?"

Karl's face screws up at my words in painful embarrassment. "I passed all my exams, I just... I didn't expect to be taken hostage on my night off and... obviously I could do with some more training."

Leaning forward with arms across my chest, locking onto Karl with a sense of urgency hoping to get the importance of silence through to his head.

“Karl, you are aware that you cannot mention what has happened to anyone? If you do, the R.O will find out.”

“Royal Order?” He asks needing clarification at my, clearly obvious, abbreviation as he tidies himself up by smoothing his shirt, rubbing the blood stain with his fingers.

“Yes, it’s like I told you. They are our leaders and you do not break any of their laws. You must keep it a secret.”

Walking into the living room to grab his coat I follow him swiftly.

No way are you walking away from me!

“Mystique, that is a little difficult to do since I was involved in a crime.” Karl says as he shrugs on his coat.

“You don’t get it! You cannot face off vampires! They will kill you! You would think that was pretty obvious to you by now, all things considering.”

“Lucy is dead! I saw her as we passed the alleyway. I saw her in the snow. I’m going to be working on catching her killers, even if they are vampires. I cannot ignore that, it’s my job. Plus, my evidence is in that building.”

“I’m sorry for her death but Karl trust me, your evidence of blood is not there! It is not.” I state, plain and simple and Karl stops, turning to me, puzzling my words.

Maybe his headache has not yet cleared. Maybe he has slowly descended into denial as we have talked. Either way he needs to understand.

“What do you mean? Of course...”

“The minions of the vampire who kidnapped you will have wiped away all evidence and burned down that building by now. How do you think they have been able to hide for so long? That woman’s killer will never be caught because the vampire who did it will just slip away.” My words sink in, possibly for the first time since he has woken up, and his denial turns into realisation.

His skin goes pale for the third time this morning, his limbs go numb as his body slowly sits on the sofa, staring into space as the reality of vampires living in a human society slaps him across the face. I move closer, whispering slowly as I see the wheels in his brain slowing down to put the pieces into place.

"Now... you finally get it. Believe me, you have passed vampires in the street more often than you think. The cases that you have worked on and have never been solved through lack of evidence or the timeline was wrong, and you *just* couldn't make things work out logically... it is possible some were caused by vampires."

Swallowing a lump in his throat, he manages to stutter out a question. "How can you physically tell ...who... who is a vampire?"

"Look into my eyes." I speak slowly standing over him, shortening the gap between us as I bend down, bringing my face closer. His cheeks start to burn as I inch closer, his breath catches in his throat.

"W-What are you doing?" He stutters, leaning back in surprise.

"I'm not going to kiss you. I need you to look in my eyes."

"Oh, right. Sorry." Apologetically smiling, he straightens up, his eyes searching in mine. The blue waves slip away like draining water to reveal the blood red irises.

"Oh fuck!" Jolting back in shock, eyes wide with a splitting look of shock and awe as his watches the shifting of colours.

"If a vampire learns to do so, they can mask their red eyes. It's the one sure way of identifying a vampire."

He studies my eyes, looking at the intensity of them. "Apart from the eyes... is there anything else?"

"Not really. The eyes are the main thing to watch out for; a bright colour that appears to be darker or lighter the next time you see them. If a vampire is camouflaging their eyes and they grow hungry, you will see specks of red in the iris." As I finish speaking, I camouflage my eyes back to bright blue as I take a seat beside Karl.

"Nothing else? That's fucking it? The colour of eyes? That is all you have on identifying a fucking vampire?!" His words escalate higher in pitch, becoming alarmed and distressed again.

"If their teeth are in your neck, that is a pretty good sign. But don't take my word for it."

"Well what the fuck am I meant to do?" His hands grab my shoulders in fear, then quickly let go as if my skin was hot like an iron.

"As long as you do not tell anyone and try to act like you have no knowledge of this information, no one will harm you. I promise. Don't speak a word about it and you will be safe; you and your son."

His heart returns to normal, blood approaching the surface of his skin once again and he calms down, his emotions clearly on a rollercoaster. I place my hand on his and speak slowly.

"I understand how scared you are. I was too, when I found out all of this. I was actually taken in by the Royal Order. The things I witnessed were things you never want to see. My head was messed up like yours, trying to understand how all of this has been able to remain a secret. But it is the painful reality. If you tell anyone, they will find out."

He nodes his head, slowly, taking in everything I have said and lets out a huge sigh of built up anxiety. "Thank you... for telling me all of this."

"I couldn't exactly lie. You knew too much. At least with you knowing you can keep yourself safe by keeping away from R. O's attention."

A nervous chuckle hesitantly escapes his throat as his hands continue to dance together. "Speaking of keeping yourself safe... How do you... I mean... where do you get your blood from? Do you do what *that* vampire did and... hunt?"

"Not exactly... I feed from the elderly. I go into nursing homes at night and feed from individuals who are close to death." Glancing at him, I can see my slightly tamer source of obtaining blood doesn't shock him any less; his mouth hanging open complimenting the wide eyes. After a few seconds to contemplate, he nods his head in understanding, grunting some words that sound like a mild approval.

"However, I cannot continue there for long. The home is closing down next year and so I have to get my blood from other sources."

"Other sources?" He questions, tilting his head to the left.

"Ever donated blood?" I ask with a smirk but he takes my joke literally, forcing his heartbeat to jump up like a coiled spring. I roll my eyes at him.

"I'm joking. I can go to another nursing home or go to the hospital and take some of their stored blood. They have so much and using it daily, they do not notice a few packets going missing here and there." Waving my hand in a dismissing gesture.

"Security cameras?" He notes, eyeing me as if I hadn't already figured it out.

"They will not pick me up if I run fast enough."

"Seriously?"

"I'll be like the wind-" I smile with humour and Karl smirks slightly, "-Plus it helps that I work there."

"You *work* in the hospital?!" His voice creeps up an octave.

"I'm a nurse... How else do you expect me to stay under the radar?"

"Fuck me." He exclaims in crude astonishment as I quietly laugh at his response.

"No thanks. You aren't really my type." My eyes catch his knee jumping up and down in chaotic nervousness. "What are you thinking about?" I ask, feeling a little concern for his mental health.

Karl puffs out his cheeks, exhaling the air before answering. "How the hell I'm going to sleep tonight?"

I can see that everything does not sit comfortably on his shoulders; it isn't an easy thing to think about. We both just sit there until Karl finally decides to head back home, promising he won't mention anything to anyone. Calling for a taxi, we sit in silence until it arrives, beeping it's horn to declare its arrival, which causes Karl to almost jump out of his skin. I walk him to the door and watch him get in the taxi, waiting until it is out of sight before closing the door on this unexpected night.

Hilary comes down the stairs, clutching her doll. "Is he gone?" Her voice squeaks from the stairwell.

"Yes." I smile encouragingly and she runs into my arms.

"He isn't going to say anything?"

"No, but I'll have to keep my eye on him."

Her sun lite hair is twisted and scruffy from sleep.

“We aren’t going to the museum this week, are we?” She asks, disappointment thick in her little voice.

“Hey, I said we would did I not? Just remember to drink lots of blood. Come on, let’s go wake Laurence up by jumping on his bed.” A mischievous smile curls up on my face as Hilary agrees with a copied look, racing up the stairs before I can, to which all I hear is a loud announcement.

“Rise and shine sleepy head!”

Chapter 6: Ignore Snow White, Like Always...

The sound of continuous ringing of the phones is equivalent to a screaming baby to Zoe as she enters onto the second floor of the police station to a scene of complete chaos. Everyone running around like headless chickens trying to deal with the press and preventing important information from leaking about certain sensitive cases. The numerous phones screaming loudly for attention as her team work on the cases while trying to warm up from the harsh coldness of the whipping wind from outside.

The room is a sea of dull darkness of red, blue and grey outfits with their identical black coats... as Zoe stands nervously in her mustard yellow coat, realising she stood out like a plastic yellow bag.

Carrying a take away tray of coffees, teas and hot chocolates, her black ankle boots leaving a trail of snow as she places the drinks down on a vacant desk. The occupant, David, is currently over by the radiator trying to warm up his painfully numb red hands. Everyone in the office is a patchwork of red cheeks, blue faces and almost purple fingers from the chilling temperatures. Zoe's brown skin with cool undertones allows her complexion to avoid this unflattering look.

"Got the daily antidote for the cold weather," Zoe announces playfully, her fruity voice singing across the room as several co-workers pounce on the offer of something hot to drink. "Careful guys, you'll give people the impression you're freezing to death." She giggles, unbuttoning her attention drawing coat.

One of them, David, picks up his coffee, his hands cling onto the warm plastic cup for dear life with his dripping wet hair as he looks at Zoe with jealousy as his nose and cheeks glow red. "We all look like freezer burnt chickens yet you look as cool and comfortable like you've walked in from a holiday. Not even your hair is wet."

Instinctively, her hand reaches up to touch the tight springs of black hair. The dyed white tips are the butt of jokes for Zoe.

"The words you are looking for is 'Thank you Zoe for the free hot drink,' and the cold doesn't affect me because I am just as cool as ice." She giggles at her own joke, pointing her finger in the shape of a gun and clicking her tongue as David grimaces in response, taking his place at his desk.

Starting to feel anxious at the thought of needing to make a statement to her team, a statement she has been practising the whole car ride here, Zoe taps her foot and fingers to an uneven beat, allowing her to build up the confidence to begin talking. Inhaling and exhaling a deep breath, she begins.

"Ok guys listen please." Zoe addresses the room, her voice changing from its bubbly self to a nervous taut as she shrugs off her coat, revealing her tall and curvy figure.

Her team continue to talk loudly, as if not hearing her. Zoe clears her throat loudly as the humming of chatter slowly quietens but does not fall to silence as she continues.

"Ok so, I know it's very cold but I need you all working at your best today. I am already aware of the situation where some information was leaked by a specific someone. That person has been dealt with. You know I don't like playing the bad guy and I *really* don't like playing 'The Boss' card, so please try and ... be more careful... and considerate..."

The whispering of secret comments by team members gradually grows to the returning hum of open conversations, causing Zoe's words to crumble and filter out as she realises no one is really listening. A stinging pain from the back of her wrist causes Zoe to glance down, to see the pinkish red irritated skin, caused by scratching continuously while she spoke.

"Ok... So, I'll be in my office... If anyone... needs me." Her words trail off as she turns and sombrely walks into her office with tears welling up in her eyes.

Shutting the door, she sighs in heavy frustration and sadness as she begins to pace around the room, trying to rid of the nervous energy scattering through her limbs. The familiar anxiety builds in her chest and she stands still, focusing on controlling the negative build up.

"I see the picture of my daughter on the desk, I hear the chatter outside, I feel the cool temperature of the room, I can smell my perfume and I can taste my morning hot chocolate."

Repeating the senses over and over again allow the anxiety to decrease and slip away as she takes a deep sigh of relief. Zoe catches her reflexion in the long-standing mirror in the corner of her office, taking in the outfit she so carefully chose to try and make her look 'like a boss'.

Tilting her head to the side and observing her reflection, Zoe knew deep down it was never going to be her black wide cut trousers that make her walk like a boss, or her mustard striped ruffle shirt that makes her stand tall and prominent. Clothes just don't factor into it as well as her natural-but-statement looking afro hair and warm amber eyes.

The office door bursts open hastily as the direct manager barges into her office, his chubby face flush from the freezing falling snow and full of annoyance, removing his hat to reveal his bald head. Zoe knew there was something wrong when he doesn't come in with his usual large black coffee and a take away bag of fast food burger, fries and a shop bought salad.

"I've just been told about a police officer telling the press about the other odd cases we have had in the past month! What the hell happened?!"

Raising her hand up to stop him, she glares at him with her shimmering eyes hoping to look intimidating.

"Don't. You. Dare, burst into my office without knocking..." The pause between the words isn't for intensity although she hopes it works, but to allow her to build her confidence back again enough to be able to talk. "- I already sent you the email explaining what happened. The person in question has been given a full warning."

The manager grumbles as he shakes off the snow from his jacket; his big belly shaking like a water balloon.

"The media are going crazy trying to get information on the other murders."

"And they won't get anything until we have more information and we chose to release it." Replying in a flat tone as she walks to her desk.

"For your sake, you better hope so! I've already had a talk with your team, all except Karl who isn't here yet. I don't want to hear another peep about the other cases from anyone. Understood?" Stabbing his finger towards me, his words hot with irritation.

"Understood Watson, sir." Zoe sits at her desk and arranges the papers in front of her as the direct manager glares in displeasure. From under her eyelashes, Zoe notices Watson take in her ombre coloured hair as his face shrivels up like he's bit a lemon.

"And why, have you not removed the white from your hair like I have asked you to do, like, a million times since you started. It's been 6 months, I think."

Biting her tongue to prevent swear words from escaping, she raises her head to meet his. "I don't believe my hair colour has anything to do with how well I do my job."

"Well according to reports, you aren't doing very well with your team right now. I suggest you try and change that." He counters with a sly grin, before straightening out his straining shirt and waddling out the office.

The ceiling fan spins round and Zoe watches it, thinking about how her team work together to complete their tasks and get cases solved. However, when it comes to holding their attention and gaining their respect, she doesn't know what she's doing wrong. She worked her way up to get to the position of detective in her old work place but was bullied out. Now she feels like it's going to happen all over again.

Zoe turns to the window of her office, seeing Karl's empty desk, the only person in this job that treats her like an equal. The only face she looks forward to seeing. The one auburn haired, scatter brained person she can relate too. Noticing the time, Zoe slowly grows concerned as it wasn't like Karl to be late for work, which he had been all week. With the snowy conditions, Zoe knew how easy it is to get in accidents. She runs her thumb over her bottom lip in anticipation, watching the door like a hawk.

After three disappointing entrances from other staff, the door slowly opens revealing Karl sluggishly walking in, his long black coat covered in snow but his stare drifts out from reality. Zoe leaves her desk and stands in the doorway, calling for his attention.

"Karl, could you come into my office for a second?"

Snapping out of his trance, he nods his head as the snow falls revealing his wet red hair as he steps into the office; snow falling behind him leaving a powdery trail. Closing the door silently, Zoe walks back to her desk and sits down, inspecting his ill features with concern for her close friend and co-worker. Karl nervously takes a seat, despite feeling emotionally drained. He wasn't nervous about being in trouble, just by the fact of being in her presence. Even now, feeling as exhausted as he did from lack of sleep, seeing Zoe made the whole agonising drive to work worth it. Karl smiles softly as he recalls her first day here. She had walked in looking nervous but determined. Her skin resembled stone, seeming smooth and cool to touch; her features and curves so beautifully balanced he was convinced she could have been carved out of marble by a Greek God.

Karl coughs, clearing his throat as he removes himself from his daydream, trying to focus. "You look lovely today Snow. Your lipstick is a little smudged though." Smiling shyly running his hand through his hair, allowing more snow to fall from his auburn strands.

Hastily rubbing the lipstick smudge off her chin, Zoe laughs nervously, trying to compose herself.

"Oh thanks! Wish I could say the same for you though, but you look like the walking dead! Did something happen?" She questions worryingly.

He shuffles in his seat, his hands clammy with moister. "Oh, I'm just not feeling right today. Think I have flu or something. Must have caught it from somewhere." His body violently jerks, holding in a moan of pain.

Instinctively her hand reaches across the desk to try and help but Karl shakes his hand in dismissal. "I'm fine, I just... shook from the cold that's all."

Pulling her mouth to the side, unconvinced at his statement and interlocking her hands together as they rest on the desk, Zoe tries to get him to open up.

"Karl you've worked here for a while now and I've seen you show up while vomiting in a plastic bin, but you still showed up on time, like the good Soldier Boy you are." She giggles, clicking her tongue.

He laughs, quickly wiping his hands on the inside of his trousers. "Well this time wasn't the case was it?"

Her eyes cast themselves over him, concerned with the dark circles under his eyes; contrasting against his pale meadow green.

"Did you sleep at all last night?"

"No..." He mutters sluggishly. "Not at all... not for the last few nights... week... The flu... keeps me up."

"You didn't say anything earlier this week... you've probably gotten worse because you haven't had any rest." Tapping her fingers on the desk, Zoe inspects him, contemplating whether to bring up a touchy subject, one she doesn't really want an answer to.

"Did your... date go well? The one you had a last week?" She asks hesitantly, ignoring the tight knotting in her stomach. "I hope you didn't have the flu on your date."

"No, I didn't. I'm sorry I don't want to talk about it, I'm just tired." He recants in a low voice.

Her hand urges to reach out and hold him close, to somehow take away this obvious pain he is trying to conceal but without wanting to hurt him further, she slides her hand back to her side, softly speaking as she does.

"... I'm sorry Karl I shouldn't pry. I worry about you." Allowing a moment to pass between them before Zoe decides to break the silence by getting on with the case at hand, she leans back in the chair, pulling out some paper from a brown folder. "Okay fine, where are we on the Lucy Benedict case from last week?" Karl jolts slightly before clearing his throat, causing Zoe to notice his discomfort.

"Well, it's thought she was tortured in the warehouse next to where she was found, but it was burned down so of course, it's only an assumption." His voice is dull and colourless which makes Zoe feel uneasy.

"Okay, do we have any fingerprints from the body or the environment?"

Karl coughs a couple of times before clearing his throat again. "Sorry, I really think I am coming down with something."

Shaking her head and sighing, she puts down the documents and smiles sympathetically.

"You are going to end up infecting everyone. Go home on sickness pay. Take the week off."

"No, don't be stupid, I'm fine."

"Go home and that's an order, Soldier Boy." The corner of her mouth turns up with teasing humour.

"Snow..."

"No buts!" Zoe interrupts as he laughs, shaking his own head.

"You are never going to let that go, are you?"

"Drop Snow White and I'll stop calling you Soldier Boy."

"Snow White suits your hair though." Karl smiles, already feeling a little better as their banter flows between them.

"I guess. Now come on you're going home and that's that." Guiding Karl to the door, offering to walk him out which he accepts graciously. "I'll ask Tina about the case; you go home and rest."

"Thanks Snow." Patting his shoulder, she watches as he slowly makes his way back through the door. Once out of sight Zoe turns to the desk of one of her team members.

"Tina, can you give me what we have on the Lucy case please?" Tina's black hair bounces as she raises her head from the desk, her thick green glasses somehow staying perfectly in place, despite looking too broad for her stick thin face. Grabbing some paper, she rubs her sleepy eyes as she skims over the printed words.

"There were fingerprints found on an empty chocolate wrapper near the victim and on the victim's watch. They came back to a guy named Andy Hall. He had psychiatric problems and had professional help for 3 years, claiming a voice in his head told him to kill." Her voice is monotone as the chewed pencil twirls around in her hand. Zoe can't help but wonder how the pencil hasn't bounced off her long hawk shaped nose.

"Ok so have you gone to look for the guy?"

Tina's expression is universal language of *do I look stupid to you?* As Zoe smiles apologetically.

"He was found dead this morning of a drug overdose. There was a suicide note stating and I quote..." She picks up a document with the statement written "- I'm sorry for everything I have done. I'm sorry for the girl by the warehouse but I couldn't fight the urge anymore. I couldn't live with it controlling me. Forgive me."

Zoe nods her head contently. "A killer who couldn't kill anymore."

"Looks that way. The autopsy said that she suffered a broken arm due to the attack and a cut to an artery on her inner leg. She lost a huge amount of blood, possibly inside the warehouse before it was burned down. Once she was outside the killer slit her throat, probably for good measure."

"It fits Andy's profile of his methods of killing." Zoe notes, with everyone nodding their heads lazily.

"The other two cases are still underway and we have new information about the Bow Street case." David speaks up as he manages to disconnect the phone from his ear.

"New information? What's gone on?" Zoe replies but fear grows inside her chest.

"Well we know, obviously, that the body was burnt to a crisp, so it was hard to figure out the time of death or the method of killing. However, autopsy revealed that the man was most likely tortured before being burnt. A hole was burnt into his leg prior to being killed."

"That's very strange." Her voice full of curiosity as her mind spins with a way to make this case work for her.

"Yes, and the strangest bit of the case is this - some of the victim's blood was recovered from the snow and it had an odd green outline on the red blood cells."

Dam Mystique, how am I going to cover this for you? Zoe couldn't help but curse in aggravation.

"Let me have a look at the report."

David hands her the report reluctantly and her eyes fly through the statement, her mind like a hurricane.

Given more time, the green aura on the blood vessels would have vanished but the police discovered the body so quickly...it will have vanished by now but it is here in black and white! Timing wasn't on my side here! Everyone will remember this odd fact. It's another little thing that can't be explained by logic... and people remember them. I will have to find Mystic and warn her before she makes another slip up worse than this one.

Zoe scans her eyes across the room at everyone working and going about their business.

If they all knew the truth to these odd cases it would cause chaos and panic... and today is certainly not a day I seem to be making friends.

Handing the document back, she quickly slips in a question. "Have they found out what the substance is yet?"

David shakes his head, confused. "No, apparently by the time they took pictures and documented it, the green colour disappeared. We may never know what it was."

"Maybe it was some radioactive chemical? I mean, what else would it be logically speaking?" Zoe replies and thankfully, everyone agrees.

How a radioactive chemical would have gotten in contact with the victim becomes the main talking point of discussion amongst the team, but it didn't concern Zoe, as long as they have a logically theory which didn't point to anything 'mythical', she's in the safe zone.

The day passes by slowly as Zoe remains in her office, filing reports and going through papers and cases and all the boring dull computer work she has to do as being boss. She looks at the clock which has just struck 3pm. Grabbing her coat and her belongings, she calls to the rest of the team, knowing full well they don't really care or even look up from their desk.

"I will be back soon; I've got to pick Danni up from school." The only person to acknowledge her is David, who looks up from behind his computer.

"Later Snow White." David calls and quickly, Zoe shoots him an expression that's meant to look serious but her big grin defeats her.

"What did I say about that name?"

"Didn't I tell you to dye the ends of your hair a different colour and then I will?" David responds half-heartedly, clearly not being fully committed to the light banter, confusing Zoe even more.

"Once Hell freezes over then I'll think about it."

"Yes Snow." He nods his head as she tuts under her breath.

Walking out into the car park, the snow quickly stops falling, as if not wanting to blemish Zoe's grace. Climbing into her red BMW, she turns on the engine to allow it to start warming up before turning on the radio, turning the volume down so it just becomes background noise. Sighing contently, she closes her eyes to try and figure out how to deal with the Bow Street case. She thought about just planting a fingerprint of a criminal who has recently died along with a fake suicide note, like with Lucy's case but no criminal would be a perfect fit. She thought about using a crazy homeless man who tried to save the girl... but then she would need to plant evidence of a cigarette lighter that could have been used to set the victim alight... And then explain how there was no footprints in the snow.

Rubbing her forehead again, her brain twinges to try and fit pieces together in order to get this case closed off... and also on how to get her team to like her. It would make her already complicated life simpler. Of course, if they knew she was fabricating evidence for some cases to help a vampire keep under the radar they probably wouldn't like her any better.

I'll just have to rely on the lack of evidence and let the case go to being unresolved; saves me the hassle of covering up Mystique's mistake. Why did I have to meet her? Why did I need to know that vampires bloody existed! My life would be ten times simpler and easier!

Slowly reversing out of the car park, her thoughts re-earth the moment when she discovered the existence of vampires and a cold shudder shook her body. Zoe makes a mental note to get in contact with Mystique, aka Amanda Field and let her know that her little justice killings are becoming more dangerous and she will be in danger of being discovered.

Chapter 7: No Sleep For Me! ...

Tap. Tap. Tap. Tap. Tap. Tap.

Adjusting his eyes to darkness, the sound of a continuous rhythm sends Karl's heart racing like a greyhound. The images that haunted his dreams fade into the night, but the eyes stay burnt into his mind like the fiery heat he felt from the venom. Mystique's words drift off into the darkness as Karl is brought back into his bedroom, away from vampires and bloodshed and the memory of that night. A drop of sweat rolls off his forehead, listening to the sound, trying to convince himself he's being foolish to get so skittish.

"It's just a branch tapping on the window."

Repeating it like a drum as the sound starts to become more normal, easing his fears as his body sinks back into the bed.

BANG!

"Fuck!" Instinct kicks in like a bullet; grabbing the hidden hand gun under the pillow and jumping out of bed, getting ready for a fight. However, Karl's foot gets twisted up in the bed sheets, causing him to fall on his face.

"Fuck. Shit! I'm coming!" Karl stammers as he kicks the sheets away, jumping to his feet. "Why the hell did I say that?" He whispers irritated at himself, as he points the gun at his bedroom door. Unwanted images run through his head of a vampire coming in through the door, appearing behind him, at the window, in the wardrobe. Creeping slowly to the door, using the nose of the gun to nudge the door open he leans out, peering down the corridor. The pain stretches inside his chest as he holds his breath, the warm sweat developing on his forehead.

The flickering of a light elevates his pulse, deciding to open the door a little bit more so he can see more of the hallway.

"Sorry." A voice squeaks from the darkness. Exhaling the pain sharply from his burning lungs, Karl moves the gun out of sight. "Jack... What are you doing?"

Picking up the broken lamp, its light finally going out, he places it back on the table and repositions the knocked table on the landing.

"I wanted to stay up and watch TV." Even in the dark Jack's innocent face is well known when presented with trouble.

"Jack you shouldn't be up at this time of night." Switching on the light, Jack shields his eyes and moans at the sudden blast of white light.

"Dad turn it off! You're blinding me!"

"Go to bed, I'll talk to you in the morning." Karl address him sternly.

With a mumble of disapproval and the utter of the words "stupid lamp", he slams the door to his bedroom and jumps into the creaking bed.

Sighing heavily and turning off the light, Karl shuffles to his bed, sitting heavily as he places the gun down, resting his head in his hands, wiping the moisture off his forehead. Regardless of that horrific event being just over a week ago the flashbacks, nightmares and visions of what Karl's death could have been like tormented his every waking moment. Images of Lucy's death cross his mind; how much agony she must have been in. The painful hole in his chest aches as a reminder that he should have looked after Lucy.

"I wish I had never asked her to move the date forward." He mumbles to himself, lying awkwardly back on the bed. Zoe appears behind his eyes, her bouncing spring locks, her joyous laugh, the way she carries herself, and for a few moments Karl finds himself thankful that he didn't have the courage to ask her out... the thought of losing Zoe was something he just didn't want to think about.

A sharp cold shudder erupts from his body as the memory of that vampire's face and the dark humour in his eyes as he played his sick game rips through the images of Zoe.

"I want your blood". His words echo like being caught in the wind.

The knowledge of vampires being about hasn't rested well Karl's mind. To try and calm his racing pulse he thinks of Mystique, repeating her name as if it would help.

"Mystique isn't like him. Mystique saved me. She saved me... Mystique." Karl replays everything she told him. Reminds himself of how normal she looked. Grabbing a handful of hair with both hands, Karl growls in anger.

“Aren’t vampires supposed to be these pale, red eyed, night walking monsters with unnatural features?! For fuck’s sake when did they become so... human?”

Turning his head, he looks at the gun he secretly snatched from a mugger, replaying the scene with an almost questionable expression. He took the mugger down a couple days ago on the job, while trying not to faint from exhaustion and lack of sleep. After a quick pursuit down the street and tackling the mugger to the floor, Karl noticed the gun sticking out of the man’s trouser waistband. Knowing no one had seen the weapon, he took it, not really sure why or what came over him. Of course, the mugger never mentioned the weapon without risking adding onto his law-breaking list of owning an illegal firearm which would have bumped his jail time up. No one would have believed his story of Karl taking a weapon also. Karl inspects the weapon closely, watching the metal shine in the dimly lit room.

Puffing out his cheeks and exhaling he closes his eyes, surrendering to the fact that he needs to try and sleep.

“Thinking about all of this isn’t going to help me.” He mumbles quietly. Glancing at the clock, it shows time of night to be 01:54am. Placing the gun carefully back in its hiding place, Karl rises from the bed in a struggling movement.

His dark blue slippers make little noise as he walks slowly down the stairs, each step creaks with a groan. The kitchen light dazzles and blinds him for a moment, as his hand reaches for the cupboard with the medication. Popping the lid and throwing down a couple of sleeping tablets down his throat, his mind relentlessly won’t drop the issues pestering him.

She could have killed me. Ripped me apart. Kept me prisoner and tortured me. But she didn’t... Maybe I can trust her...

His conscious isn’t going to let him sleep, hence the need for sleeping tablets. But the red eyes dare him; dare him to come back into the darkness so it could scare him out of his wits again. Crawling back up the stairs, knowing it’s useless to fight sleep, Karl finds his bed once again, cold and alone. For a moment Karl wishes someone was here, a woman, taking up all the covers to keep her warmth on her side. For them to have a midnight argument about the lack of sharing chores and for it to finally end with them wrapped in each other’s arms. He wishes he had someone to share his life again. Someone he can come home to. But the bed welcomes no one else.

The sleeping pills began to kick in and as Karl's head hits the cold pillow the thought of Zoe warms his cold night. Then the red eyes invade and attack, welcoming him back into the nightmare.

Chapter 8: Sudden Appearance

“Coats. Check. Scarfs. Check. Backpack. Check. Bags of blood inside backpack. Check. Hilary drinking enough blood that she feels like vomiting...” I turn to Hilary who is drinking her fourth bag, forcing it down her throat before discarding it.

“Check.” She finishes weakly, holding her stomach to try and settle the swishing liquid.

“Ok, everyone ready?” Laurence calls out to us, bringing Hilary’s pale pink duffle coat and my navy-blue swing coat.

“I believe we are, once Hilary straightens out her shirt.” I giggle as I bend down to adjust her pale-yellow plaid shirt, leaving it loose over her brown skirt.

“How do I look?” Hilary asks excitedly, giving me a slow twirl to show off her outfit.

“You look beautiful as always.” Laurence smiles widely as he hands Hilary her favourite coat.

“You certainly look ready for this.” I smile as she pulls it on, leaving it undone, as I do the same with my own coat.

“I’m a little nervous... but excited. You’ll both stay by my side, won’t you?” She looks up at both me and Laurence nervously, twisting her right foot back and forth so her dark brown laced boots squeak on the floor. Lowering myself to her level, I place her black ear muffs over her head.

“You won’t be leaving my sight, don’t worry.” I hold her hand, giving it a reassuring squeeze. Straightening up and standing side by side, still holding her hand, I nudge her leg with my foot.

“I took some fashion advice from you. Look, we match.” I wink at her as she notices instead of my normal trousers, I am wearing a dark blue skirt, paired with thick dark grey tights and black boots.

Hilary smiles brightly, glowing like the sun. “Hey look, we do match!” She giggles.

“Two beautiful sisters going out for the morning. What could be better?” Laurence smiles at us both as he pulls on his black gloves.

No longer being able to contain her excitement, she pulls me towards the front door, as Laurence picks up the backpack swinging it over his shoulder.

“Looks like we are off then.” He chuckles loudly as we make our way out the door.

The Natural History museum stands with pride and offers everyone who walks through its doors more knowledge and wisdom than ever before. Of course, there is nothing in here that will teach three vampires anything new. We are here solely for the interaction of others and to give Hilary a morning of freedom she greatly deserves.

As we arrive, I make sure our backpack is hidden underneath Laurence’s grey vest coat. We are checked by security and my white handbag is inspected, but of course no one checks Laurence, so we get in with our blood bag undetected. Hilary latches onto my arm, pulling me through the crowd to get to the main reception. Glancing over my shoulder, I spot Laurence a few paces behind us, getting caught up in the human congestion. Waving his arm, he indicates for us to carry on and he’ll catch up.

The room opens up into a vast and magnificent space with towering stairs and grand details of architecture, encapsulating the skeleton of a blue whale, floating over our heads. I seek out an empty space in the far corner, bringing Hilary with me, our hands interlacing tightly.

“I want to go and explore!” Hilary bounces on her tip toes as I bend down on one knee to meet her eye level.

“We will but I need you to remember, that if you feel like you can’t handle being here, you let me or Laurence know. Ok? We can give you some more blood to help, or we can leave.”

I wonder if her cheeks are hurting as her wide smile looks painfully stretched out as her eyes gleam with joy; the meadow green tarnished in attempt to conceal the red, leaving her eyes an almost swampy moss green. She is still learning to conceal her eyes more efficiently.

"I will, I promise, can we go now?"

"You wouldn't start without with me, would you?" Laurence approaches us, brushing off some snow from his black jumper, most likely from rubbing shoulders.

"Of course not, but I want to explore now guys, before the blood wears off." Hilary pipes up, continuously bouncing on her toes.

As Laurence reminds Hilary to not shout inappropriate things like that out loud, my attention disconnects and shifts to across the mass bodies circulating the room. The hair on my neck standing on end as I sense a danger lurking; a pair of eyes watching us whom shouldn't be. My eyes do a sweeping scan of the room, trying to catch on who this person is. No one obvious draws my attention, so I slowly turn back to Hilary and Laurence, putting on a smile to try and mask the concern growing on my face.

"So where to first Cherry?" Hilary takes advantage and guides me over to the Blue Zone, where her favourites are held.

"Look it's Rexy!" Hilary bellows as she drags me forward in front of the T-Rex, letting go of my hand to impersonate the dinosaur. "Rawr! Rawr! I am the king of all dinosaurs!"

Elbowing Laurence's arm, I nod my head to move away from Hilary for a moment, which he obeys. Ducking my head to his ear, I whisper with urgency.

"I can feel someone dangerous watching us."

Laurence swiftly moves his camouflaged brown eyes to Hilary, who is still admiring the T-Rex and stomping around.

"Whoever it is will have to be in great control of their hunger to be here." He states, looking around the room himself.

"Whoever it is, I'll try and find them. Keep Hilary close by."

Laurence grabs my elbow to halt me from walking off. "Amanda, if this person is Great Fang, I want you to be cautious."

Nodding my head, I keep my eyes trained on Hilary. "Whatever happens, take her out of here."

Hilary stomps over to us, mimicking the T-Rex. Wrapping her arms round my waist, she giggles loudly. "I got you in my jaws! You cannot escape!" She growls.

Throwing my arms up in the air, I dramatically gasp and groan in pain. "Oh no! So, this is how it ends! No!"

She releases me and then goes after Laurence, who stays still as stone.

"You can't see me if I stay still." He chuckles, gluing his arms to his size.

"Oh no! Where is he?" Hilary stomps around, growling and giggling at the same time. The danger lurks and I cast my eyes around again, trying to spot the vampire. Families, school trips and tour groups infest the room with a loud beating hum of chatter and exclaiming excitement, as the pair of eyes I search for are somehow avoiding to be seen.

Placing my hand on Hilary's back to guide her, I smile widely as I nudge her along. "Come on Miss Rexy, let's carry on stomping around."

We move through the dinosaur exhibit at a steady pace, Hilary pointing at everything and studying every feature. The bones and objects she's able to touch she does so, closing her eyes as the past images floods her mind. Removing her hand from the Tyrannosaurus skull, she smiles at the memories it brings to her.

With the sense of danger not letting up, I stand beside Hilary, guarding her but also watching her smile.

"How's your hunger? You still feeling ok?"

"I feel fine, don't worry." She comforts me while admiring the skull.

"So is our interpretation of this one correct?" I ask her as a tour guide approaches, the woman's drawn out voice repeating the script of information she must copy word from word.

"Pretty close..." Hilary admits with a smile, "-but the colour of this one is incorrect. Also, the Raptors look very different... Like big turkeys." She giggles as I pull a finger to my lips.

"Sshhh. Don't let them hear you. You'll make their heads explode."

Laurence taps me on the shoulder with a worried expression. "I've done a perimeter of the room. Whoever this person is, he is very good at avoiding us. I can smell him, but whenever I try to track the scent, he seems to avoid me without being spotted."

"We'll have to just keep aware of our surroundings." I state as Laurence's thick brows lower, deepening the wrinkles on his forehead.

"You do not think it would be wise to leave?"

I look away for a moment, wanting to hide the conflict tugging in my chest. "Normally I would say yes but... Hilary has not left the house in decades. She needs this. I cannot take it away from her. Besides, this place is so busy and crowded he cannot attack us in here without causing a disturbance. I think we'll be fine."

Turning back to Hilary, my heart drops to the pit of my stomach as she is no longer in front of the dinosaur skull. Hastily I look around the room, trying to spot her in the crowd of bustling people. My mind absorbing every movement and person in the room as my breathing deepens, my heart erratic with fear. The pumping of my blood beats in my ears as I rush and push past people, circulating the room. Laurence splits from me, taking the other side of the room.

Risking it, I call out to her, praying that she will answer me, giving me a sign to where she is located.

"Hilary? Hilary, where are you?" Over the sound of the mass of voices, my heart jumps with relief as I hear her silver voice from a distance.

"Over here." I dash over in the direction of her voice, pushing past some families until I come into a little clearing by some fossils, to see Hilary handing back a black pendant to a man whose presence and energy makes me feel on edge and draw up my hands into fists instinctively.

Approaching on high alert, the ebony man smiles as he retrieves his pendant, pushing it deep into his forest green long coat. He looks up, through the short fallen dreadlocks as I make my way to Hilary's side, placing a steady hand on her shoulder, his deep mahogany eyes examining me like a prize. His scent fills my nose and I bury a growl in my chest to try and keep calm for Hilary.

"I was just returning this man's pendant I found on the floor." Hilary explains as I glance at her with a questionable look. Her expression is one of contained fear. She must have realised her mistake once she found him to return the item.

“That was very kind of you, but you should not have run off.” As my eyes return to the man, a crowd of people scamper between us trying to follow their tour guide. I step back with Hilary, to prevent us getting trampled on as I strain over their heads to see that the vampire has now disappeared into the crowd. With my hand still firmly placed on Hilary’s shoulder, I turn us both and head towards Laurence, who has caught wind of us not too far away.

“Hilary! Why did you disappear like that?” He exclaims in fear as Hilary wraps her arms round my waist, nestling her head into my body.

“I’m sorry.” She mumbles as I pull away, placing both hands on her shoulder. “I found the pendant on the floor. When I picked it up, I saw the man’s strong connection to it. It was important to him. It was from his home. When I found him, I smelt his scent. I got scared. I froze.”

Pulling her in for a hug, I cradle her while looking at Laurence. “I think we should leave now.”

He nods his head, deeply grumbling. “I agree. For both of you.”

“Have I ruined the morning trip out?” She asks with a trembling lip.

“No sweetie of course not. I would just feel better if you returned home.”

Kissing Hilary goodbye, squeezing her tight and head of to work, leaving Laurence to take her home.

Humming of voices, alarm bells and pounding footsteps on concrete floor is all that surrounds me. The mixture of staff are running around in an almost blue blur of movement as the buzzing sound of bells trying to get answered as quickly as possible won’t stay silent for more than five seconds. The doctors are doing their rounds with the patients, their complex language of posh terminology is what identifies them as doctors; as if their training has turned them into a walking textbook of medicine and complex vocabulary.

My body is here. My mind isn’t. It’s off in another place, replaying the events of this morning and the past week. My mind is on a war path, analysing the events and breaking them down into key points.

My creator and the Royal Order assassin are the same person, as Luke stated. According to him, my creator has already been sent after me... Could that vampire in the museum have been him? If so, why was he there? What purpose did following us into a museum have for him?

My mind jumps to the policeman, Karl Cooper, who after finding his address, continued his job for another week after our encounter, before being sent home ill. For the last four days I've seen him do nothing but stay home as I monitored his activities... or lack off. This past week whenever I have been by, his blinds are drawn, his car hasn't left the drive except to take his son to and from school, his face is motionless, he looks a bit thinner and lacking in colour when I've caught a glimpse of him.

I hope the bags of food I left by his door before work is enough to cover them for a while.

"Nurse, you are starting to hurt me." My patient's voice catches my attention as I'm cut away from my thoughts to remember I am removing a cannula from my patient's arm... and not doing a good job.

"Oh, I'm sorry." Giving a weary smile as I sharply remove the tape, pulling some hairs out in the process and quickly slide the cannula out. Pressing some gauze down and adding a layer of tape, I throw the cannula in the sharps box.

"Sorry about that. Busy day." I mumble.

"Can I have a hand please?" The carer working with me is trying to calm our new patient who arrived from A&E only a few minutes ago. The man is young, only 52, but he is still drunk from his night out on the town.

"Why have you brought me here?" He shouts in a slur as I jog over to help prevent the carer getting hit.

"You are in hospital Mr Payer. You have a broken leg." I try and explain but I may as well be talking to a brick wall as the patient continues to lash out, removing the blood pressure cuff and trying to rip the drip from his arm. As he attempts to remove it, he shouts like an animal in distress. The bitter sting of the alcohol on his breath creases my nose, making my heart jump in fear but I try to ignore it.

"You are hurting me, you lot! Get away from me! Let go of my arm."

"Mr Payer we are not touching your arm." The carer tries to reason with him, to no use.

"You are hurting my arm!" He accuses as he tries to remove the needle himself. "I'll kill you! I'll throw you down the stairs."

A memory flashes across my mind, the man aggressively chasing me, his furious bear like anger as I remember the pain of each step as gravity took me down the stairs.

Shredding it up and throwing it away, I concentrate on my patient, bringing myself back into the room.

As I grab his hand to prevent the removal of the drip, I notice in his confusion he has wet himself. Within the smell of the urine, I can smell the leukocytes present as well as the rustic smell of blood, thanks to my vampire senses. As I successfully remove his hand away from the needle, the carer turns to the table to pick up a roll of tape, I quickly allow a blast of my sleep energy to just calm him, my hand faintly flashing purple, not brightly enough for anyone to notice. Mr Payer quickly relaxes as the carer puts tape over the needle sight.

"I think the drink has got the better of him," I mock as he stops writhing around. Being still, another smell reaches my nose, grabbing my attention. The bitter and foul smell of tumorous cells; more specifically within his kidneys. His consultant walks onto the ward and approaches us, chart in hand, staring at it as he mumbles to himself.

"So, dare I ask for your opinion?" He looks at me with an expression I can only describe as a spoilt child, knowing my reputation of being correct when I self-diagnose my patients.

"He has just been quite aggressive but has calmed down now. I'm going to get a urine sample from him to see if he has a urine infection. If that comes back positive for protein, I think he will need a review to check there isn't anything underlining. His notes state he is a very heavy drinker and has type two diabetes. These are all risks of developing kidney cancer so if we can get a blood test on him just to rule it out as a possibility, I would be grateful."

Holly skips into the bay at this moment, her ponytail curled within an inch of its life bounces behind her like a big red spring. The colour of her hair reminds me to go grab some blood before I leave today.

"Hey babe, can you check some medication with me?"

"Of course," Turning to the carer I address only her, "I will help you with the washes once I've done my medication round alright?" I say, drying my hands with the paper towels.

“I’d appreciate that, thanks. I’ll start washing someone.” She smiles at me with a youthful, cheery expression on her face as she walks to the trolley to get the wash stuff.

I turn to the doctor, who looks at me with an irritated expression due to me telling him what to do.

“I know you have a habit about being right about these things but one day, I’ll prove you wrong.”

Smiling innocently, I shrug my shoulders at him. “I just want the best care for my patients.”

Holly smiles and walks beside me as we make our way out of the bay and down the ward.

“How’s the new girl?” Her voice curious like a bitchy cat, clearly wanting some juicy gossip.

“She is Ok... Her makeup is a bit full on though. Looks like she needs to be wrapped up in plastic in a bright pink box.”

Holly’s laugh crackles over the noise of the busy ward. “Matron will tell her off for that.” She states as we arrive at the treatment room.

“Most likely.” I state apathetically as Holly jabs the code to slip inside grabbing the medication tray, emerging quickly to check up on me.

“Are you ok? You don’t seem yourself.” Her eyes criss-cross over my expression as I quickly check the medication on the drug chart.

“Just a lot on my mind.” My pathetic excuse doesn’t sit well with her as the noise of the ward escalates by the ringing phone continuously calling for attention. A doctor searching on the computer right next to the phone has subjectively gone deaf to the sound, no doubt waiting for a nurse to answer it or for the ward clerk to come back. We both roll our eyes as we enter Holly’s assigned bay and approach her patient sitting on the edge of the bed. We do our procedure and check the information before giving over the medication.

The door of the bay opens gingerly with a light creaking sound as we do our normal transaction. Turning to leave Holly, my feet holt suddenly as a sense of danger looms over me; my attention on high alert. A man entering the room slowly walks towards me, his eyes focusing on his feet as they shuffle in my direction. His unpleasant odour causes me to crinkle my nose as I scan over his appearance.

He's clearly homeless, or at least just unhygienic by his scruffy stained clothes and wild hair unsuccessfully hiding under a beanie hat. But his earthy skin is perfect with no blemishes, no dirt or grime as you would expect from an unkept man. Teeth pure pearl white against the contrast of his dark lips reiterating a sentence silently. My instincts are warning me there is a forthcoming danger. My mind jumps to the possibility of this person being a vampire, much like this morning at the museum.

"Can I help you sir?" Addressing him to show I've acknowledged his presence. As I monitor him, the man doesn't even look up. His hands squeezing together in an anxiety grip as his knuckles start to lighten in colour. He continues to mutter silently to himself. It's not until he is closer to me that I realise I am right as his vampire smell fills my nostrils.

The vampire finally looks up to reveal his blood red eyes are anything but human, before pulling out a knife from his back pocket.

"Oh my God! You have a knife?!" Holly shrieks in disbelief, jumping back in horror. I stand my ground, watching him in my own world of disbelief.

What the fuck is a vampire doing here?!

I examine his features, quickly ruling out that he is the same vampire from the museum this morning.

"Stay back! All of you! I'll use this!" The vampire asserts himself, swinging the knife around erratically as his body trembles with fear. Holly calls out to the doctors just outside the bay, ordering them to call security as she backs away, spreading her arms out as if somehow that would protect the other patients.

"Put... the knife... down." Stating slowly and calmly, I stand my ground, feeling conflicted in this new and overwhelming situation. A couple of the patients start to call out too, trying to aid in the situation to prevent the vampire from hurting me. Over the sound of their voices my mind races, analysing the situation.

Everyone in this hospital is in danger if I don't do something. I can't kill him openly. But I can't let anyone approach him. He'll attack them. He'll expose himself. And me.

The vampire looks at me with fear and confusion. His thick bottom lip trembles as a tear falls down his cheek. Confusion sweeps me as I examine his body language as it conveys non-threatening posture.

His voice croaks. "He... He said you could help us." From behind the vampire the doors open into the bay, as other staff dare to risk coming to my aid.

"No! Stay back!" I alert them in a fake panic tone. "Stay back! The less of us in here the less of us to get hurt. Wait for security!"

The vampire doesn't even flinch, staring like stone only at me as I raise my hand slowly, keeping my eyes on him, I take a step forward. For other's watching this will be seen as an act of bravery. For me, it's an act of aggression.

"Who is he?" I ask, taking another step closer.

"Amanda, don't!" Holly's voice squirms in fear as I edge closer, hissing under my breath for her exposing my name. The vampire fiddles with the knife, shifting its weight around his hand as his arm lowers, no longer pointing at anyone.

"Who told you I could help *you*?" I hiss under my breath again as my anger begins to surge. "Why have you endangered everyone here?"

Grabbing my arm, he jolts me forward to whisper in a quick hush as the sound of heavy footsteps stomping on the floor vibrates to us, alerting us of the security men arriving onto the ward. Holly screams in fear at the thought that I've been stabbed, until she realises he's whispering to me.

"Please, help him! Help him to achieve his goal. Great Fang! Help him! Please." Shock jolts through me at the mention of the vampire I am trying to hunt down. Anger quickly replaces it knowing I won't be able to interrogate him for information. For the sake of everyone here, I cannot let this vampire live. Grabbing the knife while I have a chance, I throw it, hearing the metal scrape across the floor. Grabbing his arm, I whisper back hastily as my power consumes him, forcing him into a deep sleep, lowing my eyes so no one can see the purple galaxy within my iris.

"You should not have come here." Stating through hushed voice as his body slumps to the floor, my hand still gripping his arm, seeming like I'm trying to catch him. The security men burst in as I deliver the final fatal dose of my power, causing the vampire's heart to stop beating. Pushing me aside, they begin to restrain him before realising he is not moving, as I channel my energy back within, my normal civil eyes returning. "He just went unresponsive. I tried to catch him!" I state to them in a fake urgent voice.

They call over to the Doctors who run in, assessing his body and declaring CPR is needed. Backing away as too many bodies surround the dead vampire, I slip away from the scene as Holly races over and flings her arms round me.

"What the HELL were you thinking girl!?" Her voice quivering with trauma.

"I guess I wasn't. I just wanted to help." I reply back in a monotone voice, not focusing on her but my own whirlwind of thoughts, trying to piece together what the hell happened. Holly guides me into the office, seating me in the chair as she insists on checking to make sure I'm not injured.

"Holly really, I'm ok." Grabbing her hand to move away the blood pressure cuff trying to latch itself onto my arm.

"Are you sure? Can I get you anything?"

The vibration of my phone excitedly shaking in my pocket catches my attention. "Yeah, can you get me some water?" I ask, pretending to clear my throat. "The stress has made my throat go dry."

As Holly leaves the office, fishing my phone from my pocket, my attention is drawn onto the words.

We need to talk. Urgent. Get back to me asap. Z

My mind races at the surprise of a message from Zoe. She only contacts me when she has to. A select number of reasons cross my mind and they all result in trouble.

What the fuck is going on today? Shaking my head in disbelief.

My fingers quickly type and hit send.

Where do you want to meet? M

Another buzz quickly answers my question.

The old antique shop. Where we first met. 5:30pm. Z

Replying back immediately, knowing now I have a perfect excuse to leave work early.

I remember. See you there. M.

Quickly hoisting myself up and standing in the doorway, I try and spot Holly in the crowded bustling of bodies to inform her of my absence this afternoon. Her bright red hair easily allows me to locate her entering the ward again and I gingerly approach her, laying on a thick trauma induced persona.

“With what’s just happened... I don’t think I can continue the rest of the day. My head is... I’m feeling really...” Without needing to utter another word, her hand rests on my shoulder with an energy of assurance.

“Don’t worry about a thing. After what you just did for us all, take off. We’ll manage. Just do the incident paperwork tomorrow. If anyone says anything, I’ll have a word with them.” Thanking her, I quickly walk off the ward, making sure I avoid eye contact to prevent a conversation. Changing into the same clothes from this morning and making my way out of the hospital, my mind replays when I last saw Zoe. Her rage towards me has always been clear, even though we have helped each other out.

We agreed to help each other in secret. So why is she wanting to meet up? What’s changed?

As I reach my car, my mind replays the stray vampire showing up. His words almost haunting me, bringing me more questions than answers. One thing is for certain... my creator... Great Fang... Is definitely out there... and I can’t wait for his blood to spill.

Chapter 9: A Cold Acquaintance For Us Both...

Zoe's grandmother's shop looks the same as she remembers it. The man who owns it now doesn't look like he's changed anything at all. Some tall clocks stand in the window, furniture and shelves with dolls and decorations still stand with pride. The pictures that hang on the walls look like they have never been moved, or even touched by a curious finger running over the surface of its paintwork. The desk still holds its stance at the back of the room, still holding onto its pride of being old but still useable. The walls the same neutral cream colour, now have lost the freshness.

Zoe locks the door behind her with the spare key the owner never asked to have back, making her way upstairs, avoiding the ghosts of her memories as each step the wooden panels creaks with pain from the pressure, begging for her feet to move quickly. Upstairs is where most of the large furniture is kept; sofas and big storage utilities, some pictures and expensive ornaments scatter around the dusty dark room. Opening a window, the dust falls off in a mist, as she wipes her hands on a paper tissue she fetches out of her handbag. Zoe knows Mystique will most likely use that one entrance; using obvious entrances was not in style for her.

The room is uncomfortably cold as her fingers hastily button up her mint green coat, the clicking of her heels echoing around the room is the only noise to accompany the faint ticking clocks.

Glancing at the one, the time is 5:29pm. Knowing Mystique will turn up on time, Zoe waits patiently, gliding her hands in her beige trouser pockets, watching the open window. As the hand of the clock moves to the six, Mystique's body glides through the window effortlessly as the clock chimes.

Zoe's astonishment in Mystique's appearance takes her back... It's been some time since being in her presence. The impact of Mystique's blue eyes standing out in the darkness of the shop, she is reminded of the power that it holds. Her appearance has not changed; no wrinkles, no blemishes, not a change in sight. Zoe's rage towards her flares up like a coiled snake, her mind racing with the memories of when they first met here along with when they met for the second, deadly time.

"Good to see you again Snow White." Mystique's smile is soft and easing, which throws Zoe's defence up; her bubbly personality fades away quickly as Mystique's arrogance shines off her in a negative vibe.

"You can't call me that. Only my friends can. I thought vampires never forget things."

"I can't remember everything Zemora. It's been a while since I've seen you. I remembered your nickname though. I like how it rolls off my tongue." Mystique speaks softly but flirty, trying to mask and shake off the events of earlier today as she wipes the dust off her skirt. Her flirtatious smirk makes Zoe angrier, pursing her lips together in aggravation.

"My name's Zoe." She corrects as she straightens up, trying to look intimidating.

"Of course... How have you been? You look well." Mystique smiles, casually placing one hand in her coat pocket. Zoe wonders how she can act so casual yet look so strong. Maybe it's a vampire thing.

In between the two women is a wooden table with flowers and swirls engraved into the edging. Pulling out the beige folder from her handbag, Zoe steps forward, holding it in the air, clearly to be seen.

"I haven't brought you here for a reunion. It's for this." Tossing the folder of the Bow Street case onto the table, it slides to her side, leaving evidence of its movement in the dust. Mystique doesn't even look at it; instead focusing on Zoe's defensiveness towards her.

"Can't we at least try and get along? I know you have anger against me but I would have thought you could be civil by now?"

"Civil?! With *you?* I believe I have been. I've kept my end of the deal. Nobody knows about vampires, or if they do it wasn't from me." Zoe's amber eyes pierce through the darkness, her words swirling with a venom taste.

"Keeping your end of our deal has kept you alive in more ways than one." Mystique takes a step forward towards the table, her voice slowly escalating in vex at Zoe's attitude.

"Well clearly you are not holding your end! Take a look." Pointing to the folder as Mystique walks over, picking it up. Opening it and inspecting its contents, Mystique slowly paces.

"Care to explain yourself?" Zoe asks, clearly annoyed at having to be here.

Her shoulders shrug, confusion spread across Mystique's face as her mouth parts slightly as she reads. "There is nothing to explain, I never knew this about my powers. I had no idea they left a trace."

"Well they do. So, you'll have to be more careful with your killings." Zoe states, resting her hands against the table.

"To be honest with you it makes sense. How it never crossed my mind I don't know." Mystique leans against a grandfather clock, catching dust on her blue coat, staring at the paper.

"My powers work the way they do by invading the human body and taking control of it. So naturally, it's taking control of every aspect; blood, muscles and nervous system. Like a virus... I guess I should have figured this out before."

Zoe nods her head in agreement. "Yes, you should have. I mean, how can you be so careless?"

Mystique snaps her head up, enraged at Zoe's statement. "Excuse me but where are you coming from criticising me?!" Gritting her teeth as the folder drops to her side, her eyes burning with rage. "If I recall you chased down a vampire and fell into his trap of luring you into a kill zone."

"He shoplifted from this very shop and ran away at a normal pace! Of course, I didn't think he was a bloody vampire." Zoe rolls her eyes and dramatically waves her arm around.

"But he was. That's why I followed him in here. I talked with you to avoid his suspicions. When it became clear that he was after you, I ran after you both. If I hadn't, he would have killed you."

"I know that." Zoe hisses under her breath, glaring at the table.

"So, stop being so aggressive with me."

Zoe abruptly laughs as she ruffles her hair. "Out of the two of us, you are the one who is aggressive."

“Out of the two of us who is being the most civil?” Mystique bites back, crossing her arms as she continues to speak. “Look, do you want to carry on working together? If not, then we can go our separate ways. If that’s what you want. But if we are to continue working together you have got to be more civil with me.”

As Zoe steps forward, she points her finger at Mystique harshly as she spits out her words. “I don’t *want* to be civil with a vampire. The only reason I co-operate with you is because the less vampires that roam about the streets the better.”

Mystique stays silent, throwing the folder onto the table, it effortlessly slides across to Zoe, positioned perfectly. Swiping it up and placing it back in her handbag, Zoe turns to leave when Mystique’s voice drifts across the cold room.

“I agree with you...” Zoe turns to look at her with a poker face, a bad one as Mystique speaks “-I know you hate me and the existence of vampires. I understand more than you know. But regardless, I am still grateful for your co-operation. If you have any more cases, drop me a text.”

All Zoe can manage is a nod of her head and true words from the bottom of her heart. “I will”.

Mystique rotates to slip out through the window, pausing as she answers. “Be careful out there... I’d hate to have to save you twice. You’d probably hate me even more.”

Before Zoe can answer, Mystique vanishes into the darkness. A sense of guilt slides over Zoe’s skin as she thinks back to that day... but she shakes her head, not wanting to tear down the wall. Turning on her heels, she leaves this unhappy memory.

Chapter 10: History Comes Calling

After seeing Zoe, I head to the care home, realising I had rushed out the hospital not retrieve any blood for Hilary but had no time to go back.

The blood in the fridge will have to last till tomorrow.

From the care home, I feed generously to relieve me of my hunger and frustration of the entire day. Hoping to race home, as I leave the traffic builds up, which is both a relief and a headache. It gives me time to organise my thoughts but it slows me down to where I really want to be.

My watch shows it is approaching 8pm and my fingers tap away frustratingly on the wheel while the radio plays some Maroon 5 song.

"The rare times I take the car and there is traffic... typical." Moaning to myself as the cars in front of me beep their horns, showing their frustration also. My mind is swimming with ways I will have to be more careful on my hunts, ways I could make sure that no trace is left behind on the bodies. It's just bad luck that I didn't know about the trace and the blood in the snow was contaminated with it. My thoughts return to Karl, then to the vampire at the museum, the one at work, my creator Great Fang who is still after me, Hilary. Rubbing my forehead with my two fingers, I try and calm the storm in my head.

Arriving home at last, I see the lights on in the house and the flashing of the television in the living room. Cutting the engine off once inside the garage, I open the car door and my whole body charges with electricity; the atmosphere is uncomfortably unsettling and the hair on my arms and neck stand on end.

Something is wrong. Very wrong.

Making my way up the stairs from the garage towards the reception, I fling open the door. Before I can step into the room, the smell of other vampires hits me like a brick wall. I almost lose my balance, needing to steady my legs. The next thing that hits me is blood, more specifically, Hilary's blood.

My legs are moving before my brain reacts and I find myself in the living room being presented with a chaotic scene; broken glass, smashed walls, broken furniture and doors are evidence of a clear struggle. A few splatters of blood here and there; some on the wall, some on the broken ornaments. I can smell that some blood is Hilary's but not all. Laurence's blood is mixed in there too.

My mind spins and for the first time in decades, I feel sick to my core. The room sways, my vision feels out of focus, my arm reaches out to hold on to anything sturdy for support.

"Hilary?! Laurence?!" My strangled voice croaks as I stagger into the kitchen, trying to find them. I call again as I find the kitchen vacant. Treading back into the living room, a note on the torn-up sofa I overlooked in a daze calls out and I reach for it, my fingers trembling as I study the words over and over and over again.

Mystique,

By now I am sure you know who I am, as I have watched you try and find me for so many decades. Well, now is your chance. I have taken your sister to encourage you, to give me something that I believe we both desire, more than anything in this lifetime. Your father failed, so now it's your turn.

If you truly are the great Mystique you have built your life and image around, finding me should be no problem. I won't bother giving you a deadline. We both know where you will find me.

See you soon.

Great Fang

My legs crumble with the numb weight of my body, for a while I feel nothing. Hollow and lifeless as the words elegantly etched on the paper slowly begin to fuel my fury like a volcano ready to erupt. My eyes can't stop themselves from looking around the room, studying the scene and imagining what happened.

A deep, agonising groan drifts through the house as I recognise it to be Laurence's voice. Shakily, I rise up and head back into the reception where I absorb my surroundings a little more clearly. Laurence's body is lay motionless in a pool of blood on the far side, facing away from me.

My anger evaporates as guilt and shock explodes inside my chest. In my overdriven state of panic, I had missed him. Racing over, cradling him as I turn him onto his back to lay on my lap. A swollen face stares back at me almost unrecognisable; swollen eyes, cut lip, a broken nose.

"What-What-What happened?!" My unrecognisable voice shakes as my tears fall like heavy rain onto his blood-soaked face. The note scrunched up in my shaking hand starts to obtain my tears and his blood, staining the paper. I throw it away from Laurence, to not damage it further.

He stutters in pain, his words barely a whisper as his shaky hand weakly grabs my top. "They... They took... Took her... Hilary... I could not... stop them... I'm sorry... I'm sorry... I'm sorry..."

Rocking him as he repeats his apology, I quietly shush him as I place my hand on his forehead, allowing the sleep energy to help ease the pain.

"It's ok, it's ok, it's not your fault. It's not your fault. I'm so sorry. I'm sorry I wasn't here. I'm sorry. Forgive me... Forgive me." My body quivers as I cradle him for what feels like forever. As my mind and body calms from the initial shock, my mind races as I stare at the screwed-up note, thinking about its markings, threatening me, as the scorching dragon rages inside.

He wants me to give him something he desires? Fine. My desire is to hold his decapitated head and watch the flesh burn like candlewax until it's nothing more than a skull in my hand... And I will make sure mine happens soon enough.

The phone rings out for the fourth time in the space of a minute. Typing in the numbers again furiously, I hear the ringing tone again and finally, after the third ringing tone, Karl answers.

"Hello?" His voice sounds a little groggy, as if I've stirred him from a deep sleep.

"Karl it's me. Mystique." My voice scorching in fury. No answer arrives for a moment. His voice is more alert once words are located.

"How did you get this number?"

"Not important. I need you and *only* you to come to the address I sent you. Once you have it written down, delete it. This is important."

"What's happened?" Sounding a little more awake, I hear the bed springs moving as if he's shifted his weight, likely sitting up now.

"I have a sister. She's been kidnapped."

The words take a few seconds to come to light. "You... have a sister? Is she... you know?"

"Yes."

"Taken by your kind?" Fear rising in his voice.

"Yes."

"Wait... was she in the house when I was there?!"

"This is not the time to ask idiotic questions! I need you here! Now!" Snapping like an enraged dragon, the phone muffles with a sound of a bang, then Karl's panty voice breathlessly comes back on the line.

"Sorry... dropped the phone. Well...What do you think I can do? You said so yourself, vampires barely leave a trace."

"Some slip up, mistakes can be made. If I can make mistakes so can others."

Sounds of wardrobe doors opening and shutting drift through the phone, shuffling of feet, the movement of fabrics. "You know I can't take evidence or anything like that."

"You can and you will. I do not trust anyone else. You have to do it."

"CSI does all the forensic stuff. All I can do is report it and..."

"We'll discuss this when you get here." I snap, getting impatient. The sound of car keys jingling chimes through the phone.

"I'll be there in 15 minutes."

"Get here quicker - 5 minutes."

"Only if I run red lights."

"Run them." I demand forcefully and cancel the call.

Standing by the front door, I search into the darkness watching out for his headlights. Laurence groans in pain as he tries to shuffle into a more comfortable position on the mattress I took from his bed. Finally, after 8 minutes and 43 seconds, Karl appears through the darkness and pulls up by the front door.

I'm not shocked by the physical change I see in him; dark shadows under his eyes highlighted by his pale skin and a slightly thinner face. His mustard jumper looks baggy on his frame as his dark brown coat looks two sizes too big. His movements seem painfully sluggish and the fear that invades his eyes upon seeing me again is as clear as a cloudless sky. With slightly hesitant steps, he walks towards me, head down and just walks into the house.

Following him inside, Karl stops and looks in horror at Laurence curled up on the mattress.

"He was attacked and too injured to move upstairs." I explain as Karl takes a shaky breath, rubbing the back of his neck.

"So... that's why you have blood on your jumper?"

His statement causes me to look down, for the first time realising I have two immense dark blood stains clearly visible on my white jumper.

"Oh, sorry. I did not... did not realise." Pulling at the fabric on my jumper, the urge to tear it off and burn it consumes my thoughts. I cross my arms over my chest to prevent myself from doing so.

"He's one as well?" Karl asks as I nod my head to answer. "So... when I was here there were actually three vampires in the house?"

"Not important Karl." I growl, making him jump as I grab his arm, pulling him into the living room. I can sense the shock and fear in the atmosphere as he surveys the scene. Hearing him swallow the lump in his throat is proof.

"Right... well there has clearly been a struggle. Blood splatter. Broken table." He mumbles to himself and I have to bite my tongue to stop a sarcastic remark firing from my mouth.

Turning to me, he begins firing questions at me; Hilary's age, what she looks like, what she was wearing last. Once twenty-one questions is over and done with, he takes photos of the crime scene; every disturbance, blood spatter, broken objects... As I stand by and watch, he pulls out his phone. A familiar number lights up on the screen.

“Do not phone Zoe!” I warn as he looks at me, baffled and alarmed by my mention of a familiar name.

“How do you know Zoe?!” Lowering his phone as dread and panic flood his face.

“Let’s just say we go back a bit.”

Not asking any more questions he puts his phone back in his pocket. “So, what do you want to do now?”

My eyes catch the broken table, a leg from the table is covered in blood, recognising the smell to be Hilary’s. I turn away in painful guilt as my mind tries to focus on what to do, to not only find Hilary but get her back.

“If you know Zoe... She could help us.” Karl speaks up, stepping towards me, glancing at the clock, showing its 8:27pm. “She never leaves the office till at least 9.”

“She doesn’t like me.” I mumble, glaring at the floor in annoyance. “She won’t help me.”

A minute or so passes in silence as my brain desperately tries to focus and piece together bits of information that I have to advance into a first step, but the logical part is drowning in a pool of guilt and fear that I cannot focus. Squeezing my eyes shut, I try and block out the emotions.

Karl’s voice appears over the noise in my head. “Right now, you can’t focus. You’re too wrapped up in shock. You need a fresh pair of eyes. Zoe is ten times better than I am. You need her help.”

Contemplating for a moment, before surrendering defeat, I walk out into the reception and snatch the note from the side table. Laurence is still asleep, slowly recovering from his trauma.

“I’ll be back soon.” I promise, placing a gentle kiss on his forehead. “Thank you for everything you did.”

Dashing up the stairs in unhuman speed, I rip the coat and jumper off as well as the skirt and tights, discarding it on the floor. Tugging on a pair of black jeans and silk fitted top, I race down the stairs and grabbing a long wool cardigan, I shove past Karl as he stands by the front door. He follows me to his car with a bewildered expression. With the note clutched in my hand, I hold onto it hoping it will bring me answers... and the death of Great Fang.

The lights of the city fly past us and the joy and party atmosphere of Friday night is alive with life; people already pissed out of their minds wobble along the streets, laughter and drunken words filling the night air. It's like the city is now mocking me.

"Mystique." Karl's voice breaks through my thoughts and I only turn my head a fraction to let him know I'm listening.

"I asked you if you were going to be warm enough in just that cardigan."

"I don't really feel the cold." I answer, as the memory of Hilary playing in the snow in the garden breaks into my mind. My lip quivers but I bite it to keep under control.

"Fair enough... Do you think this Great Fang is a part of the Royal ... Group? Clan? Whatever it was called."

"I killed the vampire who told me so." I reply dryly.

Karl swallows a lump in his throat. "Ok... So, you have a plan?"

"Yeah... I am going to tear his head off."

"Right." Mumbling in a narking manor as he indicates left and turns into a street, just missing a drunken pedestrian zigzagging across the road. Karl curses as the pedestrian flicks us the finger, I catch in the side mirror.

"You need to think this through Mystique." His voice is serious and I can almost hear the wheels working around in his head.

"I am. I'm on number 673 of ways to kill him..."

"That's not thinking it through, that's just focusing on killing." Karl answers irritated as he turns into another street.

"674... and that's all I need to think about."

His hands on the wheel grip tighter and his voice snaps across to me, "Then you are no better than every other vampire in this fucking city!"

Whipping my head around, I stare at him viciously, snarling as I do. A bead of sweat develops and rolls from his forehead, taking in a shaky breath, he starts again, but his eyes locking on the road.

"What I meant was, I thought you weren't them... Like the others."

"I'm not like them."

"So why is your attitude all about blood and death?" He questions, a hint of fear in his voice.

"A vampire's life is already decided and the path we go down has no left or right. Fear, bloodshed and death is inevitable." Silence falls among us. The car charging with tension; anger from me, fear from him. Taking in a deep breath and breaking my stare, I gaze out the window again.

"You have a case where a mother discovers someone has kidnapped her daughter. She finds the kidnapper and kills him, taking her child back. Do you see what she did as justice?"

His hands grip the wheel a little tighter again, exhaling loudly. "Personally, yes."

"So why is my case any different?"

"Your case is different because *you* and *your* kind are different."

"Thank you for pointing out the obvious." My sarcasm doesn't amuse him.

"And for the record I never said I disagree with you killing him. The less vampires there are the better in my opinion – no offence."

A small laugh slips from my lips. "Trust me, no offence is given. I agree with you."

A smile spreads across his face as he takes one hand off the wheel to scratch his head; his red wavy hair ruffling in motion.

"All I meant was, you need a plan. You can't go into all of this, guns blazing. Someone could get hurt."

Nodding my head, I catch a glimpse of a nightclub and two women stumbling out, skirts so high up they may as well be belts. "So, what plan do you suggest?"

"I'm not sure. But you need to be smart. I'm sure Zoe can come up with one."

"Let's hope so."

The station stands eerily in the night, a tall structure of justice and power to some people. For others it is a monitoring station, making sure we don't fall out of line. We make our way inside and it looks like a typical police station; officers walking about, phones glued to their ears, desks placed in a specific order, some officers clearly being made to stay behind to get paperwork done. Pictures of all the officers hang on one wall with their names beneath indicating who they are; their smiling faces beaming. I note that the people walking around here are human.

Good. No vampire officers running around the city.

Karl leads me to Zoe's office; I can already hear the pen scratching on the paper, hissing under her breath as she curses paperwork and whoever came up with it. As we approach, I look through the window, seeing her head low, focusing on her paperwork, her hair pulled up in a bun, her mint green coat thrown across the table, possibly in frustration for all the paper work she has to complete.

Karl knocks on the door as I stand behind him waiting.

"Yes?" She chimes.

"It's Karl. Can I come in?"

"Sure, sure. Come on in." Her voice is cheery and non-threatening; it's almost alien to me. Opening the door, he walks in slowly, I follow behind.

Zoe looks up from her paperwork, smiling and welcoming towards Karl, the second she catches sight of me she freezes; face falling accompanied with a mouth drop. Not with fear. Not with hate; just shock that I'm standing in her office, in her building, in her environment. Zoe looks at Karl with a mixture of wonder and concern.

"Karl knows what I am." I simply state to get rid of the unknown suspicion, in order to move forward to the importance of why I am here.

"*You* know what *she* is?!" Karl shouts in surprise, staring at Zoe with shock as his finger motions between us.

Jumping from her seat, waving her hands frantically she strides over to the office door, shutting it tightly; her emerald green poncho flailing around with her as she moves.

"Jesus Karl! Shut up! Do you want the whole office knowing about this? Yes, I've known her for a while."

Karl's face goes pale once again, making his mustard jumper stand out even more so as a thought crosses his face. "*Please* tell me you aren't one of them! Cause I swear I'll have a fucking breakdown!"

"No, she is not and will you just calm down." I turn to him, placing a supporting hand on his shoulder. This contact seems to make Zoe straighten up in attentiveness, her eyes locking onto mine.

"Invading my life in a new way now?" She asks harshly as she sits back in her seat, smoothing her black hair and fidgeting with the white ombre bun on the top of her head. Not wanting to play this game, knowing every ticking second is crucial, I begrudgingly go straight to the point.

"I need your help."

"Haven't you always?" Leaning back in her seat, she gestures the chair in front of her desk, offering me, or Karl, a seat. I stand my ground as does he.

"My sister has been kidnapped by a vampire who calls himself Great Fang." Tossing the note onto her desk, she picks it up and reads it as I speak. Karl walks to the window and turns the blinds down, blocking anyone from looking in.

"You and I have been working together for years. You work unsolved cases and find the criminal is a vampire. You tell me, I kill them. You help me with my killings and make them closed cases to lost causes. We've worked well. We don't have the warmest relationship I admit."

"I agree." Sighing, she reads the note again, more carefully.

I continue. "I need you... More than ever this time. Hilary is the only family I have left; I have protected her for all these years with Laurence's help but this time it just hasn't worked. We have done the best we can to make her ... Not a monster."

"She's already a monster. Or do you still believe you are one of us?" Zoe's words cut through me like a sharp sting as I walk over to her desk, slamming my hands on the wood, nearly splitting it in half.

"All these years I have helped you, done my best to make up for the fact- well, actually I don't know what I am making up for! I saved your life and you treat that like it is nothing! I have aided in getting rid of the monsters in your world and yet you still treat me like one of them!" I roar at her, raging like a burning fire in my voice.

Playing her best poker face, she stares back, taking a deep breath as she composes herself. "You may act human, speak and look like us, but nothing about you *is* human." She hisses the words back to my face.

"That's a bit harsh Zoe. What's gotten into you?" Karl speaks up, crossing the room to join my side.

"Not from the way I see it." Leaning back in her chair once again, she folds her arms, venomous eyes glaring back at me; her amber eyes reflecting the gold dragonfly details on her top.

"If she saved your life, you should be grateful! I'm assuming she saved you from a vampire?" He asks, as if needing clarification.

Tapping her nails on the desk, she speaks in a steady voice. "A guy came into my grandmother's shop years ago when I was there visiting her. Mystique had followed him in. She chatted with me for a bit before he grabbed one of the clocks sitting on the shelf. I pursued after him, of course. He lured me into an alleyway and attacked me..."

Hesitating, her drumming of her nails stopping short before she continues, "-Mystique showed up and saved me. When I realised, I was dealing with a threat I couldn't take down, we stayed in touch. When we got cases we couldn't solve and I suspected foul play, Mystique would step in to see if our suspect was a vampire. If it was, she would kill him."

I step in, continuing the explanation as I turn to Karl. "Zoe helped me out too. When I killed a vampire and you guys came across it, Zoe would make sure to link it to a logical explanation in any way she could. Whether that be planting evidence or drawing the suspicion to someone suitable of committing the crime. It kept me safe and vampires under the radar."

Karl's eyes are wide with shock, darting back to Zoe in disbelief. "You *fabricated* evidence?! Are you out of your mind?! If anyone finds out you'll be fired and thrown in prison!"

Standing from her seat, she leans forward, arms spread on the table. "I did what I had to do to make the best out of a nightmare situation! And what about you?!" Motioning her hand to gesture towards Karl. "You obviously know who she is! How did that happen? I'm going to link the two together and say the reason you've been so ill this past week, is because you found out about vampires and it's clearly knocked you for six! Your jumper and coat look way too big for you!" As she speaks her voice thickens with concern.

Karl's voice is alive with empathy as he speaks. "You're right. I've been unwell because I found all this out... But Zoe... She saved my life. The warehouse case, she got me out alive."

"What do you mean?" Zoe speaks worryingly as she straightens up, her attitude interchanges; her voice soft and caring as the animosity in the air fades away.

"I should have told you the truth. I was on a date... Lucy Benedict was my date. We were kidnapped and dragged into the warehouse by some vampires. If Mystique never came along, I would be dead..."

He turns to me, his eyes holding mine and for the first time instead of distress or terror, genuine gratefulness glowing like a sunlit orb shines from them. "So, I owe you my life. Not just for that night but for what you did after. The food you left on my doorstep. Thank you. Thank you so much."

Nodding my head and smiling, feeling fortunate and thrilled to hear kind words for once, I turn and look at Zoe, her eyes warmly holding onto Karl. That expression is one I've seen a thousand times by a thousand faces; one of admiration and a kind of warmth you only get from being around those you love.

Zoe's face switches between conflict and thought, but eventually gratefulness wins. However, she refuses to meet my gaze as she speaks.

"I owe you an apology then Mystique." Her hand overlaps her wrist, her fingernails scrapping along her dark skin.

"Better late than never I suppose." Silence gathered like a heavy blanket; neither one of us knowing quite what to follow up with my comment. Then Karl steps forward once again, leans on the desk and speaks softly.

"She saved our lives. Chances are she has saved lots of lives by getting rid of vampires off the street. Much like how we get bad guys off the street. We owe her to try and save her sister." Staring at each other's eyes, it was like they have a connection; an unspoken language only they can hear. Finally, she smiles a half smile as she walks round her desk stopping in front of me.

"We can be allies. This one time. After we save your sister, we go back to the way we use to... Not because I want to. I just can't look past... what you are. What you are capable of."

"I understand."

Turning quickly on her heels, she sits back down behind her desk and takes her car keys from her pocket. One small key dangles among larger ones and she uses the small one to open a draw that is locked. Pulling out a black case and using one of the larger keys, she opens it and goes through a few folders before pulling out one, filled with papers and photos.

"Great Fang is a name I have come across. He is a serial killer; grabbing people off the street and feeding off them. I managed to get a couple of pictures of him." Tossing a photo towards me, I grab it and stare at the face.

Short black dreadlocks. Black skin. Mahogany brown eyes. Stubble. Handsome features. Tattoo of a black fang just below his collar bone.

"I know him." I mumble in anger, gripping the picture so tightly it creases the sides.

"You do?" Zoe's voice jumps in surprise.

"Yeah, we all went to the museum this morning. He followed us there. He interacted with Hilary, she gave him back a pendant that he dropped and I'm a fucking idiot for not realising who this fucking vampire was! I swear if I had known I'd have torn him to pieces and now he-he has Hilary! Doing God knows what to-to her! I-I-I'm going to find him and-and I'm going to make sure he feels every ounce of pain and..." My words run faster than my voice can catch up as my chest feels heavy and my ears ring with pressure, my mind taunting me with images that I dare not look at. My feet pacing around the office to try and calm my racing thoughts.

"Woah, calm down ok! Just calm down, we'll find her." Karl places a hand on my back, trying to deaccelerate my fear.

"We will find her, I promise-" Zoe remarks before continuing, "- I haven't mentioned him to you before because I was trying to see if he was a single worker. But every time I catch him, he's with a group of his shark buddies."

"Shark buddies? That's a new way of saying vampires." Countering with a slight joke, I take the moment to salvage my mind.

"Sharp teeth. Taste for blood. Don't you think it suits you?" She asks with sarcastic humour.

"I prefer to go for the throat rather than tear limbs off." I point out, the corner of my mouth itching to smile as Zoe shrugs her shoulders in a passive gesture before throwing another picture on the desk; this time it's a bar.

"He tends to hang out at the Lost Angels bar. If he isn't there, one of his sharks is."

"I was told about this place. I was planning on visiting there soon." Staring at the picture an idea crosses my mind. "I don't suppose you were following him today were you?"

"No sorry. I got so caught up in these other cases I didn't have time."

"Worth a shot." Exhaling through my nose heavily, I try and remain positive. "This is a start at least."

"Do you think he'll be there tonight?" Zoe asks, looking at me with uncertainty.

"It is the only lead I have right now and I don't know how much time I have." Shoving the pictures into my pocket, I turn to leave.

"Slow down!" Zoe calls out as my hand touches the door handle. "You'll need back up. Let me come with you. If mayhem breaks out, I can cover you - police raid on a suspected criminal." Zoe speaks up as I contemplate the dangers.

Karl speaks up as he clears his froggy throat. "You aren't going alone."

"You aren't well, you need to be home." Zoe reflects his statement, a look of annoyance crossing her face.

"Fat chance, I'm coming," he states, standing beside Zoe in defiance. I gaze at them both for a second, before nodding my head in agreement.

"So, what exactly is your plan?" Zoe asks, hand on her hip, waiting for my answer.

Karl looks at her with a touch of concern. "Um, Zoe you know how useless I am with raids."

She smiles softly at him; her dark cheeks blushing a small pink. "I trust you; besides do you really think I am going to take anyone else?"

"Well according to Karl going in all guns blazing is not a good idea. So, what would you suggest?" I ask as I keep my hand on the handle. Zoe applies her little bit of knowledge onto a draft plan, speaking openly.

"Well its Friday, past experience tells me it is a 50/50 shot as to whether he will be there or not. If he isn't, then the most important thing is information. You need to find out where your sister is from one of his sharks. We will take it from there."

Karl smiles smugly as his hand rubs the back of his neck. "Didn't I tell you she's ten times better than me?"

The comment makes Zoe blush immensely, smiling and eyes dart to the floor as she grabs her mint green coat from the desk.

"And if he is there and I get the information... I will kill him." I state confidently.

Stopping in the doorway, Zoe turns and looks at me with wicked humour. "You'd be doing me a favour - less work for me to do in the morning."

Chapter 11: Lost Angels Of Lost Souls

The Lost Angels is a popular bar in London by everyone local. A big white building with black doors and windows stands on the corner of Battersea Park Road; it almost towers over everything. The black painted angel on the building is placed high up, as if it is guarding everyone from the dangers of the night.

I have never been into this bar, but I have heard its popularity among the locals. The food is meant to be very good; a great atmosphere is always created and the interior is meant to be very unique... Of course, a vampire there would think the food certainly is to *die* for.

We make our way to the Lost Angels, all of us in Zoe's car. I sit in the back staring out the window, Karl in the passenger seat, chatting to Zoe about a plan in case they need to go in to help me. It is obvious to anyone with two eyes that Karl has feelings for her. It can be seen in the way they move; his hand magnetising to be as close to her hand as possible, his pupils dilating slightly when speaking to her, his body even pulls towards hers. His voice always full of emotion when speaking to her, but it is also guarded. Zoe is just as obvious; the blushing of the cheeks, concern for his well-being, her eyes always looking his way, a smile present on her face whenever Karl talks.

Clearly neither one nor the other have admitted their feelings... I wonder if they ever will.

The passing night flies by the car, the colourful lights and music from the outside world continue to torment me, showing me a mirror into a world I will never know. My own world being chipped away like the breaking of glass.

"Mystique." A faint voice whispers through my cracking mind and look up to see to Karl with a stern look. "-We're here. If you need us just pocket dial either me or Zoe... And be careful."

Scanning the scene outside, rain has started to pour down, washing away the last bit of snow we had obtained for the last few weeks. The Lost Angel stands in the darkness, aglow with light, looking almost like a beacon of hope from the shadow and rain. The black angel has lights shining down on it, making it look almost angelic.

"If things take a turn for the worse, call for back up." I order, my eyes locking onto Karl, then moving over to Zoe. Karl looks unconvinced as he opens his mouth to say something, but Zoe interrupts.

"Of course. Go." Not wanting to waste any more time, pulling my teal cardigan over my head, I get out the car and swiftly make my way into the Lost Angel.

The bar is very busy as expected, the atmosphere charged with excitement and electricity from the speakers of the DJ player playing some dance songs to continue the club themed night the pub is throwing. Bodies so closely packed together it makes it difficult to move around freely. Personal space is left at the front door as different arms, torsos and backs touch you somewhere on your body.

As I push my way through, the sound of high heeled shoes on the wooden floor being almost as loud as the music, over the bopping heads my eyes scan for Great Fang. Leather corner sofas are placed around the perimeter of the room, in the corners and along the windows. Tall martini thin tables with stools try and keep their balance, but tonight they are not a good choice of seating; people struggle to stay on their seat as others brush by, knocking them slightly, the table and drinks almost toppling over.

I wonder why he likes this place?

I catch onto the old pictures hanging on the teal and cream walls, a white phone box with a typewriter inside stands to the side of the hexagonal bar. As soon as I step close to the bar, the sensation of powerful eyes latching onto my body crawls across my skin. Searching around the room, brushing past the intoxicated hormone fuelled bodies, the scent of vampires is mixed faintly in the air along with the fiery alcohol and human buzz. Counting three vampires, I get a bad feeling in the pit of my stomach. The atmosphere, though containing electricity from the party goers, has a different electric flowing in between the current; white hot danger.

Everyone is cramming at the bar, trying to order drinks. The head pulsing chatter and laughter and the music is taking over the room and almost all my senses, but I force myself to block it out, letting the scent of the vampire lead me. Swiftly diverting in between the pulsing group of friends and the chat-up experts trying their luck, all their hearts beating loudly, a small thought crosses my mind. That Hilary would never be able to do this. This would be too much for her. I hope he haven't brought her here, as much as I would love to just grab her and take her home, if she lost it here... Not one corner would be free from the warm red river. My mind focuses on her as I'm drawn to the back of the room.

I see a wall deco of stag heads painted different colours on a brown coloured wall, black leather seats in the corner and a long red rope stopping people getting into that section of seating. Two vampires are the bodyguards dressed in black trousers, black leather jackets and white t-shirts. They lock eyes with me and one throws me a grin. My hand curls up into a ball as I approach, expecting a bit of confrontation.

Beyond them, a shady figure sits confidently, looking smartly dressed and the white-hot electricity radiates from him. The one named Great Fang. His hand wraps around a cocktail in a crystallised looking glass, his wine-red shirt almost hiding against his dark complexion, his hat tilted down shadowing his eyes, part of his locks falls to the side of his face, arms brazenly outstretched on the back of the leather seat. His white teeth flash me as he smiles and the negative churning in my pit escalates.

He is expecting me.

The one bodyguard opens up the section, motioning me to go in, but not before giving me a dirty smile. Not breaking my stride, I walk straight in. Finding myself standing before Great Fang, with only a feeble table in between me and my revenge, my anger threatens to take flight as the dragon quickly glides up my spine. He lifts his face up, looking at me with admiration. "Looking as beautiful as ever." His African accent slides through his voice as his lizard tongue licks his lips, his reddish-brown eyes look my body up and down, like I am a prize he can finally claim.

He can look all he wants. He won't live for much longer so he better enjoy every last minute he has, before I decapitate his head from his neck.

His shirt is slightly open, the first three buttons not done up, the black fang tattoo on his collarbone is visible, along with the black pendant Hilary gave back to him; it's rectangle shape dangles from a black thread.

"Where is she?" I demand. Over the noise of the pub no one else will hear my question but him. Putting the glass to his lips casually, he takes a sip, places it back down and gazes at me as if looking at an old friend.

"What has the world come to where you cannot sit and have a drink with company? Please, sit." His hand gestures to the seat, his voice smooth. "I trust you had a nice morning trip?" Gritting my teeth, the dragon threatens to spit fire, but I hold back, not wanting to burn myself in the process.

"You are one of the slimiest things I have ever seen... and that's including all the slime that is on this floor."

He takes a sharp intake of breath. "Ouch. That hurts you know." Sarcasm thick in his words, he smirks at me. Staring at him, he stares back, amusement in his face. He takes another sip of his drink. I take the seat he offered, feeling like he is going to play this out.

"So, here we are..." leaning forward, hands clasp together, "-you and I. After all these years. How's the rage? Burning? Feeling a little hot under the collar?"

Aware of my fiery temper, clearly.

"Like a caged dragon. I'm tempted to cut your head off and put it on display like the wall decoration over there" I reply, pointing with my thumb over my shoulder. He smiles at my answer. A human waiter appears by me, placing an alcoholic drink down beside me.

"Here you are madam." He scatters off, to get the next drink on his list. Great Fang tips his hat towards the drink.

"You strike me as a margarita kind of woman." He winks at me and I smile sarcastically.

"And what kind of woman do you think I am Mr Fang?"

He leans forward, a twinkle in his eye. "A dangerous one."

"Correct". The clinking of glass, the mindless chatter and nonsense music of the bar becomes like white noise. We are now in our own little world; our own bubble.

He stares me down, taking a big gulp of his white Russian drink. "You really hate me, don't you?"

"Understatement."

Great Fang smiles at me, probably enjoying the fact that he has slight power over me.

He chuckles, eyes glistening. "Ok, I'm going to be straight with you-"

“Don’t you need a backbone for that?” I cut him off and he chuckles again but continues.

“-Mystique. I’ve been watching you. For a long time. I’m very impressed with this... superhero image you’ve built.”

“I’m no hero.” My voice is blank, emotionless. Not wanting to show weakness. Leaning back, Great Fang places his arms back on the leather sofa, using his hands to exaggerate his words.

“Oh, but you are! Isn’t this what you are doing? Right now? Being a superhero. Saving your sister. It’s all very heroic. Killing anyone who gets in your way. Takes guts, determination and true power. I respect that. You are very headstrong. A character trait people seem to lack nowadays.”

“So, you are some creepy fan of mine now?” Taking a sip of the drink, I try to act casual and cool, keeping my raging dragon inside best I can.

“Sort of yes.” He laughs; the sound isn’t pleasant. “So why did you choose the name Mystique? I always wondered.” Bringing his elbow up on the table, he rests his head in his hand, looking as if he is enchanted by my words, really looking like a creepy fan.

“It just seemed to fit. What kind of name is Great Fang anyway?”

Shrugging his shoulders, he parrots back my answer with a lick of his lips. “It just seemed to fit.”

Not wanting to waste any more time, I cut to the point. “So, let’s get down to why we are here. Why did you take my sister?” My fury burns his eyes as I glare at him. He doesn’t flinch.

“Ah, now see. I needed your sister so I could have you.”

Taking a deep breath, I open my mouth to speak but another waiter cuts in, taking Great Fang’s empty glass, replacing it with another full glass of the same drink.

“Here you are sir” he mumbles before walking off. Great Fang’s eyes linger on the boy as he walks away, that look is one of blood lust. He cracks a smile to himself before sipping on his drink and his eyes turn back to me.

“You don’t drink young blood, do you?” Pausing, he looks behind me at the dancing food party. “I don’t know how you can resist.”

"You resisted me-." I remark as he pauses from his second sip of his drink. "-You didn't drink all of my blood. You did not kill me. Luke told me you never changed anyone before." Silence fell among us, in our own bubble. But the bar was still loud and booming, someone over the end of the bar dropped a glass and it shattered, almost adding dramatic effects to our conversation.

"Luke was always a chatter box." Great Fang rolls his eyes to himself before taking a swig of his drink.

"Why did you leave me? Why turn me into this?" My voice is sharp now and the glass in my hand is threatening to shatter under my grip. I ask the most important question, the one I've wanted answers to most of all. "Why did you do it? Why kill my parents?"

Casting his gaze down, shaking his head and leaning back, it's clear he's mocking me, laughing as he does so. "Ah, no, no, no, no. Not so fast. You don't get the answer to those questions yet."

For the first time, my heart jumps a little bit. He didn't deny it... and I can tell... he has the answers.

"Give me the answer to one... Why did you kill my parents?" I ask again, my angry dragon growing impatient. Rolling his wrist with his drink in hand, he watches the white liquid swirl as the ice clinks in the glass.

"I suppose you deserve one answer..." He holds up a finger, "-But just one! Can't be too greedy."

I wait, stone face and burning with rage as I listen to the answer; his words slow and calculating.

"I killed your father in a moment of passion. Your mother was... collateral damage, as were you. That's why I set the house on fire. I didn't know you and your sister got out alive until I saw you years later walking around. That's when I realised, I could use you. So, I bit you. Made you like me... and waited."

I wait for a sense of relief to fill me, to wash away the doubt and burden I have faced for so many decades. Instead, the dragon in my chest burns as the pain continues to crush me. "Waited for what, exactly? What did you want from my father? What were you expecting of me?"

His eyes search within me. "Doesn't everyone expect greatness from a hero?"

Ignoring his riddle, I snap back. "You knew I was coming here to save my sister. What is the point of all this?"

His smirk tells me everything before his words confirm it. "Well because I knew you would be unable to kill me in a building full of humans, you or your two little friends outside."

Keeping a good poker face, I mask my shock of his knowledge of Karl and Zoe outside. He couldn't have possibly known that. But he did. He must have known since I showed up.

"Don't worry I won't hurt them. I just wanted to see you again before the countdown."

"Countdown?" I question as he takes another sip of his drink.

"The countdown to you and I meeting again, in the presence of your sister."

My heart jumps at Hilary's mention and he hears it. "In your note, you said you wanted something from me. Something you believed we both desired." I ask, my grip on the glass drink tightening.

"In due time, my dear. I'm not spilling everything now."

The dragon is restless, the fire building the burning pressure growing in my head. "Then why meet here? Why take my sister? Just tell me what you want."

Great Fang smirks, lowering his drink and leaning back into the leather sofa, eyes gleaming and calculating. "She is only leverage to get what I want. You see, you can't say no now. *This way* you have no choice but to say yes, because you risk losing your sister. I get what I want. You get your sister back. Everyone wins."

"So why not just tell me, right now, what you want from me."

He hums in a low, deep voice, curdling a smile as he does so. "Every good hero needs a taste of fear, to remind themselves of how vulnerable they really are." His words, powerful and certain, strike a bolt of fear down my spine. Trying to mask it, my voice stays calm.

"This will be the countdown to your death."

"I believe not. I believe it's the countdown to a better friendship... You and me." His words are full of good intentions and this makes my gut do flips.

What are you planning with Hilary? With me?

Standing up, he bows to me and finishes his drink, his other hand grabbing a black hat, placing it on his head with it tilting slightly due to his dreadlocks. "With that I must bid you farewell. Until we meet again Mystique."

The dragon breaks free, enraged with fury, demanding a fiery death. Throwing myself up, propelling across the table to grab his shirt but his two bodyguards cage my arms.

"You aren't going anywhere!" I roar loudly, my words alight with fire and rage. With that, our little bubble pops. The group of people around us notice and the noise dies down slightly except for the music.

"Don't try it!" One of the vampires tells me, but I can feel he is having to use some force with his muscles to keep me back. Pushing his hat away from his eyes, he chuckles at the scene in front of him.

"Now, now. That's not a nice way to treat the guy who bought you a drink." He mocks, looking at the spilled margarita on the table. "Even if it is now a waste."

"What is a waste is that you have survived today and taken up precious oxygen. You are not leaving until you give me my sister." I hiss quietly but knowing he can hear me.

"In due time." He winks and it sends my blood boiling.

"If you harm one hair on her head, I swear to God I'll"-

"-God will not answer your prayers. He never answered mine." Snapping back at me with his lizard eyes wide, teeth baring in an animal snarl.

"Don't start preaching about your beliefs. Tell your dogs to let go of me before I break their arms".

Gesturing with his hand, his demeanour collects itself back to his calm and cocky self, voice calm and cool. People around us are still watching with alert and curiosity.

"You'd cause a scene and put a room full of souls at risk of being devoured by three hungry vampires?" He lowers his voice to a hush, knowing I'd only hear his words. Gritting my teeth, I knew how easy this could be anywhere else. How easily I could flip his two bodyguards in the air and grab Great Fang, but the fact I am being restricted by the factors surrounding me threatens to drive me insane.

He is about to casually walk out the door and I cannot stop him!

"Good day Miss." Tipping his hat and with his blazer over his shoulder, casually, as if nothing out the ordinary, he slips into the crowd. The bodyguards release me and quickly slithers into the crowd.

Standing there, numb with anger, numb with pain, numb to my entire surroundings. My eyes stare at the spilt drink as I try and collect myself. The manager, after seeing the confrontation comes over, observing the knocked over drink and sighs with frustration.

"I hope you are more careful with the next drink you order... and make sure that doesn't happen again or else you are barred! A woman like you shouldn't behave like that."

The dragon inside me snaps again. Grabbing a fistful of his shirt, I spin, throwing him into a standing table of deserted drinks. The clattering of the noise causes the party goers to jump back in shock. An eruptive cheer breaks out as I shove my way past the alcohol fuelled drunks.

Storming out, I get to Zoe's car and slam the passenger door shut behind me, almost breaking it off the hinges. Silence looms over the car. No one speaks. They can all work out what happened and seeing Great Fang leave the bar is a good indication, before disappearing into the night. My breath is hot and heavy as my pulse rages. After a few minutes, Karl is the first to test the water.

"He gave you nothing?"

"No." I snap. "It was to mock me. Test my restraint."

"Why don't you go after him?" Zoe asks hastily.

"He knows you two are here and he has my sister. It is too risky."

"So, what next?" Karl questions in a gloomy voice.

“That’s a good question.” I reply, trying to make sense of the chaos going on in my head.

Scratching his chin, he yawns loudly. “Well look, we won’t get any answers by staying up all night. Let’s get some rest and we’ll work out a plan in the morning.”

“Sounds good.” Zoe speaks up, turning the key in the ignition. Staying quiet, I just let the world pass by the window. Hilary is all I can think of. I pray she is ok. I pray. For the first time in a long time.

Chapter 12: Unspoken Stories

The absence of my sister in the house is torture. Pure silence. I never knew how much it can brutalise a person's mind until now. I try everything, leaving the TV on, letting the radio softly play out, even listen to Karl and Zoe's on and off banter to drown out the deafening silence, but somehow it does not ease my crushing immobilising agony.

Laurence slowly recovers from his injuries as I stay beside him, keeping him comfortable, feeding him blood bags from the fridge to aid in his recovery. Karl and Zoe stay through the night, settling to sleep in the guest bedroom together.

I try to sleep, resting my back against the reception wall next to Laurence, wrapping my thick teal cardigan round me like a blanket but I only sleep for twenty minutes at the most, before waking up with a sickening emptiness within my body. The clock chimes, announcing it to be a time in the morning I do not care to know, as Laurence stirs in his sleep, mumbling Hilary's name as I try to calm him, whispering contently as I put him back to sleep with the purple haze from my hand.

The stairs creaks in a low groan, glancing up to see Karl, gingerly making his way down the steps. He smiles apologetically as he lightly steps over to me; it dawns on me his movements remind me of a deer or a fawn.

"I know there is no point in trying to be quiet. It's just a force of habit." He whispers as he approaches, his mustard jumper scruffy from sleep, revealing part of a white t-shirt underneath, wiping his left eye where his beauty mark begins to turn a little red.

"It's fine." I mumble, looking away from his warm eyes trying to comfort me.

"You know, sleeping wouldn't be a bad idea." Sliding himself next to me, bringing his knee up to rest his arm on, making himself comfortable.

"Sleep is not helping me." I retort, as the purple energy fades away from my hand as I pull away from Laurence, my fingers entwining in a dance with a stand of my hair.

"It's not going to hurt you either... How's he doing?"

"He is old, so he takes longer than most to recover. But he will be ok."

Karl smiles at my comment. "I thought all vampires were old." His humour flies over me as I keep my eyes away.

Puffing his cheeks and allowing the air to escape his mouth, he tries correcting himself, dropping the humour. "I'm sorry. I'm trying to help and I guess I'm failing. The only way I know how to help is by talking."

I don't reply, staring at Laurence for no reason in particular.

"So how did you guys meet?" Karl asks curiously.

"It is not an interesting story." I reply lazily.

"Well I'm awake, as are you. I think we have some time to share stories."

Taking a deep sigh, I quickly surrender, out of not being able to conjure the energy to argue.

"He was part of the Royal Order, one of the three leaders. When I arrived to learn more about vampires, he took a liking to my story. He found out I was going to run and decided to run away with me." My eyes scan over his beaten and bruised body, watching the cuts slowly heal; a snap of painful guilt hitting my ribs. "He told me he wanted to leave, when the Order was beginning to fail... He said that, somehow, I gave him the strength to leave, I gave him a sense of purpose."

Feeling Karl's gaze, I keep my own trained on Laurence, not wanting him to see the tears threatening to spill.

"Must be nice." Karl states as my brows cross, momentarily confused by his statement as he continues. "To be able to run away from a life you hated into a simple one that gives you freedom." The sound of his hands rubbing together back and forth irate me slowly, but I concentrate on my breathing to try and help.

"What's the story with him? How was he made into a vampire?" He asks, rubbing his hands rhythmically.

"His story is one of the nicer ones. He lived most of his life, of course. He had an education, was in the army I believe, married, had some children. One day, he witnessed a mugging, tried to stop the man. In the midst of their struggle, the man, a vampire of course, bit him. Laurence went through the change in his own home, with his wife close by. When he woke up and realised what he was, he fled, leaving his family behind. He found out about the Royal Order and believing there was no other life for him, he stayed and became the right-hand man of Edward, the leader, who calls him brother."

"Biologically?" He asks.

"No, they just became close, like family. Laurence stayed for a very long time, believing there was no other way."

Continuing to rub his hands, Karl looks confused as he speaks with a dismal voice. "I thought you said it was a nicer story?"

"No such vampire story has a happy ending, you know."

Grabbing his wrist in one quick motion, I silence his hands. "Stop it."

"Sorry." Letting his hands fall apart, he continues to try and help, turning his body towards mine, changing the topic within the subject. "So, what's your story then?"

"Much more unpleasant than his." I speak with intonation, trying to avoid that subject.

"You only have three powers?" Karl asks impatiently, trying to obtain any information he can.

Twiddling a strand of hair, I keep my eyes on Laurence. "I could possibly have more... but I have yet to find out."

Puffing out his cheeks, his eyes look around the room lazily. "What are they?" He badgers keenly.

"I do not know."

"Have you tried anything else?"

"All the information I gave you last time was not enough? I have now given you a story, please, I am not in the mood to entertain your boredom." Closing my eyes and resting my head against the wall, I try and cease the throbbing ache in my head.

"No actually, I was thinking about this earlier. When you saved me from that vampire, he mentioned your ability being split into different... umm..."

Karl snaps his fingers a couple times, wracking his brain for a word to fit. "Forms! Called your power... witchcraft? So, like, what if you can see into the future?"

"I can't." I state bluntly, tilting my head to look at him intensely, as my fingers twirl with the gold strand of hair.

Puffing out his cheeks again, he thinks for a second. "Ok what about... sense? As in, trying to sense where your sister is? You could like..." Outstretching his hand for dramatic effect, he plays out his words, "-sense her energy, aura, her spirit and track her down that way, or maybe..."

"Karl..." I interrupt, looking at him with exhaustion heavy on my face "-I appreciate that you are trying to help, but you are overcomplicating things. I only have three powers right now; paralysis, sleep and fire."

Karl looks to the floor as if searching for an answer. His voice is quiet when it resurfaces. "Hate to say it, but I think it would help us if you told us about your past."

Quickly shaking my head in hopes of shutting that idea down indefinitely. "I know everything about my past. There is no need to speak about it out loud."

"Sometimes it helps, though. If me and Zoe are going to try and find Great Fang, we need to know your connection with him."

Growling under my breath, my fingers find my forehead, rubbing it to try and relieve the pain. The ticking sound of the clocks adds to my irritability. "I know you are trying to help but even I do not know the connection."

"He must have said something to you in the bar." Persisting with his badgering voice as he runs his hand through his dishevelled copper hair.

"He confessed to murdering my father... said my mother was collateral damage... as were me and Hilary." My voice trails off as the memories of that night come screaming back. Squeezing my eyes shut, I gasp suddenly at the new pain in my chest as I try and catch my breath.

"I'm sorry... I just thought- I mean I'm throwing ideas around, trying to help..." Karl rambles, trying to correct himself as he sees the pain being inflicted. Within a second I am on my feet, the room spinning as I try and find my balance.

"-Yeah well you thought I can just spill out my whole history, like it is something so easy to do?" I snap back, tears glistening over my eyes as I try and fight them back.

"But have you ever talked about your history? To Laurence? To anyone? The more you talk about it the easier it becomes." Karl sombrely looks at me as I try to calm myself.

"Laurence knows my history. Hilary lived a part of it with me. There was never a need to revive it through words."

His own words catch me off guard. "Right now, you need to talk about it. Whether you want to or not. It may have clues that could help us."

Conflict within my chest battle to decide whether to speak or not. A few minutes pass, as Karl patiently waits for me to talk. I stay standing, opening and closing my mouth, trying to find the words, desperately trying to find my voice. The longer the time passes, the harder it becomes to speak. Exhaling through my nose in frustration, I lower my head in shame.

"I'm sorry, I can't talk about it. It is like... a fire in my chest..." Tears sting my eyes, threatening to spill. Taking some shaking breaths, I move, getting ready to leave when Karl's words snag me in place.

"My wife died in a car accident. It was hard to talk about at first. It still is. But I find it easier to share my pain with others."

My eyes scan his face, watching it change, watching the mask slip away. His warm green eyes meet mine and I see the loving ache behind them.

"You told me your wife left you." Fitting myself back into place, I sit beside him, baffled by his white lie. A half smile raises his lips. "It's a lie I tell people I don't know well. It saves me from their sad looks and the awkwardness. The word 'divorced' is better than widowed."

"What happened? If you want to talk about it, of course."

"Like I said, talking helps." He smiles a sorrowful smile, eyes afflicted as he speaks.

"Jack was only 7 when it happened. We went on holiday with friends to Paris, left Jack with a babysitter. It was a lovely holiday. We ate croissants, different cheeses, anything we could find. We walked along that bridge with all those locks on. Sarah dragged me into all the shops she could find. We were recapturing our youth, as she put it." He laughs softly, wiping a tear from his eye. "We flew home. It was raining heavily. We got in the car and started driving home. An argument broke out." He pauses, laughing softly again, wiping another tear. "You know, I can't even remember what we were arguing about. All I remember is we were raising our voices and then... I woke up in the hospital two days later."

My hand finds his, enclosing it with comfort. Karl cheerlessly smiles, looking at me before continuing.

"I was told a lorry lost control in the weather conditions. Hit us head on. Sarah was driving. She died instantly."

Tears that didn't belong to my own torment fill my eyes as I look away, the images of his story flowing through my mind as I squeeze his hand in support. "I'm sorry." Whispering woefully as he squeezes my hand back. Perusing his expression, I find myself confused. "How can you smile and tell that story?"

His smile does not wither or fade, instead he laughs lightly, his cheeks bringing his beauty mark closer to his glazed over eyes.

"Telling it brings her closer to me. Like, it revives her. I always feel closer to her when I tell the story. Why would I not smile? She always said she loved my smile."

Each word fills me with loving warmth as I smile with him. "Does Zoe know? You two seem to be close."

Karl smiles widely, his mood perking up slightly at the mention of her name. "Oh, Zoe knows everything about me. She's my best friend. We share the same sense of humour, we both like mint ice cream..."

"Zoe has a sense of humour?" I question with a laugh.

"She acts so differently around you, yeah, but believe me she does! Give her a chance. I'm so glad she gave me one." Karl nervously laughs as he scratches the side of his face, watching the clock quietly tick by.

"You obviously noticed how useless I am in dangerous situations. I was so sure the old boss was going to fire me. When he announced his retirement and Zoe took over, I still believed I was going to be kicked off the force. Time passed and every time Zoe approached me, I kept thinking *this is it, this is the end.* Instead it was always praise, encouragement and reassurance that I was doing things right. Zoe could see I was struggling and wanted to help me. That's how we became close. How we had much in common. Both of us single parents, trying to better ourselves in our jobs."

Hearing those words, I feel warmth and relief from the emptiness as slowly the aching seems to fade.

"When did you realise you had feelings for her?" I persist, not wanting this sensation to fade.

His cheeks turn pink as he rubs his hands again, tilting his head nervously. "Oh well... shit is it that obvious?"

A burst of laughter explodes from my chest; a genuine laugh. "Yeah, pretty much."

His smile reaches his eyes, almost glimmering with joy. "I guess, when I noticed little things. Like, when she wore a colour I hadn't seen her wear before, or how she clicks her tongue when she's being funny, or when she speaks most people talk over her so I step in to help."

Karl catches my expression changing, addressing it straight away. "Zoe isn't respected at our work. Cause she's new, she wasn't part of our team who worked up to that position. People feel like she was just given the job when someone already within the force could have taken it. I try to help her and talk good things, big her up, but until everyone sees for themselves what she's like they won't give her a chance."

Karl stops talking as Laurence move again, concerned we are disturbing his sleep. My own smile has not withered.

"Thank you for sharing that with me... You are really smitten with her. Why don't you tell her?"

"It's not the right time." Shrugging his shoulders, he brushes off my comment as the sound of another pair of feet steadily make their way down the stairs. Zoe appears, her clothes also scruffy from sleep, her bun no longer in place as her wild afro hair is on full display.

"Everyone is early risers I see." Rubbing her mascara smudged eye as she looks at the clock. "7am... I guess it's time for breakfast. By breakfast I mean food... not blood."

Chapter 13: Observational History

We all gather in the library once breakfast is consumed and when Karl and Zoe return from their homes for a change of clothes, talking about plans and what our next move is. I ring work to inform them I won't be available for the next few days. I lie, claiming Hilary is very ill with chicken pox and I cannot get a babysitter. The nurse on the other end of the phone seems unconvinced but I cut the phone off before any more protest can be made.

"We're supposed to be working too. What do we say to everyone at the office?" Karl asks Zoe as she ruffles her hair.

"Well... being the boss has its advantages. I've already rang David and informed him you and I are working on another case together so we need to be out the office."

"But when we go back to work, we won't have a case finished."

I watch from afar as Zoe clicks her tongue with humorous intent, smiling a toothy smile.

"Unlike you soldier boy, I plan ahead." Karl tilts his head in embarrassment as Zoe giggles at his shy flirty reaction. "I already had another case, which I have already solved, unaware to everyone else. I'll just add your name to the file later." Zoe smiles as Karl gives her an impressed thumbs up.

"No wonder you're the boss, Snow White."

Zoe lazily retaliates with a casual shrug of her right shoulder and continue going through the folder. As time ticks away, we are no closer to having any more information or answers as to where Hilary and Great Fang could be. The time passes by and my angry dragon gets restless, building more fire, simmering beneath my skin.

My hands glide the soft fabric of Hilary's doll, the scent of lavender reminding me of her platinum blonde hair, her red eyes, her sweet laughter. Perching on the sofa in the library, listening to the conversation flow between Karl and Zoe, but knowing it is pointless.

We have no leads. Zoe has barely any information on Great Fang as do I. Only that he went to the bar, had his gang with him and he confessed to killing my parents. It is making me feel twitchy.

Zoe's voice is calculating and thick with frustration, her hair standing naturally in all its pride; the white ends frizzy with her frustration.

"We have no address, no real name, no lead of any kind." Her feet pace up and down from the other side of the room as Karl sits at the desk, head down. Moving in order to stop myself from going crazy, I stand and walk over to the desk, doll still in one hand. I stare at the picture of Great Fang that Zoe has retrieved from the folder she keeps of him; sheets of paper and pictures scattered across the surface.

"He's a coward." I mumble, clutching a handful of my teal cardigan in my spare hand.

"A smart one though." Karl pipes up, lifting his head from the desk. "Zoe has put his face through the database. According to the Government, he doesn't exist. No fingerprints, no name, no place of birth."

"I'm not surprised though." Zoe states, her hand resting on the waist of her olive-green trousers. "You are the same. In fact, most vampires are. Most of you are so old you just slip away and hide. It's the new ones that are easy to find."

"Yeah how do you guys do that anyway?" Karl pipes up, directing at me as he leans back in the chair.

I shrug my shoulders, staring at one of the pictures on the desk. "I learnt how to make counterfeit documents when I needed to. It helped me survive and gain money when I needed it. Can we please focus on finding Great Fang?"

"Mystique it's like I said, we need to know your past to give us some idea about his past, and where he could be right now." Karl speaks up, trying to sound supportive.

Slamming my hand on the table, rage burning inside me, I vent my frustration. "None of this is going to find my sister! The past doesn't matter! I don't care if he was born in the sewers of London, he is keeping my sister hostage and I want her back now!"

Karl tussles his hair and closes his eyes, trying to concentrate, his greyish blue stripped shirt already creased.

“This isn’t going to happen overnight you know. We don’t have much information on the guy.” Zoe stands in, speaking up.

“Well maybe you aren’t doing your job right! You are the police! This is what you do is it not?! Find him and my sister!”

“It’s not that simple. You know that.” Her voice trying to be peaceful but it just aggravates me more.

“We have nothing to go on and he knows that! He is playing with me. He is a vampire who likes to play games. He gets off on it.”

“And winning already by the looks of it.” Zoe spits back, stopping in her stride, arms crossed behind her back, puffing out her blush pink blouse, trying to give off her superior authority vibe.

“He’s cranking you up like a coiled spring. He knows about your temper. Probably wants you to go and find him. Don’t let him play you.”

I slam my hand on the desk again. “He is not playing me! You are the ones wasting time by trying to look into the past! What good is that going to do?”

The loud bang cause Karl to jump back in the chair, the old clock chimes 9:00am and Zoe storms over from the other side of the room

“Stop it will you! This is exactly what he wants! Us to turn on one another and to get you riled up.”

Matching her anger, I shoot my words back. “Well you aren’t exactly helping me like I thought you would. I thought we would have a lead by now! Know where he lived or something. But we have nothing and my sister is still with him!”

“Because Karl is right, you aren’t telling us anything about your past so we have nothing to go on!”

“Because my past has nothing to show for it! My father was a doctor, my mother a house wife. I was married off like I was supposed to be. Then Great Fang came in and burnt my home to the...” Catching myself short, I stop dead, realising what I have revealed.

Zoe stares at me with wide amber eyes and a slow small smile spreading across her face. “Right... Ok we know your father was a doctor. That could be something... and you were married?”

Biting my tongue, I self-loath at my own mistake. "I am not talking about this." Shaking my head and turning on my heels I walk away from her.

"And where do you think you're going?" Zoe calls to me in annoyance.

"Back to the bar. Someone there must know him if he's a regular customer." As I reach for the door handle, Zoe turns and talks to Karl, who picks up a piece of paper.

"We may as well keep digging."

Scornfully, I mumble over my shoulder, loud enough to be heard. "Keep wasting your time. I'm actually going to do something about this." With that, the door slams hard behind me. Heading to the front door, I stop and turn to look at the small desk by the door, thinking of Hilary, her doll still gripped in my hand. Loosening my hand, I place the doll sitting upright on the table, smoothing out it's black hair, leaving it sat waiting patiently for my return.

Reaching the Lost Angel bar, the once hectic Friday night atmosphere has now petered away, dissolving into the morning sun. As I walk into the familiar place, it seems different now... and messier.

To my surprise the staff are still cleaning up from the previous night, moping the floors, wiping the tables and still finding bits of food and spillages from the high kited zombies stuffed down the side of chairs and behind plants. Scanning the room, my eyes focus on where we were sat, at the back of the bar in the VIP section. My feet move towards it swiftly, gliding past the staff member mopping up a sticky stain of Coke and rum. Reaching the hidden away VIP section, it was like it had been frozen in time; the glasses still stood empty and lonely, my chair still pushed back from the table after my outburst. The scene stared back at me and I seethe with anger.

Then something catches my eye, glinting in the morning sunlight stretching through the window. On the glass, smudged but useable, is a fingerprint of his, made by some black substance. Perhaps it was ink or some dirt.

Zoe only has his face to go by, but maybe a fingerprint will bring up something. Anything is better than nothing right now.

Glancing over my shoulder, the three staff members are still cleaning away, not paying attention to me apart from the fourth one who is behind the bar, finishing up wiping down the surface, his eyes watching me since I came in. Out of view, my hand carefully picks up the glass, avoiding the smudged fingerprint, I make sure to move in a way that looked like I am searching for something.

Footsteps echo towards me and once close enough I turn around, looking innocent and curious, the glass positioned behind my back in a casual manor. It is the waiter from last night I notice, his hair spiked up stylishly, his smile friendly.

"Can I help you find something?" His name badge identifies Andy.

Smiling sweetly, I play innocent. "Hi. I was here last night with a friend. When I got home, I couldn't find my phone so I thought I may have dropped it somewhere."

"What phone was it?"

"Samsung Galaxy S4 red." I lie, smiling naively.

Shaking his head from side to side, he looks at me with sympathy. "No sorry. I checked lost property 10 minutes ago. There were a couple of phones but both of them were silver."

"Oh," I sigh, pouting a little bit, my eyes catching his. "Never mind then. Well thanks anyway."

"Sorry about that. If you don't mind, I have to ask you to leave now while we get cleaned up. We closed so late last night we are trying to catch up." His hand gestures to the door.

"Oh of course, no problem." Smiling widely, I make my exit, discreetly hiding the smudged glass out of sight.

Returning home, walking past the doll and heading straight into the library, I place the glass in front of Zoe who is leaning over the desk looking from an eagle view at the papers. Karl is just coming downstairs from the bathroom.

"I got you his fingerprint ..." pointing at the black smudge "It should be usable."

Zoe's eyes stare at me in disbelief. "How did you manage to get this? He never left me a crumb, but you he leaves you a fingerprint?"

"Does it matter? Just run it will you!"

"Don't tell me how to do my job!" she snaps back at me, but grabs a tissue from the box next to her and picks up the glass "-I'll take this down to the station and get the fingerprint analysed. Once I've got the results I'll be back." In three strides she is out the door.

Karl walks in wondering what has just happened. He looks at me confused as he pulls on his navy-blue jumper, which seems to fit him a little better. "A new lead?" He questions.

"Hopefully." I reply to him, keeping a little faith.

"While we wait for Zoe to return..." Spinning round towards the familiar voice, my heart almost bursts with joy to see Laurence, standing with a tray of tea, looking still beaten down but recognisable. He places the tray down on the desk and no sooner is it out of his grasp my arms surround him in a tight, loving hug.

"I'm so glad you are ok." Mumbling into his burnt orange jumper, tears finally spilling over, staining the wool fabric.

"I'm glad to see you are safe too." His arms elope me as we embrace each other in a tight hug. Pulling apart, he wipes a warm wet tear from my cheek. "Now, how about a cup of tea for you and our guest?"

A couple hours feel like an eternity. The ticking clock in the living room shows it is 11:03am and Zoe has yet to return. The smell of eggs, bacon, toast with strawberry jam and strong bitter coffee is hanging in the air, crumbs on the discarded plate on the table in the library, evidence of a still hungry policeman. His duffle coat thrown across the arm of the sofa and the cuff of Karl's shirt peeking out from his jumper, is already stained with a small strawberry jam smudge, as he catches Laurence up with the events that happened since Hilary was taken.

I stand by the window, watching the rain droplets race down the glass, my eyes occasionally focusing on my drive way, anticipating the red BMW to appear. Showering and changing my clothes gives me a small sense of purpose as well as some peace from the silence surrounding the house; my black wool jumper soft on my torso, leaving my arms bare to the warmth of the room.

Karl switches the TV on, remarking on why I would have a TV in the library but I leave it unanswered. The program Two and a Half Men appears but he isn't paying much attention to the drunken Charlie Sheen on the screen, as his phone announces Jack is calling and is obviously annoyed that his father is working on his day off, leaving him with his Uncle.

“But dad you promised you’d come and take me to football practise today!” His voice wails from the phone as his father rubs a small jam stain off the pocket of his pebble grey trousers.

“I know Jack but I’m helping out...” he pauses for a moment, choosing an appropriate word “-a friend with something very important.”

A pang of guilt snaps through me, realising I am keeping Karl away from precious time with his son.

“I’ll be home soon. I promise. Have fun with Uncle Harry. I love you. Bye.”

“I’m sorry I am keeping you away from him. You can leave if you want.”

Karl smiles but shakes his head, shutting the phone off and putting it back in his pocket. “I have my whole life to go to his football practises and have dinner with him. That’s all because of you. I owe the same for your sister.”

Laurence pours the hot liquid into his cup, sat at the desk, watching me with intent, his grey hair pulled into a man bun.

“You know, your friends told me that you wouldn’t tell them about your past.”

Rolling my eyes, I turn back to window. “What does it matter?

“Talking about past events can aid in healing the present and providing knowledge for the future.” His wise old words flow from him so easily and instead of feeling annoyed I just smile, welcoming the fact I can still hear his advice. Minutes later, the red BMW smoothly runs up the driveway. Swiftly I greet Zoe at the front door with Laurence and Karl and immediately I can see she has some news, evident with the huge smile on her face, her cheeks round and plump.

“I got a name! Gregory Denmark. But it’s clear it’s just a fake name. His surname changes though, so perhaps that is real. He was caught for killing a man but of course, escaped jail and never found again. They took his fingerprint and, BAM, we got a name.” As she speaks, we make our way back into the library.

"Is that a smile Zoe?" I remark as she ignores my comment, pulling out pictures and pieces of information from her beige wrap coat down on the desk. "At least we have some sort of name... but is still doesn't move us closer to Hilary." I grumble wretchedly.

Zoe stares back at the papers and pictures, I can see the wheels in her head working full speed. Abruptly, she grabs a blank piece of paper from the draw and a black pen. "Hang on" she mumbles to herself, her hand writing out his name.

Great Fang

Underneath she rearranges the words to try and turn them into something else.

"You think it's an anagram?" I ask, watching her mind work, steam coming off the wheels in her head. As she tries some rearranging, scribbling through it when it didn't work, she explains.

"I tried it with your name. I kept thinking, *what kind of name is Mystique?* I was sure I could get your real name from doing it. When it failed, I moved on to looking at any records of you."

"Didn't I tell you she was brilliant?" Karl compliments her as she huffs in an attempt to hide her flattery. Myself and Laurence just glance a knowing look at each other.

After four tries, she rearranges the words and then stops, staring at it with incense. The name she kept getting didn't make much sense.

Greg Tanfa

"It doesn't make sense. Tanfa isn't a name". She scorns, hanging her head down, her black and white hair hiding her face. "Dammit, I thought I had something." Throwing the pen on the table, it rolls off the desk and onto the wooden floor, making a light patter noise before rolling towards the book shelf.

My mind is whirling with memories, information. Then something clicks, like a puzzle piece finally dropping into place.

"Wait a moment!" Racing over to the book shelf, I pull out an old history book on the fourth row, seventh one from the left and throw it on the table, besides Zoe, opening the book to the exact page I need.

"Tanfa isn't a common name, not an English name, but it *is* a name. I've come across unusual names like these before." I explain, looking through the book on the information about slavery.

Zoe leans across the desk as Laurence and Karl peers over my shoulder to see the information, looking perplexed. "Slavery?" Querying as she rubs her thumb over her bottom lip.

"Great Fang has an African accent, he's black, the 1500s was when slavery started happening and of course we are both from that time period, all of this makes sense now!" I explain, exclaiming in excitement that a part of his past is now knowledge to us.

"It says here when slaves were bought, there were documents or records made about it, like receipts. Some can be found in museums, or on the internet." Karl reads out the passage beneath my finger as it moves across the page. My eagerness for this leaps forward, charging the air with an infectious current of exhilaration.

"Turn on my computer and find records of slavery from the 1500s onwards."

Doing as I requested, sensing that I may have the answer, Karl hastily leaps to the computer at the end of the desk. It comes to life as his fingers are quick, tapping the keys in a hurry.

"I was born in this time frame. I remember as a young girl, my mother took me to an auction to see what it was like, but we never bought any of them. My mother wanted to show me how inhumane it was-." I pause for a moment, filled with sudden pride for my lost mother "-she was a woman ahead of her time." My words are quiet, as Karl focuses on finding the documents.

"Got them." His voice draws me into the screen as I stand behind him, leaning over the chair and his shoulder, as does Laurence. Zoe stays back to prevent overcrowding. We scroll through the documents and records of slaves bought, where they were from, all the signatures scribbled in faded ink on the screen.

"Can you see Tanfa, guys?" Karl asks, knowing mine and Laurence's vampire eyes are more precise then his own.

"No, but Gregory wasn't a usual name that male slaves were given." Laurence points out as the screen continues to scroll through.

"So, what is Tanfa?" Zoe wonders out loud, but I have pieced it together already.

"That was his name... from his tribe. The name he was born with." I say it again, to get the taste on my tongue. The name of the monster who has destroyed my life...who is risking my sister's life. "Tanfa."

Zoe speaks aloud, the whole scenario of what we now know as she rises from her seat, treading carefully around the room. "So Tanfa was possibly involved in the slavery trade. He was shipped off from his tribe somewhere in Africa to here. He must have been bought by someone... and somewhere down the line he was changed into a vampire."

My hand curls up into a ball once again, as the realisation of a dead-end sinks in as I speak with frustration. "But not his involvement with my family. We had nothing to do with buying slaves."

We all look at one another, concerned and confused. Turning my back, I walk away from them, resting my hand on one of the book shelves, feeling the immense sense of failure shrouding me.

"We are practically back at square one." I mutter in vex. Feeling a hand sturdily fixate on my shoulder, I look to see Laurence smiling softly at me, his lip still cut and red, not spreading widely across his face as normal.

"I think you need to explain your past, for them to try and find how this all fits together."

Inhaling and exhaling deeply through my nose in resentment, I turn back to face Zoe, her eyes calm and unjudging, for once. Karl looks at me with curiosity. Reluctantly, I surrender. "Fine, what have I got to lose now?"

Taking a deep breath, pushing all my effort to voice my words, for the first time in decades, my story breathes air.

"I was born in 1512, here in London. My father was one of the best doctors around so we had a comfortable life. I had a normal education for that time. Poems, literature, music, Latin, French... I won't bore you with the details." As I pause, the discomfort in my chest swells up but I ignore it, pressing on. "When I was eighteen, I was betrothed to marry a man, Thomas Miller..." A stabbing pain shoots through me as I say his name, needing a moment to catch my breath, my hand clutching the denim fabric of my jeans.

"I did not love him, but this is the period where woman had no power, no voice for our own futures. I married him out of not wanting to bring shame to my family. He... was not a nice man." Instinctively, my hand rubs my arm as if the bruises are still present. Retrieving my hand back into my body, I continue. "My mother announced she was pregnant soon after the wedding. I was so excited to be a big sister. The day Hilary was born, it was like she was my own. Joy and protectiveness filled me up like a cup in a rainstorm." I laugh nervously at my own description, noticing everyone else smiling at my poetic words.

"However, this spurred the idea for children of my own from father. He wanted grandchildren..." Regaining my breath, my hands begin to tremble as the memories play out in my head as my words try to come alive.

"We had been doing what was necessary to conceive children but it was not often. Thomas liked his drink. I would do my best to avoid it; shuffling away from that toxic fog that coated his breath as his hands fondled unlovingly... There were times I had to give in and as the saying went, lie back and think of England. There were times I was able to avoid his advances before he passed out cold on the bed."

Karl, taken aback in horror, bites his tongue as my story only deepens. Zoe gazes at me with commiseration.

"That night his advances were different. He overpowered me. My tears unnoticed, my screams ignored, my shaking body violently disregarded. As soon as the ordeal was over, I could not move; numb from the trauma, I guess. It felt like... my voice was lost inside my chest, imprisoned. The one and only good deed Thomas gave me was the tremendous relief of rolling away and going straight to sleep."

Karl interjects with horror. "But that's against the law! He was forcing you into it!"

Laurence interjects, allowing a moment to myself to collect my words as Karl looks on in horror. "There were no laws against marital rape at that time. In fact, rape inside of marriage was just... not a thing. It did not exist. It was expected of a wife to sleep with her husband whether she wanted to or not."

I continue, not going unnoticed how fragile my voice sounds. "Somehow I found the strength to move my limbs. I was in a daze, I felt...unhinged. I found myself in the kitchen. The thought of baring his child crossed my mind. That thought of carrying his seed made me want to rip open my womb and remove it myself. A child being brought into this world... with him as a father wasn't a world, I wanted my child to live in..." My words trail off, watching Karl mortified expressions go through different stages of grief for my experience.

Pausing to allow the tearing agony to cease, I take some more deep breaths as Karl braves to look me in the eyes. "So... what happened? To Thomas?" He asks, his words cautious.

I look back at him as I speak the fatal words. "That's when I saw the knife."

Zoe looks at me with sympathy and no judgement on her part, as Karl jumps up in disbelief. "You mean to tell me, you killed before you were a vampire?!"

Before I can even protest, Zoe shoots him a deadly glare, metaphorically standing toe to toe with Karl, seething with woman's fury.

"She was *surviving* in a world that was dominated by men who didn't give woman a fighting chance!" The room is silent as Karl stares like a dear caught in headlights at Zoe's truthful honest words. Swallowing the lump forming in his throat, he mumbles a response with a guilt-ridden face.

"I only meant that I didn't picture her being a killer when she was human."

"Sorry to disappoint. Put yourself in my shoes... What would you have done?" Querying his mind, I wait for a response but of course one does not arrive as Karl looks at me with remorse.

"So how does Great Fang play into all of this?" Zoe treads carefully, trying to rope more of my past out into the open.

Squeezing my eyes shut, I cannot find my words. They have taken the opportunity to scatter, hiding away.

A pair of hands grab my arms, strong but gentle and Laurence's low humming voice projects to the room, as I keep my eyes closed, not braving to look at anyone.

"That's enough. Reliving trauma can be very painful. Give her time and she will unburden herself when she is ready." The pain eases away as Karl is the first to speak up about a plan.

"Ok, look... maybe there is a link somewhere. We will find it soon. One thing is for certain, he is a vampire. He needs blood, right? Won't he be hunting today?"

We all raise our heads to him, instantaneously remembering the crucial part of vampires. My eyes lock onto Laurence, who seems to read my mind, nodding his head as he speaks.

"Great Fang will likely be hunting, yes. We can search the streets. We may find him, or one of his followers."

"It's worth a shot." I agree, staring out at the gathering black clouds consuming the sky. "With the weather this bad, it will be difficult to track him, but it works both ways. He will not see us coming either."

"We'll split up. More ground is covered that way." Zoe announces as Karl gravitates towards her, showing his desire to stay close.

"I agree, but not you two together. Karl you go with Laurence, Zoe can come with me. Laurence can take my car; we will take Zoe's."

"Ok just so we are clear. What's the plan exactly?" Karl asks, seeming very uncomfortable, almost skittish.

Laurence answers for me. "Find information, whatever you can that will lead us to Hilary, so we can bring her home."

Chapter 14: Examination Of Trust

The storm is heavy, leaving nothing untouched in its path. The rain floods the streets quickly, the wind showing its force on the umbrellas used by the darting pedestrians trying to shield themselves as they take cover, turning umbrellas inside out and some being left abandoned in the street, their mangled corpses being taken away by the wind. The rain is relentless as the wiper blades just about giving Zoe a clear sight of where she is going on the road as we travel down Bow Street, the a/c on full blast, giving us warmth. The pinging of Zoe's phone causes her to pull up on the pavement, to check the message.

The droplet bullets on the roof are loud and unwelcoming but we ignore it, focusing on the task at hand. Zipping and buttoning up my coat, I watch as Zoe replies back to the text, listening to the hum of the engine.

"Karl's text me, he's on the other side of London with Laurence. He'll let us know if they spot anything."

"Can I ask, what is with the name Soldier Boy?" I smile at her from across the car with a knowingly smug look that I cannot hide. Zoe tries to hide her own flustered smile but struggles, instead she gives a closed off answer.

"It's just a nickname to wind him up."

"Like your nickname is to wind you up, yes?"

Zoe pulls her lips into a pout at my comment but nods her head in agreement. "Yeah, it's what friends do. You wind each other up."

"Me and Hilary do that all the time. Once, she put hair dye in my shampoo bottle, turned my hair neon purple!" I chuckle as I tell the story, remembering the events. "She had ordered it online from my card and I did not notice. For weeks she was wary of me, in case I got her back. I did, of course, months later. We had a water balloon fight for her birthday and I made a special one with neon orange dye."

Zoe laughs, a genuine, fruity sounding laugh and it brings a smile to my face.

"How did you get the dyes out?" She asks as the sound of the rain pellets on the roof are now droning out along with the humming of the engine as our focus evolves round our conversation.

"Oh well, with Hilary having to stay indoors I had to keep her entertained as much as possible. We learnt everything from hair dye to make up, sewing and making clothes, you would be surprised on my cooking skills too."

"Must be nice to have a sister... to have someone." Zoe's voice wavers, dipping into a downcast tone. Deciding to help her, I take a shot.

"But you have Karl? How long have you had feelings for him?" She looks at me with a shocked face, but quickly throws up her steel wall, fiddling with the buttons on her blush pink raincoat.

"I don't know what you are on about. I don't have..."

"Don't act like I'm an oblivious blonde."

She looks away, not meeting my gaze, almost hiding behind her wild hair. "I have nothing to say."

"Your rise in heart rate and blushing cheeks says everything, even though your dark complexion hides it well." I reply, almost seeing the heat come out of her ears. "Look, I'm not wanting you to give me a love story fit for teenagers, but all I am going to say is this... in light with what is happening... please don't let pride get in the way of..."

"You're going to talk to me on pride?" She forces in, words like venom. "Everything you do, you believe you have the right. You don't stop for one minute and think about others."

"And how would you know? I only told you half my story, don't assume you know everything about me." I retaliate, raising my voice with the heat of the car blasting in, as the windows begin to mist up, obscuring anyone's view of looking in.

"I'm sorry for what happened to you, but it doesn't excuse you. You think you can sit in your gigantic house and just hide from what you are?" As she projects, her hands tighten on the wheel, turning her knuckles a lighter shade in colour. My own ball up and not being able to contain myself, I snap at her judgement and ignorance.

"What is the alternative? Why are you so threatened with me trying to be the bigger person? I do the best I can to save innocent people-"

"-But when it comes to your sister you would happily watch them die. If you had to choose between us or your sister, I don't doubt for a second you would choose her." She interrupts harshly. The sound of the rain is now almost too loud in my ears as it pounds on the metal of the car.

"You truly believe me to be that big of a monster?" I ask the clearly rhetorical question. Silence wraps around the car like a coil, sucking the air out of it as we sat in silence, feeling the tension. Zoe's voice is harsh still as she speaks.

"You take joy in killing. Karl told me how you killed that vampire. I've been sorting out your killing scenes for a good while. You think I haven't noticed how you torture all of those vampires? You are still a danger. We are allies only until we get your sister back." Releasing the wheel and turning off the engine, folding her hands on her lap, her fingernails begin to scrape the back of her hand as her breathing shakes with conflicted emotions.

"I... I just... can't accept what you are. At times I forget that you are dangerous. A monster. At times I forget... and I can laugh with you... joke with you... trust you." Her warm amber eyes scan mine, as if searching for something... possibly something human. "But then it comes flooding back, like now, hunting for blood and all. It floods back that you are a monster. A killer. An abomination outside the laws of our society."

Not wanting to let this tension continue for either of us, I speak quickly, torn in anger and aching pain at her words.

"I do not know your past; therefore, I hope you never have to go through what I did. I have had to keep my sister safe all the while playing to our society's laws and regulations as best I could and I admit, at times I failed. I try to be as normal as possible... But cannot have a family of my own..." I pause as I feel my eyes begin to water, feeling the pang of loneliness snap inside me. "I cannot have a friend or a lover... all I have is Hilary and Laurence to comfort me, to guide me, to make my life somewhat normal, giving me sanctuary and right now..." Trailing off, my words fade out, shaking my head in disbelief that I have rambled on like this, acting out of the ordinary.

"All I was trying to say in mentioning Karl, is do not let pride get in the way of love. It can be a lonely world when you have no one to hold." Leaving the words hanging in the air, I step out of the car, pulling my hood up and head into the storm, walking down the road leaving the car with the still open door to fade into the misty haze of the storm.

Not many people are around, most have taken shelter from the storm, jumping into taxi's or running inside for shelter. I let my boots walk me to wherever they want to go, in any direction. The rain is strong and fresh, reviving in a way, as it covers my body it is washing away the tension from the conversation. With the smell of the rain it somewhat masks the other scents around. Keeping my eyes alert for any signs of Great Fang or his buddies, but so far there is not a vampire in sight.

As minutes drift by, my mind wonders to Hilary and all the things I miss about her. My hand feels empty, alone, like a part of me is missing. My fingers should be laced with hers, her body should be close to mine, my heart aches for Hilary as my hunger grows, urging to sink my teeth into warm flesh. The rain is not showing any mercy with easing off, as I walk through puddles and down the streets, through alleyways and back streets, I hear no vampire or commotion. Every now and then the sound of a human skittishly run from one building to another, or people at the bus stop mumbling about the weather drifts to my ear over the noise of the rain.

As time slips by, the rain erodes my strength, my wall in my mind to avoid the darkness and negative thoughts begin to crack and weaken. My body begins to feel numb again, a gaping hole present in my chest. My coat losing against the rain, starting to get heavier in weight.

The sound of a heavy body slamming onto the concrete floor snaps my head towards the west. Two vampires I count based on movement, before racing towards the sound of the impact. I find myself heading back into Bow Street, racing round the corner, seeing Zoe's car in the distance. The noise of the body being dragged on the wet concrete floor points me to an alleyway just a few feet from where I am standing, with my heart racing.

My energy charges strong and bright as I run into the alleyway in a red blur as my hand wraps around the warmth of the flame. The first vampire is completely unaware as I shoot the ball of fire into his back as I charge in, as he stands over his victim. The painful noise escapes him as he turns, glaring at me; eyes blood red with his jacket now scorched and stained black. The body lies motionless as the other vampire crouches beside the victim, protecting their meal. Recognising that one to be the same one at the bar when meeting Great Fang, he too recognises me and we lock eyes for a millisecond, bodies tense and minds spinning with what actions to take.

He chooses flight instead of fight, running down the alleyway but I already predicted this, throwing myself up behind him and landing a kick into the back of his knee so he falls to the floor. Twisting his body, the vampire throws a punch but I block it, grabbing his neck and dragging him to the other side of the alleyway, pushing him against the wall so it cracks under the force. The other vampire runs towards me to help his friend, but my eyes change to purple as the aura emits from my body as he slams into me with force, pushing me only a few inches back. The energy consumes his body and mind and within a few seconds, collapses onto the floor in a deep sleep. My eyes don't unlock from the vampire in my grasp, instead of returning to their normal blue, I allow my true vampire eyes to be revealed.

"You are going to tell me where Great Fang is." I demand, my eyes burning into his.

"Hello to you too sweetheart." He mocks, a sly grin on his face. "Great Fang was quite impressed with you."

My steel arm presses into his neck, cutting his airway as I speak, directly staring into his eyes with all my anger radiating from me. "Tell me. Tell me where she is. I will spare your life if you tell me."

His breathless laugh mocks me. "You must be desperate." He chokes out, his body beginning to jerk with lack of oxygen. Ripping my arm away, I throw his body across the alleyway, sliding across the rough gravel, scrapping his bare skin with the sting of my rage. He rises onto his feat quickly, wiping the dirt of his face as he coughs violently, his eyes gleaming in the pouring rain. "You must be very desperate."

"You will tell me." I demand, walking closer to him, the rain not letting up, landing like bullets and shrapnel on the gravel. Stretching his arms, preparing for a fight he smirks at me with confidence.

"I am going to enjoy this." He charges at me like a bull. My feet move efficiently, avoiding the blows the vampire tries to throw. Suddenly one of them hits my stomach. I buckle under the pain, as a front kick sends me into the floor, tearing the material on the left side of my coat. As I jump up and throw a punch, I miss and try and kick out instead. The vampire blocks it, sending my foot over my head, flipping me onto my back, hitting the floor once again.

"Someone's off their game." He mocks, his red eyes shining. "Someone missing their lil sister?" His back foot shifts his weight just slightly in the wrong direction, I take advantage of it, swiftly kicking his leg underneath him, his weight drags him to the cold floor with a loud thud. On top of him in a heartbeat, hand caged round his throat as my knee pins his one arm, as my other hand pins his other arm.

"Now, I am going to enjoy this." I slowly replay his words, as the vampire stares at me with a mixture of shock and fear. "Tell me... where my sister is." The rain bombs us with heavy fire as I watch the vampire's expression merge into a sinister, wicked smile and his deep laugh sends a cold shiver down my spine.

"Great Fang wondered how far you would go to save your sister and how far you will go to save ...humans." Uneasiness consumes me as over the sound of his voice, an electronic crackle from his pocket makes itself known. Removing my hand from his neck and fishing into his pocket, I pull out a phone, already on the line with an unknown number. A scream of terror from the other end sends another shiver down my spine.

"I will give your sister's location; however, my other friend is hungry. She's going to feed on a random human in... 30 seconds and only then will I give you this information. The choice is yours. Save a human you don't know, or your sister." Another scream explodes from the phone as I clutch it tightly, staring at it with internal conflict. The vampire watches me, gauging my response. Seconds go by, I place the phone down looking back at the vampire beneath me, trying to hide the remorse in my decision.

"I cannot save everyone. But I will save my sister." Trying to keep my voice strong, the vampire gives off a short chuckle.

"Well you are desperate." The 30 seconds goes by, the sound of a woman screaming in terror shoots from the phone before falling silent; the sound of a vampire drinking can faintly be heard.

"You promised you would give me the location."

He smiles a devilish smile. "I lied. You now have 20 seconds before my friend kills that ginger boy who is with the old vampire."

I freeze at the mention of Karl, momentarily paralysed by his words, unable to mask my fear. Grabbing the phone, I redial Laurence's number. The phone rings out. I try again, with the same result.

"God dammit!" I growl, squinting in the pouring rain. Throwing the phone away, I growl again. "He will be safe. He is with a friend." I do a quick scan around the alleyway, a penny dropping inside my head.

"Great Fang is watching, isn't he?" My words seethe out in hot anger. "He is trying to find more weaknesses. He is testing me again?"

The vampire's crooked smile is accurate to my statement, but I feel my knee jerk beneath me. Within an instant, his arm hoists my leg up, causing me to lose balance, falling onto my back with the vampire trying to overpower me. Bringing my knees into my stomach, I kick my legs out into the vampire's abdominal area, sending him flying back into the alleyway. Once on my feet, I turn and run, wanting to get away from Great Fang's sight. As I run out into the open street the vampire catches up, grabbing the tear in my coat, the material ripping even more as he spins me round, as I try to defend myself. His fists impact my stomach, doubling me over as he then makes contact with my face as I try to throw a punch, breaking my nose, my eyes streaming with tears as I crumble to the ground.

The vampire, in the midst of the rain, laughs in a demonic way. "Great Fang wants you? Look at ya. Pathetic. Weak minded little..."

BANG! The vampire's body collides onto the bonnet of the car before coming to a harsh stop on the ground. Zoe jumps from the driver's side, staring at the vampire for a second before looking at me. "You seemed a bit off your game."

Scrambling to my feet, holding my broken nose, I furiously yell at her. "I thought I told you to stay in the car!"

"No, you didn't."

"Well... it was implied!"

"And yet here we are with your broken nose and a car crashed vampire on the ground."

In three strides I am over the vampire, grabbing his arm to hoist him up, allowing my paralysis to consume him to keep us safe. "Why would you help me if you think I am such a monster?" I shout over the sound of the pouring rain.

"You saved Karl. We're even. Now can we go? My hair is getting wet!" She shouts back, pulling her raincoat over her head, which only protects half her hair.

"God's sake... open the car door, will you?" Instructing irritably as I begin to heal, my nose stinging in eye watering pain. Zoe's face drops like a pile of bricks when she does what I ask, watching me sling him into the backseat.

“Are you out of your goddam mind?!” She exclaims in horror, jumping into the car with me. Ignoring her, I phone Laurence on my own mobile, he picks up on the first ring.

“Don’t worry, we are both safe. I saw the female vampire before she spotted us. We’re heading home.”

“We will meet you there.” Putting the phone down, I breathe a sigh of relief.

“We have another vampire joining us! Oh great!” Zoe proclaims in sarcasm as she turns the engine on.

“Shut up and drive!” Wiping away the tears using the sleeve of my coat as well as to wipe the blood from my top lip.

“Bloody vampires.” Zoe mutters under her breath, shaking her head as we pull away from the curb, making our way home with the temporary extra group member.

Chapter 15: Vampire Intervention

"Fucking great! Now what?!" Karl projects with a mixture of anger and alarm as he situates himself as far away from the new vampire as possible, regardless of the fact that he is still paralysed, tided to a chair, with myself and Laurence to protect him.

"He has information about my sister. What else could I do?" I shout back, as Laurence rubs his beard, still dripping from the rain, watching the vampire as he just sits there, watching us all shout amongst each other.

"So, get the information from him already." Karl responds as he keeps himself back against the wall. "I don't like this energy he's giving off. He looks like he wants to eat me."

The vampire scoffs, rolling his eyes. "You are like a twig... Now... Now that girl over her." His eyes direct themselves to Zoe as she pulls a disgusted face and crosses her arms, her hair slowly becoming frizzier as it dries.

"Do not go making threats you can't keep." I snap back, walking over to the vampire and pushing him back into the chair. "Listen closely. I am *very* hungry right now for two things. One of them is information. You will give me my sister's location and then I will have the second thing I want."

The vampire curdles his lips as he looks back at me with a confused expression. "You have young blood here. Why...Why take mine?"

Lowering my lips to his ear, I whisper with urgency. "Your blood will satisfy me more knowing it split to save my sister."

He smiles back. "You know my friend is out there... right... right now, killing human after human. She won't ...stop." He stutters his words as the paralysis contracts all his muscles, making him twitch and squirm.

"I cannot save everyone." I reiterate, glaring at him as strands of my fringe cling to my forehead and feeling my hair latching onto my back like a wet blanket.

"Yet it kills you... not being able to. I can... can see it." Stuttering his words, the vampire tries to laugh but it comes out in a choking noise. "So... how do you... you plan on getting this... information?" He asks, a flash of fear behind his blood-stained eyes. I smile, grabbing his jaw in a cage within my hand, allowing my eyes to burn into him.

"For every human I cannot save, I torture and kill a vampire. Tonight, I will start with you, then I will go looking for your friend."

"Mystique." Zoe's voice drifts gingerly across the room. I turn to see Zoe and Karl side by side, looking at me with concern at my actions.

"What?" Snapping with irritation as I eye them impatiently.

"Can we talk to you for a moment? Away from him?" Karl nods his head in the direction of the door as Zoe waves her hand to approach. I comply and walk out with them as Laurence is left alone with the vampire.

"What do you need to talk to me about that is more important than finding Hilary?" My words breathe like fire as they both give each other a concerned glance.

Karl is the first to speak. "How about your sanity? Mystique I know you are worried about Hilary but you are pushing yourself into a place that you've obviously battled against for a long time."

"What are you talking about?"

"Your eyes have been red since you fought that vampire! You haven't bothered to hide them." Karl points out and I scoff in rejection of his concern.

"It is not a big deal, I just forgot that's all." My eyes keep to the floor allowing my fringe to conceal as Karl continues his speech.

"It is to you. The person who saved my life is changing. You have a different energy about you. I can see it, so can Zoe and I'm pretty dam sure Laurence can see it too."

Zoe speaks now with her hand on her hip, her trousers stained a darker shade of green from a rain patch.

"Don't think me and Karl haven't noticed how you want to be different. You do everything within your power to separate yourself from them. Keeping your eyes blue, only feeding from the fatally dying, having a day to day job. When you talk about vampires, the Royal Order, you identify them with what they are... Yet when you talk about yourself, you don't acknowledge it. You avoid it."

"What has all of this got to do with my sister? All I care about it finding her and I will not let anything stop me!" I scream back, breathing fire from my throat as I stand toe to toe with Zoe, hot rage burning within my chest, my irritable dragon screaming fire, fuelled by my blood lust hunger.

Zoe says nothing, uneasiness filling her face as Karl's shoulder slides in front of hers, trying to force a gap between us with him as a shield. Karl speaks calmly as his hand rests on my arm.

"I have never truly believed you would harm myself or Zoe... Right now, I am terrified you will. Back off."

Hissing in rage, turning on my heels and marching back into the library, I disown every word that came from their mouth, my only concern is ridding the anger and vast emptiness within me. As I re-enter, Laurence is kneeling in front of the vampire, his hand on the vampire's leg.

"Thank you for sharing that information." He smiles widely, almost playfully as he removes his hand and stands up. The vampire, hunched in the chair, is angrily cursing at us all.

"You tricked me... You... little..."

Scepticism crosses my face as I stare in disbelief at Laurence as he chuckles. "It's amazing how a slip of the tongue can change the course of events."

My mouth hangs open in shock. "Are you... You have powers?!" I bellow in astonishment.

"You mean you didn't know?" Zoe questions in amazement also as they join us back into the room.

"You mean to tell me after all this time... You had powers? You can control people's emotions? And you never *told me?!*"

Laurence looks at me with a sceptical expression, raising his bushy eyebrow. "This is not my power. I am just very good at drawing the truth out of people. While you guys were arguing, I talked to him" Turning back to the vampire he smiles with a smug look. "He let slip her location."

"I have nothing more to say, so you may as well kill me now!" The vampire blatantly states, unmoving and stone like, realising there is no point in fighting. Striding up to him, my hand grabs the back of his hair, forcing it to tilt, exposing his neck. "Sounds perfect to me." Exposing my teeth, I go for a bite.

"Mystique!!!" Laurence bellows with shock. "Not here! Not in front of them." He indicates towards Zoe, who stares at me with disgust and Karl, keeping his head turned away.

"Lead them out of the room then." I bark back. The atmosphere is damp like a wet rag as Laurence's expression is desolate and fearful but I ignore it. My hunger grows with passing seconds and I need to silence the hungry screams. Laurence leads them out and as soon as the door closes, my teeth sink into the vampire neck, warming me with the flow of his blood.

The hot damp rag washes away the blood from my neck as I clean myself up, my sleeveless black jumper saved from any staining. As I wash out the rag watching the blood swirl down the sink, I catch my reflection in the mirror. Two big ruby red eyes stare back at me with horror as I step back in fright, only then remembering it is my own reflection. Concentrating, I change the colour, watching the red fade and be replaced with the calming blue.

My mind jumps to the three of them; their words of concern and their fearful expression but I shove it to the back of my mind, snarling as I walk away from the mirror. Drying my hair takes time, with the length of it, as I concentrate on that, keeping my mind from wondering. My eyes catch my discarded coat on the bed, its tear dangling from the navy-blue material. I make a mental note to throw it away. Once my hair is dry, I leave it loose, allowing it to sway behind me. Heading down the stairs, I find everyone huddled in the library, the vampire's body removed by Laurence. Their muttering is like a buzzing of electricity but I do not bother to listen closely as I enter the room.

"Where did the vampire say Hilary was being kept?"

They scatter away from each other with Laurence speaking first, clearing his throat. "The Tower of London."

"Trust him and the Royal Order to pick somewhere so dramatic. Right, let's go." I state, walking towards the front door. Within a second Laurence is blocking my path, stopping me in my tracks.

"You will not... leave. Not like this." His voice deep and strong as he stares at me, turmoil swimming in his eyes.

"Do not make me move you." I threaten, staring back.

"I want Hilary back as much as you do. I love her like my own grandchild as I look on you as my own flesh and blood. But I will not risk your life and everyone else's lives when your mind and heart are travelling in a storm, clouded by revenge and hatred." His words hit me like bullets, leaving a stinging pain seeping through my body. I disconnect from his eyes, looking to the floor in shame, gritting my teeth in grief and anger.

"The day you walked into the Royal Order I knew you were different. Someone who did not want this life but you were going to make the very best out of a bad situation. I will not lie and say I have agreed with every single choice you made, but I have understood your meaning behind them all; to protect." His hands stand sturdy on my shoulders, pulling me into a warm embrace. My anger begins to melt away, my dragon drifts into a slumber, freeing my mind as I inhale his scent.

"I love you with all my heart. However, I need you to calm the storm within your mind and allow tranquil thinking. We need a plan and we have more allies to help us. A little help from friends can make a difference."

Allowing my anger to wash away like the running of a stream, I calm myself and slowly pull away from Laurence's warm embrace, bringing a smile to my face.

"Are you sure you do not have any powers?" I question with a grin.

"I never said I did not. Quite frankly, you never asked." He replies, raising his eyebrow again. Turning to Karl and Zoe, I smile apologetically as they approach me.

"I am sorry for how I have been acting. Can you forgive me?"

Karl smiles, his beauty mark almost touching his eye as he surprises me with a hug. "As long as you don't scare me like that again, we'll get along just fine."

Zoe glares at me, pulling her mouth to one side with arms crossed. "I'll decide once we save your sister. I'm not sure yet if I'm ready."

"That's fair enough." Pulling away from Karl, I look around at our group and take a steady breath. "So, what's the plan?"

Karl smirks as he looks at Zoe with a mischievous grin. “Can we do something with Zoe’s panda hair first?” He laughs teasingly as Zoe slaps his arm at his witty joke.

Chapter 16: As Long As My Sister Breathes, You Aren't Safe, Stupid...

The brick walls of the dungeon cell are damp and the stale conversation of the two vampires outside the door can be heard echoing through the darkness. No windows for light, no vents for air. The only draft Hilary feels is from the cell door. Bringing her knees up to her chest, hugging them not really for warmth, just for something to hold, she waits patiently for Great Fang to arrive with some blood, as he promised he would a couple of hours ago. Her stomach growls as she growls with it, impatient for his arrival.

"When is he getting here?" Her voice calls out into the darkness, aware of the two bodyguards confiding her in the cell are sat out there, playing their cards and chatting about the football game.

"Relax girl he'll be here." The one lazily calls back, the sound of his cards shuffling in his hands faintly heard by Hilary. She has tried to escape numerous times but to no prevail due to the one vampire's strange power.

"So, Medusa, turn anyone to stone recently?" The female vampire mocks, laughing nasally as the other growls.

"Stop with the Medusa thing! I'm a man and secondly, I freeze people's bodies not turn them to stone." He throws a card down, as the woman laughs again; the high nasal laugh is like torture.

"Ok... how about Medusio?"

"I'm hungry over here." Hilary calls out again, irritable with the growling noise from her stomach.

"So am I but you don't see me barking on about it." The irritated vampire shouts back, shuffling in his seat.

"Feed me or I'll hurt you!"

“What are you going to do? You can’t escape, you’ve tried, you’ve failed. Several times.” The male smugly mocks as the other laughs loudly, her nasal laughter squeaking harshly into the darkness. As the laughter dies down, Hilary buries her head into her knees until the clicking of the cell door snaps her head back up in attention. Through the darkness, a single candle is being held, reflecting light onto half of Great Fang’s face; his expression calm and poised. His grey cloak shrouds his entire body.

Hilary scrambles to her feet, back against the wall, watching him with alarm in her small eyes. His steps echo in the cell, as he pulls his hood down, revealing his entire face.

“How are you child? I have something for you.” Digging deep into his pocket, he pulls out a plastic bag full of blood. Throwing it towards Hilary, she grabs it eagerly, gobbling it up in a matter of seconds as Great Fang watches with interest, lowering himself onto the floor, crossing his legs. Once Hilary drains the bag, she stares at him cautiously.

“You don’t have to be afraid. Come, sit, sit. Sit by me.” His hand waves in the air, gesturing for Hilary to come closer. But she stays in place, against the wall, the space between them the only safety she knows.

“What do you want with my sister?” She tries to sound scary, but instead her voice weavers.

“I admire that with you. Both of you, protecting each other. It is nice to see.” His voice bouncing with his accent, gives off a false sense of comfort. His eyes trying to calm her nerves only encourages her fear.

“What do you want with my sister?” Hilary asks again, impatient for a true answer.

“Have you not figured it out girl?” Great Fang tilts his head, his short locks falling to the right side, partly shadowing half his face. Hilary lowers her head, her short hair pulling together like a curtain, hiding her face as she strokes the lining of her coat, feeling the damp material against her fingers. Her voice brittle as she speaks.

“When I touched your pendant, I saw your tribe. You were taken away on a boat. Back to England.”

Nodding his head as Hilary speaks, the candle flickers in the darkness. “What else did you see?” He asks, mockingly smiling as Hilary wipes a tear from her eye in fear, her bottom lip quivering.

"Don't cry. No tears. We want no tears."

Regaining control over her lip as her hands curl up into balls, she takes a shaky breath, lifting her head up so the candle light flickers against her cheek.

"Go on. Tell me my story. My reason for doing all of this evilness, as you think that it is." His arms open out, inviting Hilary to answer him truthfully.

"You want to serve in God's army yet burn your enemies with the Devil's fire." Hilary's poetic words cause Great Fang to inhale a sharp breath, taken back by her wise words. He stares in shock at her young but mature mind, before composing himself.

"Adult words from a child mean nothing." He sniggers back with a dismissive smile.

"I'm a vampire, idiot. My body may be twelve but my mind is as wide as yours. And FYI, even human twelve-year-old children aren't bloody stupid." Hilary states with a wave of confidence as she takes a step forward, trying to assert herself.

He laughs roughly, rubbing his jaw line with a toothy grin. "Of course, I do forget at times." Standing up, he towers over Hilary, in the candlelight he illuminates danger and darkness, feeding fear into Hilary's heart as she braves speaking again.

"I saw your pain. I felt your anger. Maybe we can help you. When I touched your pendant, I saw how religion is important. How it fights inside you, when you kill people." Even in the dim light, his red eyes glare at her in fury for mentioning something so sensitive. His chest rises and falls heavily as he snarls, curdling his lips to show his teeth.

"My Gods sent me on this path for a reason. I have suffered for a purpose."

Hilary continues, raising her voice in hope that it makes her sound brave or that perhaps her words are heard. "You believe in a God but murder is a sin. Every day you live in sin. Today, you could change that. Let me go. If you let me go, God would forgive you."

"Quiet." Great Fang mutters with building rage.

"Isn't God forgiving? If you let me go, I'm sure God would forgive you..."

"Do not speak as if any God's tongues are in your mouth!" He hisses, his red lizard eyes scowling in fury. "What do you know of the Christianity God, child? God took me away from home. Took me away from family. He threw me into Hell and I am trying to save, not just myself, but everyone!" He steps forward, his shadow eclipsing Hilary's stature as she tries to stand her ground, though her legs tremble. "Your God has burdened me with Devil's fire to save humanity in His glorious light."

"What do you mean?" Hilary questions, narrowing her eyes as his words circle her mind. "You said, Christianity God, your God?"

A quick huff from his throat shapes into a chuckled laugh as his tongue licks his lips, rolling his eyes, his words carefully measured. "Child, I worship many Gods, orishas, deities, whatever you may call them. My land and home worshiped many. When I arrived here, I was forced to mask my own Gods with your *Christ worship.*" He says the words with an over exaggeration of repulsion, sticking out his tongue as it scraps against his top teeth like it left a bad taste in his mouth. "As far as I am concerned... your God and Devil are one and the same." His hand rises, finger outstretched, pointing to Hilary through narrow eyes.

"And what did you mean by 'to save humanity'... save us from what?" Hilary questions with a rise of fear.

Great Fang steps closer to Hilary, lowering himself to her level, smiling as cold as the stone walls around them, licking his lips again. "This is why I need your sister. She is the crutch of my plan. I could not risk her saying no." His long fingers stretch out to move Hilary's hair from her face. Slapping his hand away, she snarls fiercely like an animal.

"My sister will save me and you will die." Hilary states with a sneer as he retracts his hand back slowly.

"I am surprised you do not hate your sister. I have watched you both for a very, very long time. She controls you..."

"No." Hilary snaps back as Great Fang continues, undisrupted by her voice.

"-Controls you by keeping you inside the house, away from friends..."

"No."

"-Away from having a life of your own."

"She protects me, like she should. That's what families do. That's what big sisters do."

Tilting his head, he pouts with his bottom lip, looking at her with condescending sadness. "Yet, you are isolated."

No words come from her as the truth of his own repels Hilary to look away, being confronted with a truth she doesn't want to admit. But Great Fang leans in, his pout turning into a shrewd smile.

"But of course, with your track record of killings... I suppose you have to be."

"You won't win! My sister will save me! She will protect me! *Dum spiro spero*! That's what she said to me. Know what it means?" She yells, staring him in the face, hands balled up in anger.

"I don't speak another language." He states with irritation.

"While I breathe, I hope. So as long as we both breathe, we will always find each other." Hilary declares with loving enthusiasm dominating her voice.

"Charming words. I will remind her of that when she arrives. Won't that be a lovely reunion?" His honeyed words thick with false pretences as he storms out the room, slamming the door shut, the whisk of the draft removing the light from the candle, leaving Hilary in darkness once again.

Chapter 17: Planning Adversity

The tapping of the keyboards chatters away as we congregate around the desk, trying to think of a plan to get us in there unnoticed. Laurence makes us all tea, as usual, placing a tray down and handing us all a cup. No more rain falls from the sky, instead the snow has returned, covering the ground with a slushy mix of water and ice.

Karl searches the internet for a floor plan of the Tower of London. He finds it, printing it off and sliding it onto the desk for us all to see as he speaks hastily.

"Right ok, we don't know exactly where they are keeping Hilary, and the Tower of London is obviously very big and also guarded. I think me and Zoe should disguise ourselves as guards and look around the perimeter to see if we can find her..."

"Woah, stop! No! No way are you and Zoe going in there. You will be spotted a mile off and blow the plan up within minutes." I intersect as Karl looks at me with shock.

"Did you just say woah?" He asks naively as I reply with an expression of a blasé look.

"If the guards are vampires, they will spot you with your human scent." I explain intensely.

"She's right Karl." Laurence clarifies, handing him a cup of tea, as if it will solve all problems.

"Surely not ever guard in the Tower is a vampire?" Zoe queries, running her thumb along her bottom lip, the pale pink lipstick somehow not smudging.

"Most likely not. But I would hedge a bet and say the night staff are." I answer as Karl rubs the back of his neck.

"Ok but look guys we need a perimeter search to try and locate Hilary." He asserts the still lingering problem.

"I can do that. I will be much quicker than you two. Once I think I have an idea of where she is, I will radio you both, you come up with an escape while I grab Hilary and we get the hell out of there." Confirming the plan, I watch their reactions change simultaneously, as a hunger pain hits me, causing my hand to rest on my stomach.

"Hey, what about me? Do not think you are leaving me behind. I can search with you and cover more ground." Laurence speaks up, lowering his cup and looking annoyed I have left him out.

"I cannot have you hurt again. You can guard over these two to make sure they are safe."

Zoe taps her fingers on her crossed arm, looking concerned. "You realise this is most likely a trap?"

I nod my head, determined and unafraid. "That is why you both are not entering, under any circumstances. Understood?"

Zoe glances at Karl, her expression a cocktail of uncertainty and fear before looking back at me with severity. "And if myself and Karl happened to be caught up in the fight, what would happen to us?"

Laurence breaks into the conversation with objection before I can compose an answer.

"You are not doing this alone." Laurence scowls, placing his cup down on the desk. "I know you have this belief you are alone, that you must do things all by yourself. But look around you. You have friends, allies who can help you. Use us and let us help you." His arms widen to showcase the room, to showcase all three of them with his grin beaming on his face. I wonder if he even realises myself and Zoe are not specifically what you would call friends.

I smile sadly, placing a hand on his shoulder. "You have risked your life for me the moment you left the Royal Order. You have been beaten close to death, twice now. I cannot risk losing you again. If something happens to me, you must take care of Hilary."

"Nothing will happen to you..." Laurence tries to reassure me but I cut him off.

"-IF something happens to me, you will take care of Hilary. Promise me."

Laurence gives off a short chuckle, pulling me into a hug, my arms just about going around him as his body shakes with his laugh. "You have no need to ask such an idiotic question." He replies, hugging me tighter until pulling away.

"Great, so we have a plan, but I'm still not happy with me and Zoe sitting on the side lines. We could do more." Karl opens up, looking a little annoyed.

"You said it yourself, you do not handle yourself well under danger." I reply as Zoe touches his shoulder in reassurance.

"I know you want to prove yourself but now isn't the time. We can help them to escape, without putting ourselves in danger. Let's go back to the station and grab the radios." Zoe speaks with strictness in her voice, as she nudges his shoulder for him to leave with her.

"Once you are back, we will head there. While you guys are gone, I will go to the nursing home and feed." I nod my head to them as they nod back, all of us in agreement. As Zoe and Karl leave, I breathe a sigh of relief that they are out of my presence, taking my place in the desk chair, to relax my stress aching muscles. Laurence watches me as he drinks his tea.

"You seem stressed." He states.

"You do not say." Rolling my eyes as I rub my forehead, feeling the hunger for blood growing. "I always need more blood when I am stressed."

"I mean with Zoe. She still hasn't warmed to you, has she?"

"No... In the car, she told me she thinks I would abandon her and Karl to save Hilary! She really believes I am a monster."

"Would you?" He asks, as his lips leaves his cup, his eyes watching my own. "Would you sacrifice them to save Hilary?"

"Does saving both their lives mean nothing anymore?" I shout in frustration, my hand slamming on the desk with a loud bang. Laurence does not flinch, as he speaks. "You saved both Karl and Zoe when Hilary's life was not in danger. Tonight, you were lucky I spotted the female vampire after us."

Turning away from him, arms crossed over my chest, I try to keep calm at his words. "She is concerned that if you had a choice between them and Hilary, you would let them die."

I keep my head turned away, blocking out the impact of his words, I stay silent, not wanting to address any of this... out fear for the answer.

"That will be a choice I will not have to make, as long as you watch over them and make sure they do not enter, no matter what. Please promise me you will stop them from entering the Tower. Promise me you will not come to help me. If I am captured, injured, about to die you do not help me. You grab Hilary and run. Promise me again Laurence."

The intensity of my words forces my eyes to greet his, to see no hesitation within the red, to hear no apprehension in his voice as he looks back, almost mirroring the gravity of my intentions to this fatal situation. I speak again, allowing the significance of words to settle. "You do not save me. You save Hilary."

Laurence only bows his head in acceptance, despite the clear breaking of his heart, as I look away, watching the snow fall on the world outside.

Chapter 18: Is Now The Right Time? I Can Never Tell, I'm Really Bad At This...

Karl's hands dance around themselves again as Zoe drives towards to the station, making light conversation on the snow or how Jack has been, as well as her own daughter, until the conversation turns to banter again.

"At least your panda hair is looking better." Karl smirks as Zoe shakes her head, her black and white springs dancing around her.

"Stop it will ya! Leave my hair alone." She laughs, turning down the street towards the police station. "Right, we're here now. If anyone asks, we are still working on the case, we're just picking up some stuff we need. Don't go into too much detail."

"Right, ok no problem." Pulling up outside the station, they race to get inside, trying to avoid gathering too much snow on their coats. The sound of the snowy slush squelch beneath their shoes as they run up the steps. Zoe's high heeled boot slips on the unstable surface, almost falling over completely as Karl grabs under her arm and pulls her close, using his body to stabilise her balance.

"If you break your ankle you still have to drive." Karl jokes as Zoe laughs at herself, straightening up and pushing against Karl's side.

"You are a bastard you know that?" She jokes back, as she goes to open the door. Karl steps in front of her, opening the door before she can.

"Watch it, be careful, walk slowly or else you'll fall again." His arms spread eagle as they enter, his humorous acting like she's delicate and dainty just makes her laugh even more. Zoe feels a rush of warmth to her face, unsure if it's caused by Karl or the sudden change in temperature.

The station is busy as usual, the same ringing phones, the same work chatter about different cases, the tenacity of the weather and the vulture press pecking at their heads. Quickly calming down from their banter, they focus on their plan, trying to avoid any unwanted conversation, heading straight down the corridor towards the police equipment room.

Karl jabs in the code to unlock the door, as Zoe tries to keep an eye out for anyone they know who will approach them.

“Shit, what’s the code again?” He asks, embarrassed.

“How long have you worked here?” She replies, a tone of sarcasm in her voice.

“How many bloody codes do we have? Personal ones and for work? I’m not a memory file...”

“David’s coming!! Quick get in.” Zoe jabs the correct code in as Karl darts over his shoulder to see David walking towards them with his head in a folder. Her hand grabs his jumper, pulling him into the room and slamming the door shut.

The room is eclipsed in blinding darkness, the stale smell of the room and the noise from outside is their only working sensory they have to rely on. Her hand glides up to Karl’s mouth, covering it quickly and shushing him quietly as they press their shoulders against the door, waiting to see if anyone tries to get in.

Even in the darkness, Karl hopes Zoe can’t see his bright red cheeks glowing, even though he’s adamant she can feel the heat beneath her fingers. The smell of her perfume stings his nose; too strong a fragrance for his sensitive smell but is somewhat distracted by the fact he is in a room in close proximity to a woman he harbours strong feelings for.

Zoe prays that in the silence Karl can’t hear the heavy thumping of her heart banging against her chest. Putting her hand over his mouth was just an instant reaction, now she finds herself frozen in place as she realises the small gap between them is urging her to come closer... but she’s certain she’s the only one to feel that.

The silence wraps them both in a hot blanket of mixed emotions, as Zoe carefully moves her hand away, fighting the urge to step closer.

“I think it’s safe.” She whispers, placing her hand on his arm, feeling the pattern woven in the cotton.

“I think so.” Karl answers, with his mind a blank sheet, unsure what to do.

"Karl?" Zoe whispers again, her voice sounding soft but urgent. His brain clicks, as it plugs itself back in at the realisation of needing to switch on the light.

"Lights. Yeah lights, let me find the switch." His hand blindly searches along the wall, trying to find the switch.

"Yeah, I think, I think it's on your side." Zoe answers just as the lights pop on, its yellow dim light glowing up the room, revealing the rows of metal bookcase shelves around them with all the equipment and just how close they are to one another.

Karl jumps back first in shyness, rubbing the back of his neck. "Well, we have light. Shall, shall we start looking for those radios?" He chuckles nervously as Zoe smiles a half warm smile, her amber eyes almost glowing.

"I think they're over here." Zoe points as she turns, walking down a narrow space towards the radios. Karl follows, feeling ludicrous at his mishap to look like he isn't an incapable idiot all the time.

"Here they are." Zoe calls back to him, finding the shelf with the radios, picking one up and turning it on, making sure it works.

"Zoe, since I have you alone, do you mind if I talk to you? Seriously, for a moment?"

"Sure, what's on your mind?" Turning to face him, she allows the floor for him to speak. Karl notices the colour of her cheeks turning a little red beneath her cool dark complexion.

"How have you been?"

The question amuses her, laughing lightly as she brushes the dust off the radio. "I'm fine, thanks for asking."

"I'm serious... How have you been with all of this? Did you get much sleep?"

"We shared a room."

"I know, but I was so tired I fell straight asleep. You slept though, yeah?"

"Yes, I did."

"We need to make sure you get some more food before we go on with this plan." Karl picks up another radio, copying Zoe's actions.

"What's gotten into you?" She asks.

Shrugging his shoulders, he tries to play off his concerns. "I just want to make sure you're alright... I know how all of this can be a bit of ... well a bit of a strange situation." Karl plays with the radio in his hands, moving it back and forth between them.

"I've known about the existence of vampires longer than you. Really, I'm ok." She states, steadily holding the radio in her hand.

"How?" His voice deepens, with every word it sinks deeper into a cold darkness that Zoe suddenly feels a chill. "How are you ok? Cause I'm not. I can't function properly. Can't sleep..."

"You've seemed ok with me."

"That's because I'm with you." Karl replies hesitantly but sweetly.

"Glad I can help." Zoe replies quietly, placing the radio back onto the shelf, taking a step closer as Karl continues speaking.

"I'm filled with this dread that something bad is going to fucking happen. Not by Mystique but by others."

Eclipsing her hands into his, she holds then tenderly, thinking for the right thing to say, to calm his fears, but her mind comes up empty. Squeezing his hands as her shoulders slump, shaking her head in defeat.

"I... I don't know how to help you. I'm only your boss, there isn't much I can..."

Karl butts in, with a flashing expression of insult crossing his face. "You aren't my boss, you're my best friend! I'd be completely lost without you, you know that right?"

Zoe looks at him in a moment of surprise until her cheeks bulge from her face with a joyous beam of being thought of as a best friend. An idea pops into her head, just a method to try and help with his negative whirlwind of emotions. Keeping their hands clasped, she glances at him, noticing his smile has not appeared and how much she wants to see it.

"I have an idea. I know this method, which helps me with my anxiety. It's a grounding technique, when I feel overwhelmed. Maybe we can try it." Zoe suggests, hoping it works for him as it does for her.

"Ok, sure I'll give it a shot."

"Name something you see, out loud."

"You." The corner of his lips turns up as he answers.

"A little obvious but ok. Name something you can hear."

"Your voice."

"If your phone goes off, you can say Soldier Boy." Zoe giggles as Karl snorts humorously.

"You will never let me forget that."

"Who still uses that song as their ringtone?" She giggles again. "Ok, um, something you smell."

"Your perfume. It's really strong." He answers, wiggling his nose and lips as they scrunch up.

"Hey! It's my favourite."

"It's nice smelling, just you're wearing too much."

"Ok, ok we're off topic. Something you can taste."

"Erm... coffee I guess."

"Something you are touching."

"Your hands." Karl answers, giving her hands a little squeeze again.

"Keep going down that list until you feel better." Zoe instructs, watching and waiting as Karl repeats the list, closing his eyes for a short while to soothe his fears. After what feels only to be a short while, Karl seems to relax as Zoe notices the creases on his face smooth out as he relaxes, his tightened shoulders resting naturally and his hands just ease up on his grip slightly.

"Did it work? How are you feeling?"

"Better. Thank you." Opening his eyes as his famous smile takes its place, Zoe breathes a sigh of relief.

"No problem."

The atmosphere grows in warmth, the romantic rope pulls them closer and for a moment they are tempted to take it, but Karl breaks the rope first, dropping back into the reality of their ongoing situation.

"Radios... we need to grab the radios and get out of here."

"Yes, yes of course. Come on." Grabbing two each, they slip out the room and out the station, unnoticed, leaving behind their little moment, pushing aside their feelings and focusing on the plan ahead.

Chapter 19: Tower Entanglement

The snow continues to fall, coating the ground in its winter cloak as Karl and Zoe return not long after I do, looking a little tizzy from something, but I ignore it. Laurence throws some blood bags into a backpack, slinging it onto his shoulder.

"If we find Hilary, she may need it."

"We *will* find her." I promise, not just to him but myself too. We all bundle into my own car with Laurence driving, and make our way towards The Tower of London. Karl and Zoe sit in the back seat, connecting the radios to the same frequency, getting prepared for the evening ahead.

We go over the plan a couple times, keeping in mind that the route to escape may change at any given moment. Karl pulls out the floor plan, studying it for a back-up escape.

"By any chance do you know any secret tunnels hidden away?" Karl asks curiously.

"It's known that London has many hidden tunnels and passageways spreading all over the place. The Tower of London is not an exception and even to this day not all secret passageways have been discovered. There is a legend that Cromwell ordered a Lieutenant to hide 20,000 gold coins. They still haven't been discovered." I state, pulling my hair out of my coat, letting it fall naturally.

"Thanks for the history lesson." Zoe rolls her eyes, before continuing. "For murdering your husband, wouldn't you have been held there? Maybe that's why he's holding Hilary at the Tower? Some twisted sense of immoral justice, maybe?" Zoe questions, pondering the unimportant questions.

"The Tower of London was not the only prison. If I was captured, I would have gone to Newgate prison. The Tower was only for people of high importance or who posed a very big threat on the royal family." Correcting her inaccuracy, my fingers rub my forehead, the pulsing irritation running riot inside my head.

"How were you able to escape being caught? As a human, I mean?" Karl asks, copying Zoe's useless ponderance. Knowing we are still a bit of time away from the Tower, I humour them with my own history, feeling more comfortable to tell this part of it.

"I just stayed low, kept out of sight best I could. A family friend eventually took me in, believed I was innocent, told me how I could still get my inheritance from this horrible lawyer he knew. He owed him a favour of some kind. Met him in this seedy tavern, he was a very ghoulish man, I remember."

"So, you got your money and bought yourself a place, right?" Zoe implies, naively stuck in the present times.

"No, women could not own property until 1800s. I had no choice but to stay with this family friend. He gave me work as a maid which helped in keeping me under his roof and away from the streets, until my manhunt died down. As the King did what he did and married on and off again, the watchmen, or police as you would know them to be, became more concerned with the riots caused by politics of the royal family. I was almost forgotten-"

The sound of a car horn harshly blaring causes us to jump as Laurence shouts in anger as an impatient car cuts us off, flipping us the finger in the process. "Your urgency doesn't exceed ours! Bloody twat." Laurence's choice of words causes me to chuckle under my breath.

"Almost forgotten?" Karl asks, leaning forward, resting his hand the back of my seat.

"An incident occurred, I spilt tea on a visitor who seemed to recognise me. I left, with Hilary, to avoid being caught, moving from family to family as a maid until the day came that changed my life forever." The snow continues to fall as I watch the snowflakes blanket every surface on the streets, watching the sky grow more concealed as we drive deeper into London city. The citizens passing by in a colour mass blur as Laurence speeds up whenever he can to get us there sooner.

"How did Hilary become a vampire then?" Karl asks, the question firing from his mouth without thinking.

"A story for another time. All I'll say is I did what I could to make sure we both survived."

He looks at me in silence, rubbing his hands as he thinks. "So, all your life, you have just protected and survived?" Karl contemplates, his question not needing an answer. "Protecting Hilary made you strong, made you brave."

In the rear-view mirror, I notice Karl's eyes glance to Zoe, who has overtaken looking at the floor plan, seeming now lost in her own head, tapping her fingers against her thigh.

"All of us are capable of bravery. Those who feel lacking, are the ones who have the most. The rarest diamonds are those that are buried deeper." Laurence adds his wise words into the conversation, as he turns the car into a street, following the sign posts for the Tower indicating the route to take.

"I guess." Karl mumbles, his brows frowning together as Zoe gives up looking at the floor plan, pushing it away from her.

"I can't think of another escape plan other than the obvious entrances." She grumbles, resting her elbow on the window as her hand disappears into her black and white mass of hair.

"As long as we keep in touch, we will find a way out." Trying to assure her, I glance at Laurence who is holding his stone face, hiding his worries.

Finally arriving at the Tower of London, it stands tall and still looming, holding onto its power and authority within its stone walls. Laurence pulls up the car just outside the main entrance. Grabbing a radio, I slip it into my inner coat pocket, swiftly getting out of the car and watching it drive off as planned. Wasting no time, I head inside with it being a couple of hours before closing, giving me time to search. I pay for my ticket and head inside.

The walls tower over me as I make my way into the centre, taking in the sheer coldness of the day. Every breath I take sends my lungs shivering, plunging my chest into aching coldness. As my boots crunch on the snow, I am mentally clocking all the guards, identifying their vampire scent as I walk by, careful that I am mixed in with a crowd of humans to try and mask my own scent, keeping them unaware of my presence.

Using the groups of tour guides to blend in, I sway from crowd to crowd, trying to find any clue or sign of where Hilary could be. Deciding it's probably better in the centre and work my way out, I go into every door, building and tower I can find, careful to not draw attention. After that, I work my way outwards, going into the different towers along the perimeter, trying to find hidden passages or any clues to Hilary's whereabouts. Further and further I begin to get closer to the outer walls, checking all the towers, even the famous ones with no other escapes as I can find or any clues to where Hilary is being kept, away from public eye. Everything is in order, nothing appearing out of place or strange.

My boots crunch on the snow, my breath like fog in my face as I walk steadily towards Salt Tower, leaning just outside the entrance, peering over the side, away from view as the radio cackles in my pocket.

"Any luck?" Zoe's voice crackles harshly.

"Not yet, I have done a perimeter search. No signs of another way out yet. No signs of Hilary." Answering her question as my fingers push the snow off the iron moulded knight protectively standing to the side.

"How many towers and buildings have you look at?"

"About half, no sign, no scent, nothing yet." I growl, turning away from a small family who walk by, into the entrance of Salt Tower, holding my phone in front of me, disguising the radio as a phone call on speaker as I position myself by the barrier. The smell of their blood tugs at me, as I realise all this stress is causing me to gradually grow in hunger.

"What about guards?" Zoe continues her wheels of questions, reminding me of when Karl did the same with vampire myths in the kitchen.

"Most of them vampires." I inform crossly, feeling the ice-cold barrier beneath my hand, brushing off the small piles of snow. "Stick to the plan. It will be closing time soon."

"Keep us informed."

"Will do." I sigh, the white haze drifting from my mouth as I hold onto my faith of finding her. Looking up at Salt Tower, I march in, muttering our little Latin saying as comfort.

The room is about average size, with some information about the history on the one side, some kind of interactive door on the other. Stairs going up the tower try to invite me; however, I know she is not going to be held up in a public viewing with no access to any secret rooms or tunnels. The echoes of the family rush down, their blood still tugging at me. Turning my attention to the basement, which is much more promising, being sectioned off by a metal gate with the slightly pointy spikes on top. The gate is just taller than average height, with a gap between the gate and the roof which is just fine for me. Jumping up and propelling myself over, using the gate as support I get over. However, a sharp pain in my palm causes me to cry out in a short burst as I land on the top step with a muted thud, which echoes slightly down the stairs. Checking my palm, a long but narrow cut sits shining red. Of course, the cut begins to heal as I move forward, heading down the steps, a short descend into the dull basement.

Somehow it feels colder then outside, the large brown stone walls feel cold and damp to touch as my hand glides on the wall as I enter. The vast room is empty, plain stone walls with only a few crates scattered around. Two dungeons are present next to each other on the one side; unfulfilled and vacant. My steps vibrating off the walls as I step and scan around. There is nothing here, at least to the naked eye there isn't.

Slowly walking around the room, my hands caress for anything unnatural on the walls; an uneven surface, a different texture to the stone maybe. Circling the room, I come back to where I was, nothing catching my attention which causes me to grit my teeth. The sound from more visitors drifts down from above as I take another walk around the room, trying again in case I missed something. As I walk to the far right, my steps change in tone and depth. Baring down beneath my feet, a very small shift in weight happens as I lean on my feet either side. Stepping back and analysing, a faint perfect outline deep within the floor, right by this wall. Not wanting to wait around to find a button or trick in opening this, I dig my fingers into the edging, managing to grip beneath the surface, and rip the floor concealment out over my head, revealing a long and narrow passage down beneath the ground. The radiating pain in my fingers cause me to glance at them, watching the ripped skin and muscles begin to quickly repair themselves.

The shocked and worried voices of people above catch my attention but I ignore it. Looking into the tunnel, the smell of vampires hits me in the face like a wall of heat as I submerge myself into the darkness of Hell.

My eyes adapt to the darkness, being able to see without the need for a torch, I head down into the tunnel. The vampire stench cannot be avoided as I make my way through, my mouth uncomfortably dry from the cold air I've been breathing in since arriving. The only sound is my boots treading on centuries of dirt and rocks as the tunnel goes deeper into the ground. Reaching an opening, a familiar scent jolts me into a run, straight into the room, tunnel vision to everything else except the open cell door. Reaching the doorway, my hands clinging on for dear life, digging into the hinges as I stare at the vacant room; Hilary's scent potent within the cell.

"I knew it was her blood on the gate!" Spinning on my heels, with my eyes stinging with tears, two vampires dressed in guard clothes stand adjacent, watching me with wide red eyes paired with surprise as their lips curl up in a slow smile. Their expression is almost excitement, or glee, as if they are happy to see me.

Now I notice the string of lights hanging up on the walls, another tunnel entrance next to the vampires and two empty chairs and table to the one side.

Asserting myself into a fighting stance, I growl at them both.

"Quick grab her!" The dark male shouts as the female wastes no time, charging forward. Grabbing the door frame above, I pull myself up as the female guard misses me, stumbling into the cell. Dropping down I pull the door shut, locking the bolt down, quickly using my fire power to melt it just as the male grapples with me. As I pull my paralysis energy forward towards my hand, I thrust my arm out to grab his shoulder or arm but he blocks it, securing my wrist in a lock. In another attempt, I begin to channel the energy to the rest of my body, but the vampire locks onto it, catching onto my plan.

"I'm sorry." He mutters; his tone and expression similar to the vampire who approached me in the hospital. Before I can work out his apology, he throws me into the table and chairs and as I hit them, a sharp breathless pain jolts through me. Looking down as I struggle to get up, a thick piece of broken wood from the table has lodged itself into my left side, through the fabric of my now stained coat, watching the blood slowly seep from the wound. Instinctively, I grab it, preparing to pull it out so it can heal but the vampire's boot crushes my arm in place on the ground, preventing me from doing so as I cry out in pain, thrashing my arm to try and free it.

"Please, stop fighting! We will take you to see him and your sister!" The male explains, but I hiss sharply, kicking out, using my other arm to fight, but the wound weakens my strength. "We will take you to her." He tries again, as I slowly stop thrashing, taking heavy breaths as the pain brings new tears to my eyes. The female vampire finally breaks down the door; the loud crashing almost symbolic to the pain I am feeling.

"Please, just listen to what Great Fang has to say. He wants to help you. To help us." She adds in as I hear her footsteps approaching calmly.

Shaking my head as the pain slips deeper into my body, I manage to sharply hiss out some tangible words as the pain unsettles my mind; being reminded that without my healing how much I *hate* pain. “No, he wants me dead.”

“I have to do this, please forgive me.” As I look up, his fist makes contact with my head, dropping me into darkness.

The first thing my mind thinks of is the pain of the harsh blinding lights, consuming my world, as my eyes slowly and weakly open. The second thing I notice, unavoidably and unfortunately, is a high-pitched ringing in my ears, to match the intensity of the gleaming white light.

I am not dead; Heaven would never accept me. I am alive. Yes... alive.

It takes me a minute to gather myself, my fingers caressing something smooth, as my right cheek is pressed against something cold. As my mind adjusts, the ground that I am lying on is no longer dirt and soil, but smooth concrete. Slowly moving my fingers up towards the wound as I begin to come around, remembering the impact, my fingers prod the ragged wood still embedded in my body. While gaining my faculties, my hand grips the wood, violently heaving it out. My cry of pain cries back to me, as well as the sound of my coat ripping more, as I throw the piece of wood away across the room. Breathing a huge sigh of relief, I lie unmoving on the ground, with my eyes closed, trying to control my ragged breathing. I wait for my body to heal, feeling the open wound slowly close up.

Taking this moment to get a sense of my surrounding, no scent of any vampire is in the room with me; I am alone. The only thing I hear is the sound of air vents, allowing oxygen to flow into the room. The next thing I feel, once the pain fades away, is how hungry I am for blood. My mouth still dry, my tongue feels rough against my cheek as I pull myself up onto my feet, taking in my surroundings. Every inch has been cemented; large electric lights fixated onto the ceiling show the vastness but also the strangeness of this place. It looks like a secret hideaway; large bookcases stand from floor to ceiling, a large desk with a huge TV stands on one side with stacks of papers and folders dotted around in some organised chaos. A large wide door situates on the one side, seeming to draw my attention. Glancing behind me, there is another door, identical, which must be the way I came in.

My attention falls onto a large board which sends a continuous chill to my bones, almost freezing me into stone as I stare in disbelief. Pictures of me, Hilary and Laurence fill this unnatural sized board, hundreds of pictures in black and grey through to colour, pictures spanning through decades, through most of my own timeline. I spot a very recent one; the day trip to the museum.

My stomach twists into a knot as the reality hits me. I have known Great Fang and the Royal Order have been watching for so long, but seeing it physically in front of my eyes, it is no longer a thought; something I can casually throw into the wind. My fist shakes as my blood boils, with my hunger for blood and revenge growing with every second. Standing in the centre of the room, staring down the door, my hands and feet twitch, fighting the urge to break it down, kill Great Fang and grab Hilary.

"Come on then!" I shout, knowing Great Fang is going to be here, somewhere close by. "Come on I'm here! Come and get me, you pathetic excuse for a creature!"

I stand my ground, waiting, my heart aching but my anger flaring as I watch for the door to move.

After what feels like an eternity, the door budges open. My breath catches in my throat as the first thing I see is Hilary, looking terrified, still in her little pink coat, trembling as she walks in.

The second thing is wires around her stomach, a bomb clearly strapped to her chest.

The third is Great Fang's face; a small snake like smile slithers as he waves a remote in his hand, pointing it towards the bomb on Hilary's chest.

"What a glorious day to make history!" He gleams with some twisted pride as he waltzes in with Hilary, his grey long coat swaying behind him. Hilary spots me, her red eyes filling up with tears as her voice cracks and trembles.

"A-Amanda..."

My boiling rage stays stagnant as I analyse the situation. I cannot make it to Hilary before he presses the button. I cannot make it to him before he presses it either-

"I can see the wheels clicking in your head. Stop wasting your time. You can't save her without me blowing her up so don't bother."

Trying to stay calm, my hands twitching in negative emotions as my hunger craves blood, my protection craves Hilary's safety and yet I cannot have either. Taking a deep breath, allowing some anger to escape through my nose as I exhale, I keep my eyes on Hilary as I speak to Great Fang, wanting to try and comfort her in some way.

“Why are you doing all this?” From the corner of my eye, I see his lips curl up.

“You mean you haven’t figured it out yet? Smart girl like you?”

“I will be honest with you. I do not care.” My eyes move to his harshly, wishing I could kill him with the daggers in my eyes as my voice graduates volume with building rage.

“I know part of your backstory but I do not care to know the rest. I do not give a dam about what purpose or motive you have conjured, into believing what you are doing is right, justified or for the greater good. All I care about is family. You will tell me why you killed my parents; you will tell me why you turned me into a vampire and you will release my sister, or so help me I will rain down on you with all the power I have.”

Licking his lips, he looks to the floor, then back to Hilary before meeting my gaze again, looking unconcerned and almost blasé with every word I spoke, which ignites my anger. “The problem with that, is I am not a person who does something for the sake of it. This is where you and I are the same.”

“We are nothing alike, I told you that!” I spit out my words with rage, taking a step forward.

“Can you not even guess as to why I’m doing all of this?” His hand grasps Hilary’s arm, locking in place.

Rolling my eyes and baring my teeth, I growl at him. “I already know I just do not care. I want my sister back.”

“Go on, tell me why.” Nodding his head up as he speaks with a spark of excitement wrapped in his voice.

Exasperating a sigh, I spit out in irritation. “The Royal Order want me in exchange for money, so you took my sister as a bargaining tool. Your plan is to take me to them, where you can then collect your reward. So fine, take me! Just let her go!”

His expression changes suddenly; his brows rise up in stunned surprise as his head tilts up too. “I thought you said you knew my story?”

"I do, I know your name is Tanfa, I know your slave name is Gregory, you followed me for centuries and I know *you* killed my parents!"

His eyes narrow at the mention of his other names. "All true, clever girl, apart from the misinformation that, I do not work for the Royal Order."

"What? Of course, you do! That's why you took Hilary! Why bother lying?" I snarl as he shakes his head, before leaving it tilted on one side, his dreadlocks naturally in place on the right side.

"You are so blind to your own flaws. You only see what you want to see. You want to know the reasons without learning why, because it is the *why* that holds the emotion and you..." His finger stabs the air in my direction, wetting his lips again, "-cannot handle the truth that you are not the only person who has suffered."

My chest burns with fire as his words try and attack me. "You're lying! You work for the Royal Order!"

"No, my dear, I am not. I have nothing to do with them."

My anger boils again; his words are a waste of time as I go through what I know. "I was told by two vampires; one I hunted down and the other was Luke. He told me you knew him."

Great Fang nods his head up as he speaks, gripping Hilary's arm once again. "I knew Luke, but I never told him I was working for the Royal Order. I am afraid you have been misinformed." His dark hand grips tighter on Hilary's arm, making me hiss a warning snarl towards him.

My mind flashes back to Bow Street, the vampire I interrogated; his words exactly play out in my mind. "A vampire I killed told me the Royal Order had sent someone after me..." My mind goes back to Luke, what his exact words were, "-and Luke told me you will work for them if given a price. Hilary was taken by you soon after. It all fits."

He shakes his head, his dreadlocks swaying in the motion. "I *use* to work for them when I needed money to survive. But that was decades ago. I am not after your reward; I have not done this for the pathetic excuse of money." His face scrunches up, looking disgusted that I would assume something so trivial. Then it lowers, his face changing into false concern.

"You made the assumption of my entire plan based on what two vampires told you? I thought you were more thorough than that?"

My mind spins with chaos and confusion as I realise I have been wrong, I simple assumed the assassin was him and pretty much ran with it... then my stomach ties into a double knot as I feel like a punch in the gut has just been delivered.

The assassin who is after me is still out there.

Great Fang moves the remote around in his hand, watching me intently as I try and focus, getting my head back into this situation. Hilary watches me with concern, tilting on her tiptoes, eager to race towards me.

"What is it that you want?" I ask sternly.

"Allow me to clarify..." Great Fang begins to speak, but he halts suddenly as three guards enter the room heads low, marching in and standing behind me, all smelling of vampires, one of them having wild hair with white tips peeking out from the hat.

I play my best poker face, staring at them with internal horror as my heart crashes to the floor.

This was NOT part of the plan! What the hell are they doing?!

Great Fang snarls in annoyance. "What are you three doing? I told you I was to have Amanda alone!"

Karl breaks first, looking up in shock, eyes wide. "So that's your name!"

Zoe is the second to look up, removing the tall hat in annoyance. "Not really important right now, but can't say I'm not pleased to know". She flashes a half smile in my direction. Laurence breaks last, removing the hat also but looks at Great Fang with an intense glare as he notices the bomb on Hilary's chest.

"What the hell are you guys doing here?!" I shout in disbelief.

"You didn't radio us back. How were we meant to know if you were in danger?" Zoe replies, removing the jacket also.

"Laurence decided to look around. He caught whiff of your blood, so beat up three vampire guards and took their clothes, to get us in and mask our scents, of course." Karl announces, standing close to Zoe as always.

I turn to Laurence in a fit of rage. "How could you let them do this?! What were you thinking?! What in God's name were you thinking?!"

Laurence turns to me with a stern and determined look. "This is a battle for family. Family should fight together."

"I wasn't going to be left behind either, we are a team after all." Karl smiles, giving me a look of determination.

"You two shouldn't be here!" I shout at them, enraged at their carelessness.

A strong cough from Great Fang pulls us back as he stands looking bored, arms folded, giving us a blank look. "I'm sorry to ruin this lovely family moment, but I need to explain what this whole event has been about, since Amanda here, is clearly wrong."

I stare at him with locked on seriousness, thinking back to the Lost Angels pub, to the note he left me.

"You said you wanted something from me that you believed we both desired. What is it?"

His eyes lock onto mine, careful and calculating. They almost twinkle with joy. "You hate being a vampire, I can see it. How it pains you to be the way you are, to watch your sister have no life... I want the same thing too, to be rid of this curse. That is why I need you. Your father failed."

"What do you mean failed?" I press, feeling like my closure is finally nearing.

Twirling the remote to remind me I am still in an impossible situation, he finally brings alive the mystery of my past. "When I was brought here against my will, I was sold off to a man. Except he was no man. He was, what I now know to be, vampire. He bought slaves and when he wanted, he fed from us. One day, he tried to feed off me, but he was interrupted. Never found out who it was. My owner killed him and fed, while he did this, I had the strength to run."

We stare at him in silence, my eyes flittering from him to the remote in his hand, silently contemplating a plan on getting Hilary out of here, using this time to think.

"I thought what he gave me was a disease. I thought because I had been taken from my homeland, that because I was walking on foreign soil, the God Babaluaye was punishing me."

"The God of illness and disease." Zoe speaks out quietly, but enough that we all hear her. Great Fang smiles a warm soft smile.

"You know the African Gods, child." He states, a hint of glee bouncing in his voice. "It is not often I meet a modern African who still has knowledge of the deities."

"Of course, Africa is my roots. Even my name."

"Which is?" Leaning forward, his eyes dancing with interest.

"Zemora."

His voice, though bouncy and thick, seems to purr. "What a lovely name."

"So, you sought out my father." I add in to draw Great Fang's attention back.

"Yes, your father was meant to be the greatest doctor in all of London. I went him, begging for help. He was so curious that he declined payment, hoping he would become famous for discovering and curing such a strange disease. He promised but failed. I confronted him a number of times, the last he told me to pray to God." His laugh starts off small, growing in volume until stopping abruptly, staring with an open smile. "You people with your God... I had to pretend to worship that false Christian God in order to worship my own. I blame your God for doing this to me because it was *you* who took me from home. When your father said that, I snapped. That's when you walked in."

The memory of that night plays out in my head, my heart feeling like it is being squeezed in a vice grip as tears I can no longer hold back fall.

"You killed my father in the name of religion?"

"No, I killed him in the failure of medicine."

"You said me and mother were collateral damage." I snarl.

"Well, you walked in and then your mother did. What was I to do?" Shrugging his shoulders dramatically, like being in a panto show, the urge to kill him grows, but the remote in his hand restrains me.

"I never thought you two would get out alive. So, imagine my surprise, when a few short years after, I see you walking down the street. You and your sister! That's when it struck me." Taking big steps, he parades around the room, using large gestures with his arms, staying close to Hilary, to prevent her from running off.

"It struck me, that you are the doctor's daughter! If you had the disease, you could find a cure! So, I found you, bit you, watched you, waiting to see if you would make this cure, naturally."

Karl steps forward, his brows crossed, the lines on his face deepening with disbelief.

"You could have just asked her! You didn't have to bite her!"

Shrugging his shoulders again, he looks at all four of us as he speaks, his one hand caging Hilary's shoulder. "What use would that have been? Her father failed because he didn't have the drive to do so. She needed to suffer to understand." His eyes lock onto me as he squeezes Hilary's shoulder, causing her to whimper.

"As years went by and it became clear you had no intention of making a cure, instead running around and building a reputation of hunting vampires, I went ahead and tried to make a cure myself. I got scientists and lab rats, doctors and nurses and everyone I could think of but nothing worked. So, I fell back onto you."

Raising his hand with the remote, he points it to me, licking his dark lips. "You want a cure as much as I do. Help me and I will release your sister. You both can have this cure and be human again."

Watching my breathing, I find my rage entangled with another emotion, but I shove it away, not needing the distraction and complication.

Karl steps forward, taking a deep breath. "This cure isn't a bad idea, I'll admit. But kidnapping her sister and putting a bomb on her chest is not the way to fucking do this!"

Great Fang glares at him, baring his teeth. "She left me no choice."

"Let my sister go! There is four of us and one of you." I shout, trying my best to keep the moral up on our side.

He opens his mouth into a wide grin before chuckling a deep laugh. "Unfortunately, two humans cannot harm me..." He only glares at me, ignoring the others, "-Two vampires will never be quick enough to stop me pressing this button if you do not co-operate."

My mind is slowly unhinging as the dire situation starts to look bleak. "If you kill my sister, I will never make this cure for you." I state with strong venom.

"Don't give me a reason-GAH!" A loud bang explodes through the room as Great Fang's hand violently jerks, the remote flying across the room, landing away from us all. Turning our heads simultaneously we stare at Karl, holding a gun, still aiming with a look of fear being washed over with realisation to what he just did.

"Where the *hell* did you get a gun from?" Zoe shouts in both rage and concern.

"Does it fuckin' matter? Go!"

Taking the unexpected opportunity, I dive for the remote, as does Great Fang. My hand grasps it, but Great Fang knocks it out with a swift kick, wrestling to prevent me from gaining it. Over his shoulder I see Laurence race towards Hilary, but the bursting of a door announces three vampire guards dashing in; the female I fought clasping onto Hilary in a vice grip as she screams. Laurence fights with the other vampire trying to reach Hilary, while Zoe and Karl stand side by side, with Karl shooting towards the male vampire I recognise.

"I wonder what you will do now." He growls as we lock into a hold, both our strengths matched. "Save your sister, or your friends?"

"I can save them both." I reply as he suddenly unlocks us, swiping a punch towards me. Moving out the way, I channel my energy, grabbing his shoulder to paralyse him.

"You've just made a mistake. Did no one tell you?" His red eyes gleam with excitement as it dawns on me in horror; watching his eyes slowly shape from red to green. A surge of energy escapes from my skin as he consumes my power, as I had been warned, absorbing it, strengthening the ability to a scale I never could.

Throwing me to the floor, the mental pain derails my mind for a moment, disorientated and confused as my blurry eyes begin to sharpen again. Great Fang smiles widely as he brings the paralysis power forward into his hand; the energy stronger and more unique.

"This tickles a bit. It feels nice." He chuckles to himself; the flashing green glowing against his dark complexion. Without warning, he stretches out his arm, the paralysis energy shoots like a beam from his palm towards me, having no time to move.

A golden shroud of energy barriers me from the attack, as Great Fang exclaims in surprise. Looking towards Laurence, his arms outstretched in a stance, his face in full concentration as he reveals his powers at last. The vampire he fought lies dead on the ground beside him.

I scan for the remote, finding it in one of Laurence's small shield between Hilary and Great Fang. Thinking on my feet, I pull up and run towards Laurence, still being shielded from the beam that Great Fang continues to shoot.

"Seriously?! All these years and you can create force fields?!" Angrily stating as I reach him.

"I never had a need to use it until now. We need to get Hilary." Growling in pain, as his concentration starts to slip, showing as his shield begins to crack with the power of the beam. Looking through the shield, I can see Hilary still being held by the female, as I turn behind me to see Karl and Zoe struggling to keep the male vampire back; the gun going off every few seconds.

"Can you move the remote over to us?" I question quickly.

"Not unless the object itself moves, like you did."

Contemplating a poor plan, I make a quick decision. "Take them and get out of here."

"We are not leaving you!" Laurence yells, as Karl and Zoe sprint over to us, trying to use his shield to protect them from the male vampire.

"Guys we are out of bullets!" Karl shouts over the noise of battle, panic stricken.

"We have no time to argue. You promised me. Now, go!" I scream at Laurence, baring my anger down on him.

"We are not leaving you, are you mad?" Karl tries arguing with me, but I stare at him with the weight of my conscious.

"Do you want to know where bravery really comes from?" I question him with sheer intensity. "Strength from bravery is only a spark, fear will fuel it. You will either defeat your fears or watch them come to life within the flames. The choice is yours."

Karl stares at me with shock, until the point of my words sink in, his face falls into solemn understanding.

Great Fang stops the beam, heavily breathing in tiredness. The energy changes; fire smoulders from his hands, snaking into a long whip of flames.

“Save them now!” I yell towards Laurence as Great Fang snaps the whip forward, snagging the thin shield, shattering it like glass. The three of them draw back as Laurence quickly kills the other vampire that was attacking them. Over the mixture of noise, I hear Zoe decline to leave, as Karl tries to pull her back, arguing they can no longer help since the gun has run out of bullets.

With Laurence’s focus now shifted, the shield guarding the remote vanishes. I lunge for it, as the fiery whip tries to stop me. As the flames wrap round, I remove my coat to use as a substitute for the whip to snag, as I slip my body down under the lines of fire. Part of the flames lick my bare arms in a searing pain as my plan pulls off, burning the coat as I dash forward.

Great Fang pounces on the remote, snagging it in his grip, exclaiming in brief excitement that he got the remote before I did; only to look up and freeze in dismay to see me killing the female vampire and ripping the bomb off Hilary’s chest.

“No!” He roars, as I see his thumb move towards the button. Reacting immediately, I hurtle the bomb across the floor towards Great Fang. As the bomb slides, I take in the position of where he is, close to the back entrance of where Laurence was trying to take Karl and Zoe to safety; except Zoe is not as far back as they are. She has slipped from Karl’s grasp as Laurence holds him back, with Zoe running towards me in an attempt to help me somehow, not seeing the bomb before it is too late. My heart stops, watching the bomb go off, in close proximity to Zoe and Great Fang.

The shockwave of the bomb sends them both hurtling through the air, as I shield Hilary with my own body. The room trembles with the aftermath, as the room fills with rubble and debris. All I can see is dust hurting my eyes, a ringing in my ears hurts my head and the smell of blood quakes my muscles.

“Zoe?!” I call out, as the dust thins out, spotting her body lying on the far side of the room. Hilary’s hands grasp my arms in a tight lock grip, holding on for dear life as she smells the blood too, trying to prevent herself from going after it. Laurence is by my side; grief stricken and concerned as we both stare at her body, frozen in shock.

My voice speaks, evidence from the scratchy pain in my dry throat, but I do not comprehend what I say as Laurence nods his head. He picks Hilary up, who claws at my arm screaming in agony to be parted from me as he takes her away. As my hearing returns to normal, over the screaming of Hilary I hear Karl's voice; agitated and frantic, concerned for Zoe's safety as Laurence drags him away too.

The sound of the ceiling cracking under pressure, I realise I do not have much time. Racing over to Zoe, I kneel before her, cradling her in my arms; her limp body unmoving, a deep cut on her neck from shrapnel pours with blood. As my hand touches her back, the warm liquid coats my hand. My hunger claws at my stomach, waters my mouth with saliva and at this moment in time, it sickens me. I cannot even grieve for my friend without my bloodlust making itself violently known.

Lowering myself to touch our foreheads together, I stifle a scream, a cry, an explosion from my own chest. It is then I notice the sound of a heartbeat.

"She's alive!" I gasp shakily, my hand moving her curls from her face, stunned into hope. Without a second thought, whisking her up into my arms as the creaking ceiling begs to cave in, I go to leave but a tug stops me. Gritting my teeth, I try to leave again, but the tugging of an emotional rope holds me back.

Knowing my conscious isn't going to let me leave, I turn to see Great Fang's body, lying motionless on the other side of the floor, slowly healing his wounds; his grey coat now marked in deep blood stains.

Laurence reappears, his face disturbed by the crumbling room and my presence still being here. "You need to leave now! This room is going to..."

"-Collapse I know! Where is Hilary?"

"I gave her the blood bags to calm her. She's with Karl in the car."

"Ok, take Zoe." Shoving her into his arms, he does not argue, racing out the falling room. Hastily, I grab one of the dead vampires and take as many mouthfuls as I can muster to dull the screaming blood pains before dash over, slinging Great Fang onto my shoulder and racing out the room. From behind me the exploding sounds of the ceiling caving in, under the pressure and weakening of the bomb shriek down the tunnel as we escape.

Racing out from Salt Tower as it trembles, with hairline cracks spreading out like fine webs, deep down both me and Laurence knew this may come back to haunt us. However, we had our own urgency to deal with. In the distance sirens can be heard but as the general public scatter from the alarm, we head out, ignoring staff's protest to check on us or demand to know what happened as we jump into the car and speed off, leaving the Tower of London with its new mystery.

Chapter 20: Corrupt Settlement

It is amazing how a familiar environment can turn into an unsettling place, when circumstances change. The noises I became accustomed to and zone out are like screeching vultures now; pecking away at my vulnerability. The whirling of the machine as it pumps fluid into Zoe's veins, as the beeping of the blood pressure machine starts its fourth reading within the hour, as the sound of her breathing is exacerbated by the oxygen mask; it is all suddenly intimidating.

Standing at the end of the bed, not baring to sit down, I watch with a broken heart as Karl holds onto Zoe's hand in a grip that will not be moved, as he watches her closed eyes; every passing second hoping she will open them, revealing her warm sparkling amber once again.

Laurence sits on the opposite side, watching the blood pressure machine in silence, shoulders heavy with grief as he rests his arms on the bed. Hilary hugs me from my side, staring at her, eyes wide with worry for this stranger's health, a stranger who tried to save her.

"Amanda, who is she?" Her voice squeaks from below, her hands gripping my jumper tightly.

"A friend." I explain, as a hot tear rolls down my cheek. Dr Gale knocks on the door to the room lightly before entering, giving me a saddened smile as he enters, Holly accompanying him; her bright hair seeming dull now.

"Are you guys friends of Zoe?" He asks, as Holly glides past him, wrapping her arms around me in a supportive squeeze.

"I heard you were in ICU but didn't believe it, at first! Are you ok?" She mumbles into my hair as I nod my head while looking at Dr Gale, momentarily wishing I had fed more before arriving here; everyone's blood is causing my hunger pains to rise again.

"Yes, we are." Karl replies, his bottom lip trembling.

"How is she?" I ask, pulling away from Holly before the temptation rises. Dropping her hands, Hilary moves away from me, sitting on Laurence's lap; her way of saying she needs to be away from humans.

Dr Gale pulls a face I recognise too well; the face of bad news. My heart stops for a second time.

"She will live, let's start there. The good news is she will live." He discloses as Karl breathes a sigh of relief while I hold my own in anticipation for the blow. "However, the shrapnel hit her spine. It caused a lot of damage, nerve damage. It's unclear how much damage has been done until she wakes up. But I have to warn you, and Zoe when she wakes, there is a strong chance she won't be able to walk. I'm sorry."

Silent shock vibrates the room as we all take in his words; Karl drops his head, placing it on Zoe's hand, hiding his agony from everyone, Laurence closes his eyes and looks away and Hilary allows tears to fall, squeezing her eyes shut, letting out a whimper of sorrow for the woman who tried to save her. I stay silent, going through the stages of grief all in once and then reverting back to anger.

"How did this happen?" Holly questions, making me realise she is still in the room.

"We were in the Tower when the bomb went off, Salt Tower, it just went off in the basement." I replay our story, excluding certain details naturally.

"I'll leave you alone for a moment." Dr Gale expresses before exiting the room.

Holly looks at me with concern, her eyes watching my face. "Amanda, are you ok? You really don't seem yourself."

"How do you expect me to be right now?" I snap at her as her blood sings to me, teasing me for a taste. "I need to go. Laurence, bring Hilary home when you are ready, ok."

Laurence gives me a half smile, holding Hilary's hand gently as she looks at me with new worry.

"Where are you going?" Hilary asks, leaning forward in Laurence's lap.

"There's something I need to sort out. I'll see you at home." Announcing sullenly as I leave the room, trying not to slam the door behind me.

Not stopping to feed, not stopping to ease my hunger, I race home, marching through the front door. Through the reception, through the living room, ignoring its mayhem and chaos, into the kitchen, to find Great Fang sat at the dining room table with a wet bloodied cloth to his head.

"You know, in all my years, this is the first bomb recovery I've had to do. It takes longer than I expected to heal." He grunts with a twinge of pain as he places the damp cloth down, pushing back up the dark purple sleeve that slipped down his arm.

"I should kill you, right now. I want to." I state intensely.

Shrugging his shoulders, he dismisses my remark sarcastically. "And yet, here I am!"

"This cure you wanted... why did you have to do all this? Take my sister, strap a bomb to her chest..."

"-because you..."

"-force me to remove the bomb and hurl it across the room..."

"-because..."

"-for it to almost *kill* my friend! Tell me, why did you not just ask me?!" Standing over him, my hand coming down the table, denting the wood as I finish, simmering with all the fury I contain as he stares at me, calm and poised as ever.

"You don't listen, do you? You would not have listened to me, with that temper of yours. The only thing you would have seen, are my eyes. Indicating, *vampire*. That is all you would have seen, and needed to see, before killing me, not giving me a chance to explain. This is really your fault. You just don't want to admit it."

Snarling as I turn away, pacing back and forth in the room as the dragon fills my head with smoke and a whirlpool of emotions threaten to drown me as I take in every detail, every option, every path I can think of to take to try and make this whole thing better.

"How is your friend?" He asks, playing with the rag.

"She will live." I reply dryly.

"That's good news."

Staring at him, with venom and rage, I feel torn and twisted. His eyes watch me, almost as if he knew how I was feeling, gives me a sympathetic smile.

"I never truly intended to hurt your sister. I was backed into a corner, I needed you to hear me out."

"When I removed the bomb, you pushed the button."

"I panicked."

Scoffing as I turn my head away, my fingers caressing my forehead in a circular motion, the whirlpool of emotions and my angry dragon begin to settle, allowing me to think with a clearer head. Making a decision, I turn back to him.

"This cure, how far did you get?"

His smile changes into a wide grin; a grin I do not trust. "Well the bomb buried the documents I had on it, so we can't retrieve that. However, I have it all to memory. As I said, we didn't get very far."

Vigorously approaching him with a handshake out, Great Fang looks surprised by my gesture, looking at my hand like I have just offered him a piece of human food.

"It is called a handshake. I'm sure you remember one of those. Here's the deal. You and I will find a cure, once we have it, you use it first then myself and Hilary will use it. If anything happens to Hilary, Laurence, Zoe or Karl, at any point from now till then, I will send you back to Africa..."

"How nice!"

"In pieces."

"Oh not so nice."

"Is that a deal?"

Looking at my hand for a moment, his red eyes look into mine. For a second I see a flash of sincerity. Taking my hand in a firm grip he shakes.

"Deal."

"This does not mean I trust you, or like you."

"Of course not."

Releasing my hand, Great Fang inhales a sharp breath, licking his lips before asking a hair-raising question. “So... since you destroyed my home, where am I sleeping?”

My blank, stone expression answers his question. “What now?”

For you to read my book is like finding a gold coin. To have a new fan is like finding treasure. If you liked my book please leave a review on Amazon!

A.J.Woolfenden

You can also find me on:
Instagram/aj_woolfenden
Twitter: ajwoolfenden
www.ajwoolfenden.wordpress.com

FICTION FROM APS BOOKS
(www.andrewsparke.com)

AJ Woolfenden: *Mystique: A Bitten Past*
Davey J Ashfield: *Footsteps On The Teign*
Davey J Ashfield *Contracting With The Devil*
Davey J Ashfield*: A Turkey And One More Easter Egg*
Fenella Bass: *Hornbeams*
HR Beasley*: Nothing Left To Hide*
JW Darcy: *Ladybird Ladybird*
Lee Benson: *So You Want To Own An Art Gallery*
Lee Benson: *Where's Your Art gallery Now?*
Lee Benson*: Now You're The Artist...Deal With It*
TF Byrne *Damage Limitation*
Nargis Darby: *A Different Shade Of Love*
Jean Harvey: *Pandemic*
Michel Henri: *Mister Penny Whistle*
Michel Henri*: The Death Of The Duchess Of Grasmere*
Michel Henri: *Abducted By Faerie*
Amber J Hughes: *An Injection Of The Unexpected*
Hugh Lupus *An Extra Knot*
Ian Meacheam: *An Inspector Called*
Tony Rowland: *Traitor Lodger German Spy*
Andrew Sparke: *Abuse Cocaine & Soft Furnishings*
Andrew Sparke*: Copper Trance & Motorways*
Phil Thompson: *Momentary Lapses In Concentration*
Paul C. Walsh: *A Place Between The Mountains*
Michael White*: Life Unfinished*

Printed in Poland
by Amazon Fulfillment
Poland Sp. z o.o., Wrocław

53793423R00119